Adored

Also from Lexi Blake

Adored

A Masters and Mercenaries Novella

With bonus content
Sweet Child o' Mine

By Lexi Blake

1001 Dark Nights

EVIL EYE
CONCEPTS

Adored
A Masters and Mercenaries Novella
By Lexi Blake
1001 Dark Nights
Copyright 2015 DLZ Entertainment, LLC
ISBN: 978-1-940887-33-3

Foreword: Copyright 2014 M. J. Rose

Published by Evil Eye Concepts, Incorporated

Author Acknowledgments

Thanks to Liz, MJ, Jillian, Pam and the whole crew at Evil Eye. It's always a pleasure to work with truly creative people. As always thanks to my own crew – Chloe, Riane, Stormy, my husband and my son who will likely yell at me because of all the italics in this book. And to the amazing Steve Berry who I owe for the inspiration to make Mitch a lawyer. I also owe him five dollars.

This book is dedicated to the parents out there. No matter how it happens children change our lives, our marriages, and our souls for the better.

Sign up for the 1001 Dark Nights Newsletter
and be entered to win a Tiffany Key necklace.

There's a contest every month!

Go to www.1001DarkNights.com to subscribe.

As a bonus, all newsletter subscribers will receive a free
1001 Dark Nights story
The First Night
by Lexi Blake & M.J. Rose

One Thousand and One Dark Nights

Once upon a time, in the future...

*I was a student fascinated with stories and learning.
I studied philosophy, poetry, history, the occult, and
the art and science of love and magic. I had a vast
library at my father's home and collected thousands
of volumes of fantastic tales.*

*I learned all about ancient races and bygone
times. About myths and legends and dreams of all
people through the millennium. And the more I read
the stronger my imagination grew until I discovered
that I was able to travel into the stories... to actually
become part of them.*

*I wish I could say that I listened to my teacher
and respected my gift, as I ought to have. If I had, I
would not be telling you this tale now.
But I was foolhardy and confused, showing off
with bravery.*

*One afternoon, curious about the myth of the
Arabian Nights, I traveled back to ancient Persia to
see for myself if it was true that every day Shahryar
(Persian: شهریار, "king") married a new virgin, and then
sent yesterday's wife to be beheaded. It was written
and I had read, that by the time he met Scheherazade,
the vizier's daughter, he'd killed one thousand
women.*

*Something went wrong with my efforts. I arrived
in the midst of the story and somehow exchanged
places with Scheherazade – a phenomena that had
never occurred before and that still to this day, I
cannot explain.*

Now I am trapped in that ancient past. I have taken on Scheherazade's life and the only way I can protect myself and stay alive is to do what she did to protect herself and stay alive.

Every night the King calls for me and listens as I spin tales. And when the evening ends and dawn breaks, I stop at a point that leaves him breathless and yearning for more. And so the King spares my life for one more day, so that he might hear the rest of my dark tale.

As soon as I finish a story... I begin a new one... like the one that you, dear reader, have before you now.

Chapter One

Mitchell Bradford stared down at the phone and wondered if he could somehow manage to reach through it and strangle the man on the other end of the line. His office was cool, but he could feel the temperature rising with each word he heard. He was certain Kai Ferguson would tell him he had anger issues and should come in for a session. Then Mitch could kill the fucker in person. "What do you mean you paired Laurel with the new Master? Which Laurel would that be because you couldn't possibly be talking about Laurel Daley, my paralegal. I believe I told Big Tag that she was to be refused admission to Sanctum."

Kai chuckled over the line. "Oh, you know, Big Tag has a soft spot for a well-meaning sub."

He took his cell off speaker and pressed it to his ear, as though bringing it closer would make his point more clear. "The only thing Laurel means by joining Sanctum is to push me into a jealous rage. She's manipulating me. That means she's manipulating Tag, too. Deny her application, Kai."

Laurel Daley was rapidly becoming a pain in his...damn it. Thinking about the gorgeous, not even thirty-year-old brunette made his cock hard. She was stunning. Smart and capable, he'd thought about firing her more than once because his brain shut off the minute she walked in a room. He'd hired her sight unseen because she was his best friend's sister. She'd needed a job and he'd needed help.

His best friend. There had been times Will Daley had been his only friend. Will had picked him up and dusted him off and made sure he didn't kill himself with booze. How did he tell his best friend in the world that he wanted to fuck his sister so badly he dreamed about it every night?

He might have been able to deal with the entire situation if Laurel hadn't lost her damn mind and decided she wanted him, too.

One of them had to be sensible.

"I can't deny her application. She's perfectly sane." Kai was his other friend. He and Will and Kai had taken to hanging out together. Unfortunately Kai was also the gateway to Sanctum. He was the club's resident shrink, with the power to approve or disapprove membership applications.

"You wouldn't think that if you saw how pissed off she gets at fictional characters. The woman yells at her e-reader. She threw it across the room the other day and her only explanation was that someone named Joshua Lake was being a butthead." He'd narrowly missed having his head taken off with the damn thing. Luckily, the e-reader seemed pretty tough. The thing hadn't had a scratch on it and she was right back to reading after she'd finished the first draft of the contract she was working on.

Kai chuckled over the line. "Those women are serious about their book boyfriends. If that was a sign of insanity, I would have to get rid of most of the submissives at Sanctum. Face it, Mitch. You're going to have to deal with her."

Laurel would soon be running around Sanctum, likely wearing very little.

Sanctum was his sanctuary. It was a BDSM club, a very exclusive one. He'd had to pay through the nose and give Ian Taggart, the owner, a massive discount on legal services in order to get in. Apparently all his paralegal had to do was bat her eyelashes. His stomach turned and he wondered if he had any antacids. He wasn't exactly sure what he would do if he couldn't spend his nights at Sanctum. His friends were there. It was how he blew off steam.

So take her and train her. She wants to learn about D/s and you want to find out how tight her pussy is and how she'll whimper when you fuck her hard. You can have her sign a contract. This is actually perfect, dude. Stop thinking so much and let me take over. Have I ever steered you wrong, buddy?

"Mitch, is your penis talking to you again?"

He should never have admitted that to a shrink. He tried to move the conversation back to the point. "Why did you pick Master T? He's obviously wrong for her."

He wasn't going into the fact that his libido was sometimes a voice inside his head. And fuck you very much, penis, but yes, his dick had led him astray on numerous occasions leading to two disastrous marriages.

Twice he'd been forced to start his life over again with nothing. He'd had to build not one, not two, but three businesses from scratch, and he wasn't doing that again. No matter how well intentioned he would be going into a casual relationship with Laurel Daley, he knew how it would end up. It would start with amazing sex and end in divorce because the only thing stupider than his dick was his heart.

"Master T has become quite proficient at all aspects of D/s. I think he's a good match for training Laurel," Kai explained in a very logical voice.

Master T. They were all using the alias, but Mitch happened to know that Master T was actually Tennessee Smith, disavowed CIA agent in deep cover. He didn't have all the specifics of Ten's new mission. He only knew that the handsome agent was dangerous and that meant Laurel should stay away from him. Ian was planning to use Sanctum to run some kind of operation in the next couple of months, and Mitch didn't want Laurel anywhere near Smith when he got to work. Hell, he didn't want her anywhere near the handsome ex-agent for any reason.

"What about the married Masters?" It was how things were done at Sanctum. The married Masters tended to be the most experienced. They and their submissives often trained both Doms and subs for several months.

There was a pause on the line. "She's worked with Ian and Liam for six weeks. They think she's ready to move on and so do I."

He stopped, the phone heavy in his hand. "She's been going to Sanctum?"

"She comes in on Thursday nights for training and works the nursery on Saturday nights."

Well, that explained it. He didn't go in on Thursdays and there was no reason for him to ever visit the nursery. "And no one thought to tell me my paralegal has joined the club I attend?"

Kai's voice went a bit hard. "I'm only telling you now out of courtesy because Master T prefers to train on Friday nights. The confidentiality of our club members is very important, as you would know."

"But she's Laurel. You know what she means to me," he rasped into the phone. Laurel was all he could think about half the time.

"Then you should have claimed her, Mitchell. She's done waiting for you and I think it's the healthiest choice she's made in the time I've known her. I applaud her for taking control of her life and deciding what she wants. She wants to explore D/s. You won't train her."

"You know why I won't train her." He'd already fucked up his life beyond repair. Twice. He wasn't about to screw up hers, too. He was too old for her. He was too rough and hard for her. She was a kid starting out and he'd run through all his chances.

"Yes, I fully understand all of your psychological reasons for pushing her aside. That is your choice. This is hers."

"She's trying to manipulate me. She thinks if I have to see her with another man, I'll come around."

A long sigh came over the line and Mitch could practically feel the weight of Kai's disappointment. "Then this is your chance to prove her wrong, Mitch. You should thank me. Master T will be taking responsibility for her. I believe they're signing a month-long contract. If it doesn't work out, I've got a couple of Doms looking for permanent partners. You don't have to worry anymore. She'll be taken care of. She won't bother you once she's found a proper top."

She wouldn't bother him? Seeing Laurel was the best part of his day. He'd hired her six months before and every second of every day since had been about catching sight of her or arguing some point of law with her or trying to keep his hands off her. The idea of her with another man...

"Let me find her a Dom. It can't be Master T. He's too old for her. He's too cold."

"He's too much like you?" Kai's voice had softened, was almost sympathetic.

"She deserves better." He was ten years older than her and about a hundred years wiser, though much of his wisdom was made of things a sane person would avoid. "She's a bright light, Kai. She's one of those people you can't help but adore. She shouldn't be with a Master who will grind her under his boot. She needs someone young and positive."

"Does it help if I tell you her contract forbids sex for the first three weeks? They can decide afterward if they want to take the relationship further."

Did it help? Not really. "She needs more. Even during training. Have you thought about Theo Taggart? I know he's in the program. Or Michael Malone?"

He hated the idea of either man laying hands on her, but he had to stop being a selfish prick. She was lonely. He wanted her to be happy. Theo Taggart had a ready smile and a positive outlook on life and Malone came from a wealthy, loving, completely functional family. Neither man had been married before so they didn't have three tons of baggage they dragged through life.

"Mitch, will you listen to yourself? This is ridiculous. She wants you. She's made that plain."

"She's a little girl with daddy issues."

A sharp gasp had him turning around pronto. Shit. Why hadn't he closed the door? Laurel Daley stood there, a clipboard in her hand and her face about three shades paler than normal. "Kai, I'm going to have to call you back."

"She's listening, isn't she?" Kai sounded almost excited at the prospect. "I can be there in twenty minutes for a session if you like. I think if we all sit down, we can find a middle ground..."

He hung up. Kai could go on and on about therapy, and Mitch wasn't interested. He set the phone down. "You could knock, you know."

Yes, arrogance worked in situations like this. No wonder his wives always left him.

Laurel's jaw tightened. "Sharon was at lunch so I was watching the front desk. You have a walk-in. Do you want me to tell him to go away? He claims it's urgent."

Urgent was way better than dealing with her wounded eyes. "What's his name? Or rather company name?"

He was an expert at corporate law. He'd specialized this time around, taking on no partners who could potentially fuck his wife and then take his business over. He was a high-priced consultant. His only real courtroom work anymore was when his friends needed him. He'd recently dealt with a tenancy issue for Sean Taggart's restaurant, Top, and managed to get Case Taggart's speeding tickets taken care of. Dude needed less road rage. So he didn't get a whole ton of walk-in clients. It was usually Big Tag trying to get him to sue someone who had pissed him off. He only tried the lawsuits because his wife, Charlotte, had forbidden assassinations.

Yep, this was his world. He wasn't sure sweet Laurel Daley fit into it. No. That wasn't right. He didn't want Laurel in it. She should be married with a few babies, depending on a husband who loved her and only her and had never made the kinds of mistakes Mitch had made.

"He's with a firm called Dixon Technologies."

It didn't ring a bell, but he often dealt with tech firms. They constantly had intellectual property issues. "Send him in."

"All right. I'll try to put aside my daddy issues long enough to go out there and give him directions to your office."

When she turned that smart mouth on him his cock pulsed, but then it pretty much did that whenever she walked into a room. He was thirty-eight. She wasn't even thirty. Why couldn't his dick pick a more appropriate focus?

Because I want that one. God, just fucking look at her, man. Look at those breasts. Firm. Round. So sweet. And that bratty mouth. Come on, hands. Aren't you itching to smack that pretty ass?

"Laurel." He put a little bite to his tone.

She turned immediately and her eyes slid to the floor before coming back up. She steeled herself as though she needed to remember not to defer to him. Yeah, his dick liked that, too. He'd realized his mistake about five minutes after she walked through his door. Laurel was a natural submissive. She deferred to those around her, sometimes to the point of burying her own needs. It was exactly the kind of thing a well-meaning Dominant partner could help her with. A Dom with good intentions, who loved and cared for her, would protect her and teach her how valuable she was.

"What?" Her chin came up and a stubborn glint hit her eyes.

He knew her well enough at this point to know this was Laurel trying to shove her emotions deep. He'd said something that hurt her. He should gather her up and put her in his lap and stroke her hair while he apologized. Unfortunately, that would lead to fucking her on his desk, so he settled for words. "I don't suppose you heard the part of the conversation where I talked about how I wanted you to be happy?"

She was obviously unmoved. "Nope and I know you have a very creative mind so I'll suspend my disbelief." She stopped and her mouth softened slightly. "I take it you found out about me joining the trainee program at Sanctum."

"I don't think it's a good idea. I don't think it's professional for the two of us to be at the same club together. I count on that club, Laurel. The few friends I have in life are there."

"All right. I'll let them know I won't be coming anymore." She took a deep breath and there was a hollowness to her expression he despised. It was only there for a moment and then her face was a polite blank. "Do you need anything? Coffee? You skipped lunch. I could get you a sandwich."

"Just like that? You'll leave it like that? I expected more of a fight out of you."

She shook her head. "I didn't join to cause you harm or to take something away from you. I joined because I wanted to explore that side of myself. Since you've made it plain that my presence takes away from your enjoyment of something you need, I'll leave."

How did she do this to him? She'd had him in knots since the moment he'd met her. "Could you give me a couple of minutes to catch up? I didn't even know you were interested in the lifestyle."

Now her inner brat made an appearance, those pretty blue eyes rolling. "Of course you did, Mitchell. That's a complete cop out and unworthy of you, counselor. If you're going to defend yourself at least do it properly. You've known I was interested in D/s since the moment you hired me."

He had. He'd found books by Sanctum's resident authors, Amber Rose and Dakota Cheyenne. Silly pen names for Serena Dean-Miles and Laurel's sister-in-law, Bridget Daley. Bridget was the one who had sparked Laurel's interest, though he'd rather thought it had all been a means to an end. "I thought it was really me you were interested in."

She stepped back in his office. The whole place had been redecorated. It had been a dull beige with brown carpets and fixtures from the seventies when he'd bought it and he'd done nothing to update until Laurel had taken the project over. Now the whole office was modernized, with the exception of his desk. Laurel had tried to get rid of it, but he'd put his foot down. His crappy old chair had been replaced with something ergonomic. A week in he'd noticed his shoulder didn't hurt anymore after a long day. He'd also noticed how the brighter colors had livened up the place, given it an elegance and grace that matched the woman who had overseen its design.

"You've made it very clear that you're not interested in pursuing a relationship with me, Mitch. You made it clear that night. I've stayed away since then."

The night he'd gotten slightly drunk in Hawaii and kissed her. It had been her brother's impromptu wedding that had done it. He'd been Will Daley's best man and watched as his friend married the woman of his dreams. Sure Will had some surly, mouthy and bratty dreams, but Bridget was also creative and funny and kind.

A lot like Laurel.

Watching Will get married made him wonder what it would have been like if he'd met Laurel before. Before his divorces. Before life had ground him down. When she'd joined him on the beach, he hadn't been able to resist pulling her into his arms and finally tasting her mouth. He could still feel how soft she was, how her body had fit perfectly against his. And he could still see how hurt she'd been when he'd pushed her away.

"That night was a mistake. I shouldn't have kissed you."

Her eyes slid away from his. "Yes, you've mentioned it a couple of times."

"So why join my club?"

"Because it's the only one I'm allowed to join. I tried to find another one. My brother took exception."

Mitch felt his stomach drop. "You went to another club?"

She shrugged. "I knew you wouldn't like me going to Sanctum. Honestly, I thought it was weird going to a club with my brother, too. So I found another one out in the suburbs. Horrible, actually. Anyway, I went twice and Will found out and he showed up and hauled me out. It was horrifically embarrassing. I spent some time on a website, but nothing panned out. Bridget invited me to Sanctum and then I think with all the babies they needed subs who were willing to work the daycare, so I signed on. I might still offer to work with the babies. I've grown quite fond of them."

He was stuck on the fact that not only had she gone to some club he knew nothing about, but she'd spent time on the Internet. "What did you do, Laurel? Did you upload a profile at FetLife? Maybe advertise on Craig's List for a Dom? Do you want someone to murder you? Because that's pretty much what you're asking for."

Her jaw firmed, eyes flashing, and he was pretty sure this was one of those times it would have been better to take a step back and measure his words. "I wanted to figure myself out, you giant ass. What right do you have to tell me what I can and..." Another deep breath. "It no longer matters. I'll let Mr. Dixon know you can see him now."

"Laurel, we're not done discussing this."

Her eyes narrowed and he was sure she was about to tell him where he could shove it when a thin man with wire-framed glasses stepped into the doorway.

"Mr. Bradford, thank god. It's imperative that I speak with you."

He wasn't done with Laurel. He needed to make her understand that the way she was going about this wasn't good.

And how should she go about it? He'd told her she couldn't go to the safest place. Then told her she couldn't go anywhere else either. She was trying to figure herself out. If she meant those words, how could he hold her back? Didn't she deserve the same chance he'd had?

No. Laurel is supposed to be normal. Laurel is supposed to not need the rough stuff because she's a sweet princess. Wake up. This is what you do. You put a woman on a pedestal. You aren't sexually liberated. You're still the same pathetic boy who wanted his father to take two seconds with him.

Now who had daddy issues?

"Mr. Bradford?" the man asked.

"Laurel," he said, more softly this time. "Can we please discuss this further?"

She shook her head. "There's no need. I'll keep my private life private from now on."

"Hey, I'm serious about needing to talk," the man said, his shoulders straightening.

"In a minute, buddy." He needed to talk to Laurel. He didn't like the look in her eyes. In that moment he realized the only thing worse than having Laurel around was not having her around. If she quit, he wouldn't be able to watch out for her. He wouldn't know where she was or what she was getting into—like offering herself up on the fucking Internet. "Laurel, let's talk."

"No. I need to talk, damn it." The thin man had turned a brilliant shade of red and sweat had broken out on his forehead. "You have to listen to me, Bradford. My brother is going to kill you. Harvey has sworn to not stop trying until you and everyone you love is dead."

The room seemed to chill.

"Okay, then. Why don't you sit down?" It looked like his talk with Laurel was going to have to wait.

* * * *

Thank god for crazy people and their death threats. Laurel Daley sat down and was very aware that most people wouldn't be happy that their boss had been threatened, but it was a well-timed announcement. She'd been about to cry and she'd promised herself she wouldn't do that over Mitchell Bradford anymore.

Besides, it certainly wouldn't be the first time someone had threatened to kill her cantankerous boss. Hell, she thought about doing the deed herself about ten times a day. She was thinking about doing it now.

What right did he have to tell her she couldn't go to Sanctum? Asshole. Selfish prick.

She's a bright light, Kai. She's one of those people you can't help but adore.

Selfish prick who said the sweetest things when he thought no one was listening. He was also a selfish prick with serious insecurities, with a truckload of baggage it looked like she wasn't going to be able to plow through.

"I understand your brother is angry with me," Mitch was saying. He was back behind the massive desk he hadn't allowed her to get rid of. It was a refugee from the 1960's, when apparently men compensated with large oak desks instead of sports cars. At least she'd been able to get rid of his crappy chair and replace it with one that wouldn't mangle his spinal cord. "I'm a lawyer. A lot of people get angry with me."

"It's in his job description," she quipped.

His dark eyes moved her way, and it took all she had not to fall to the floor in a submissive pose. But she wasn't going to. Nope. Not for him.

"As I was saying, my line of work tends to bring out the worst in people, but I'll admit I don't remember your brother. You said his name was Harvey? Harvey Dixon?"

"We don't have a file on him, sir," Laurel said, knowing damn well that the "sir" would get his motor running, and that was why she merely meant it as a politeness. She wasn't even thinking of capitalizing the word the way she would with Master Ian or Master Liam. If Mitch wanted the relationship professional, then he better get used to a lowercase *s*.

He frowned at her, his handsome face going all gruff in a way that somehow managed to make him look more masculine. "How do you know? Do you have the files memorized now?"

She could have them memorized if she wanted to, but that would cut into her reading time. "Nope. I checked my tablet. I scanned in all the files and where they're stored about a month after you hired me. We're fully automated."

His brows formed that *V* he got whenever something confused and disturbed him. "No one told me. I don't think that's a very good idea."

He was often like the old guy on his lawn shaking his fist at those young people. For a superman of not even forty, he was very adverse to change. "And that's why I didn't tell you."

She often had to go around her gorgeous grump in order to get anything done. Mitch had a smoking body and the finest legal mind she'd ever met, but he also had a few quirks, and he could be a massive ass when he wanted to be.

"You can't go around destroying my files."

"Good god, Mitchell. I didn't destroy the files. I scanned them in. Please tell me you don't think that involves the computer eating the files or something."

"Of course not." The look in Mitch's eyes told her he would have a discussion with her after this was over. Which was good since she intended to have a discussion with him, too.

He turned back to their guest. "Why do you believe your brother intends to kill me?"

Patrick Dixon shifted in his chair, his hands nervously moving along the arms. "Well, my first indication was when he told me he was going to spend the rest of his life trying to rip your heart from your chest, eat it and then...well, the rest is all digestion but he used much more crude language."

"He wants to shit my heart out?" Mitch asked, his eyes rolling. "Like I never heard that one before. Is there a reason he wants me in his bowels?"

"He shouldn't given how much red meat you eat. It might be harder to pass than he thinks." She tried to force him to work a salad in every now and then.

Dixon ignored her. "My brother considers himself quite the inventor. Over the years he's been awarded twenty-two different patents. He's a brilliant engineer, but he prefers to work for himself, and the patents have never panned out, if you know what I mean."

"Just because you patent something doesn't mean you're going to make money from it," Mitch replied.

"Exactly." Patrick sighed as though this was something he'd thought about long and hard. "Some of his inventions didn't have much use or purpose in the real world. We managed to get a few of his ideas to market, but it wasn't enough for Harvey. He always thought about the ones that got away. A few of his more brilliant ideas were taken by large companies."

Mitch shook his head. "Was he working for them at the time? Are you trying to say they stole his patents?"

"No. While my brother is very smart, his processes can be a bit convoluted, difficult to understand."

"Ah," Mitch said with a nod. "So someone swoops in and refines the idea, changes the process so it's easier to produce the wanted effect."

"It's not fair," Patrick said, his hands forming fists.

Mitch shrugged. "A patent applies to a process for bringing about a result. It doesn't apply to the result itself. Otherwise, we'd have monopolies all over the place on manufacturing. If someone took your brother's ideas and made them simpler, easier to get to market, then they win the prize. It's Edison vs. Tesla."

This was why she'd hung around. Mitch was brilliant and all that law knowledge seemed to have taken up the majority of space in his brain. He didn't have a whole lot of tact. He obviously couldn't see that Dixon was on the edge of an emotional outburst.

Laurel leaned forward and patted the man's arm. "I'm so sorry to hear that. It must have been very frustrating for him."

Dixon immediately calmed, his eyes sad now but resolute. "It is, Miss Daley. It's hard to watch someone you care about struggle. I have to admit that my brother isn't the most stable of people. He's brilliant but not stable."

She couldn't say that about her boss. Yes, he was gruff and he obviously didn't put any stock in chemistry and wouldn't know the prefect sub if she bit him in the ass—actually she hadn't tried that—but Mitchell Bradford was stable. Since the day she'd met him, he'd been the man who walked her to her car every day, even if it was afternoon, even when he wasn't leaving himself. He was the one who wanted a text to make sure she'd made it home all right. Mitch was the one who flipped out when he realized her car had a warning light that had been blinking away for six weeks. He was also the one who took her car down himself because he didn't trust mechanics to not take advantage of her.

"None of this explains why I'm his target. Or why he has a target at all," Mitch said gruffly.

Dixon leaned forward. "You have to understand that Harvey has always had big dreams. He would make a little money and then spend it all on the next invention because he didn't want to simply be comfortable. He wanted to be rich, famous. He's had many offers over the years for stable employment but he turned them all down because his wealth was always right around the corner."

Laurel understood the type. "He was always swinging for the fences because getting on base wasn't enough, right?"

Dixon nodded. "Exactly. That seemed to work during his twenties, but he got involved with drugs at some point and it went downhill. He became paranoid. He worked less, but was angrier about the failures. Then two years ago he started working on a way to store solar power."

"The Bentley Industries project." Laurel immediately pulled up the file. As solar energy became an actual option for individual homes, the issue of storage had become a problem. Engineers had been trying to find a way to store up energy for longer periods of time so the houses with the capability could be more self-reliant rather than having to switch back to the electricity grid. So sunny summer days could be saved to power winter days. Bentley Industries had recently filed for a patent on a system that would allow for solar storage of up to a month and had confidence they could refine the process to go much longer.

Mitchell Bradford was their attorney and stood to gain a percentage of the profits. He'd also been the spokesman for the company when they'd done the talk show rounds.

"Yes," Patrick agreed. "I don't even think Harvey was close to anything, but he's decided this was his last shot. He's back on drugs and he believes that Mitch somehow stole his idea. I tried to go to the police, but they said there was no proof and when they talked to Harvey, he was in one of his lucid stages. He can be very convincing when he's like that. I've been his partner for twenty years and I've never seen him so angry."

"What makes you think this isn't just talk, Mr. Dixon?" Mitch asked. If it bugged him that someone wanted him dead, he didn't show it. His gorgeous face was as passive as it was when he talked about the weather.

But once it had been animated and fierce. She couldn't forget the possessive look that had lit those dark eyes as he'd lowered his lips to hers and devoured her like a starving man.

She shook her head because every time she thought about their one and only kiss, the room seemed to heat up. It had been months, but she could still feel the way his hands had tightened on her body as though he would never let her go.

He had, of course, and now he was quite good at evading her web of seduction. Or maybe she wasn't any good at the seduction part.

"It's a feeling," Patrick was saying. "I know that something is off with him. I truly believe he's going to make an attempt on your life. You have to be careful. I don't think I'll be able to stop him."

The poor man was shaking. Laurel leaned over and put a hand on his. "It's all right. We'll look into it. Thank you so much for telling us about the threat. I can't imagine what it cost you to come in this afternoon."

"He's my brother." Patrick sniffled slightly and that sent Laurel running for a tissue. Naturally Mitch didn't have any. He tried to pawn off anyone who looked like they would get even vaguely emotional on her, so she excused herself. She kept a box in her office.

That was when she saw the man in the lobby. A hoodie was pulled down over his face. He stood in the hallway outside their doors. The building housed several businesses. This particular floor was shared by their office, a dentist, and an accounting agency.

He was probably looking for the dentist. He was dressed too casually for business.

She grabbed the tissues off Sharon's desk and was about to turn when the man suddenly shifted toward her.

The hoodie covered his eyes, but she wasn't really looking at him anymore. Nope. She was standing stock-still at the sight of what was in his hands.

A gun.

She managed to scream right before he pulled the trigger.

Chapter Two

"Derek, I want this asshole found. Do you understand?" Three hours later, Mitch could still feel his heart pounding.

Harvey Dixon had taken a shot at Laurel. He'd shot at her through the ceiling to floor glass windows the real estate agent who had sold him on this building had sworn gave the place a professional feel.

They gave the place a clear line of sight to shoot into it. He was done with that shit. Steel-enforced walls. He would have them put in as soon as possible. Surely Big Tag knew some crazy doomsday preppers who could outfit his office with everything one would need to keep out people who shot at his paralegal.

"He understands, Mitch. You've yelled at him for an hour," Laurel said with a sigh.

Derek Brighton, a lieutenant with the Dallas Police Department, merely shook his head. "He can yell all he likes. He's had a scare."

"I was the one who nearly got shot and no one even offered me a lollipop." Laurel looked sulky at the thought.

The EMT had offered her more than a lollipop, Mitch was sure. The kid couldn't have been much past twenty-five and he'd flirted like mad with Laurel before declaring her perfectly fine.

"And I want another EMT. She needs to go to the hospital." That was what people who got shot did. She'd almost been shot. Maybe the kid had spent so much time flirting with her that he'd missed a gunshot wound. It could happen. Adrenaline could make a person ignore pain.

He wanted to run his hands over her himself. It had been his first instinct. He'd needed to feel her skin under his palm, to make sure she was warm and alive. He'd pulled her up, but before he could get her in his arms, she'd stepped back, keeping a professional distance between them.

"I think I might send you to the hospital, buddy. You look like you might have a heart attack. Why don't you sit down, Mitch?" Derek was a friend from Sanctum. He'd shown up with the first responders, having recognized the address. "You're going to wear a hole in the carpet."

"I don't want to sit." He still might have a damn heart attack. Since that moment he'd heard the glass cracking and realized what that sound had really been, his heart had kicked into overdrive. He'd run out into reception only to find Laurel on the ground. It had taken him a moment to realize she wasn't hurt. Before she'd turned over and reached a hand up, he'd thought she was dead.

Hollow. The world for a moment had been so utterly hollow.

"All right, well, I think we have what we need. I hate to tell you this, but it wasn't Harvey Dixon. I just got a report that he's in a rehab facility and has been for the last two weeks. I informed his brother and he's already on his way over. Turns out he hadn't talked to him lately. He found some stuff Harvey had written in a journal a couple of months back. Besides, we've got this guy on camera. He's a good twenty years younger than Harvey Dixon. The dentist next door says he's had some trouble with break-ins. Kids come looking for drugs. He claims to have complained to the landlord but apparently the landlord is a difficult asshole. His words, not mine."

Mitch sighed. He was the freaking landlord. "Trust me. I'll have a new security system complete with those eye scan things. No one's getting in here again."

"That could be bad for business," Laurel said with a sigh.

"Yeah, well, I don't care about business anymore." Except he better because until his new ventures started coming in, he had one ex-wife who would haul him in front of a California judge if he missed her alimony check.

Derek held out a hand. "I'll get this kid. He was probably high. I already have some officers canvassing the area to see if he's local. I'll check with the other buildings. I saw some security cameras up and down the street. We might be able to get a better view of him. You want me to give Big Tag a call?"

Big Tag had recently had a set of twins. Another reason to never get a woman pregnant. Sometimes they gave birth to litters. "Nah. If Harvey Dixon is actually locked up in rehab, I suppose we're all right. Can someone inform me if he checks himself out?"

"I've already asked the facility to let me know. He's there on court-ordered rehab, so he can't leave unless he wants to spend his time in prison instead. I'll monitor the situation and let you know what I find out. I'll also check phone records and see if he's called anyone, but Dixon was fairly certain he was after you, so I don't see why he would take a shot at Laurel." Derek gave Laurel a smile. "I'm thrilled you weren't horribly murdered. If you're still up for it, Karina and I will be at your place at eight on Friday, okay?"

Laurel paled. "Oh, actually I'm not going to be able to go, but thanks. Please tell Karina hello for me."

Derek's eyes narrowed. "You all right?"

Laurel nodded. "Yes, something came up. I can't go on Friday."

"Okay, but if you change your mind or you want to go on Saturday, we'll be there. With Will and Bridget at that conference of hers, you call me if you need a ride." Derek nodded and strode out.

Everyone had known about Laurel's foray into submission with the exception of him.

Sharon walked in. His secretary was in her mid-fifties and was much more worried about her grandkids and their myriad of social activities than she was about working, but every time he tried to fire her Laurel intervened. She was his tenth secretary in the last four years and it looked like he needed a new one. "Okay, I called the glass company and they're sending someone out tonight to fix the glass. He can't be here until after six and I have to be at Afton's school play, so someone's going to have to stay to let them in."

The poorly named Afton was actually a boy, but that didn't matter to Mitch. "I didn't give you those orders, Sharon, and I don't want glass."

"No, I did and I've already approved the amount. We are not turning this office into a steel-reinforced bunker." For a woman who had recently been shot at, Laurel was surprisingly on top of things.

He should have known she would plot against him. This was what life with Laurel would be like. Every day was a minor war between the two of them. He wanted steak and potatoes for lunch and she ordered in some kind of salad. He wanted a filing system he understood and she computerized everything. He wanted her to not be shot and she made arrangements for windows and possibly hunting blinds throughout the office. He wouldn't put it past her. She would do it to challenge his authority. He was putting his foot down. "We're closing up the windows and that's that."

Sharon smiled and utterly ignored him. "Okay then, Laurel. I'll see y'all tomorrow. But not too early. I want to go with Denise and the baby to her doctor's appointment. I'm going to be a grandma again."

She walked out and he was left shaking his head. "How many does that make? Are her children rabbits?"

"Seven," Laurel shot back. "She has three kids and seven lovely grandchildren. They're all very sweet."

Another reason to step back from Laurel. She wanted babies. He didn't want babies. The last thing he was going to do with his life was ruin some kid's. His childhood had been a long series of short-term stays with his mother and her revolving door of boyfriends, and the occasional card from his father. No. He wasn't going to inflict that on anyone.

"I don't want windows. People can shoot at you through windows," he said. It looked like it would be a long night. He started after Sharon. The woman could move when she wanted to get out of work. She was down the stairs and out of the building before he knew it. "And that woman is fired."

Laurel followed him, her heels clacking on the stairs. "You can't fire her. Why would you even want to? Because she's not coming in until late? You don't have a single appointment tomorrow. You should be happy. You've scared everyone off."

He liked not having appointments. It made his day much nicer to not have to deal with people. "I'm firing her because she took too long for lunch. If she'd been at her desk, she could have handed you the tissue and then you wouldn't have spooked the crackhead. So she's fired." He swiftly locked the door and set the security alarm that was getting a serious upgrade in the morning.

When he turned, Laurel was standing on the bottom step. They were completely alone in the building he'd bought with pretty much everything he'd had left after the divorce from Joy, aspiring actress and expert at manipulating men. If she'd been half as good at auditions as she'd been in the courtroom, she wouldn't have needed half his assets and three grand a month in alimony.

"I should call your brother." Now that he was alone with her, his heart was still pounding but his dick was pulsing too. He couldn't forget how still she'd been, how there'd been blood on her arms from the glass cutting her. "I would feel better if he looked you over instead of that hormonal puppy who practically humped your leg instead of properly examining you."

"Mitchell, he was gay. We were talking about how much he liked my shoes."

He frowned. "Really?"

"No, not really. He asked me out, but the truth of the matter is it's none of your business and we're not calling my brother because he's with Bridget in Chicago. She's at book convention being worshipped for the goddess she is. I'm fine. You should head home. I'll handle the contractor. They're coming in with pre-cut glass so it shouldn't take them long at all."

"I'm not going anywhere and I'm serious about reinforcing our doors."

She turned and sighed. "We won't get any of the natural light from the skylight if you do that. You'll turn the entire reception area into a gloomy cave. It will utterly ruin everything the decorator did in the last six months."

That was where he had her. "Yeah, well it won't matter because I'm filling in the skylight, too." There was a massive glass structure on the roof that filtered light down through the building. The four-story building had a courtyard style setting in the middle and glass elevators that ran up the back. That glass over his head might be pretty, but now he was thinking of all the ways assassins could break through and enter, and his security system wouldn't protect anyone at all. "I'm calling Taggart in the morning and having him redo security for the whole building. I'm going to need you to make a couple of those lemon cakes he likes. Even with a discount the big bastard is ridiculously expensive."

She turned and her face was in a fierce frown. Her golden brown hair was slightly disheveled. Sex hair. It looked like she had sex hair instead of almost-got-murdered hair. "I am not going to help you do something like that. Do you know how hard I've worked to make this a nice place? Do you even care?" Tears shone in her eyes and she shook her head. "You don't. You couldn't care less that the office is beautiful now. Nothing I do matters. You know what? You can keep Sanctum. I'll find my own place and Will is going to have to be all right with it. Hell, maybe I'll talk to Master T and he'll train me privately."

She pivoted on her heels and started back up the stairs.

His gut rolled with anger. He was doing everything in order to keep her safe and she was treating him like this? "Laurel! Stop right where you are."

She kept moving. "I don't have to. You're not my Dom. You're not my boyfriend."

"I'm your boss."

"Not anymore. I quit. I'm not staying in a place where I work my ass off but my boss doesn't care. You don't want me but you won't let anyone else have me."

They were going to do this here? He started up after her, his blood pressure ticking up every second she didn't turn around and fight with him. He stepped up the pace because they weren't done. He knew even as he thought it that it was perverse. He knew he couldn't have her, knew he should be happy that she was leaving and taking temptation out of his path. But all he could think about was the fact that if she quit, he wouldn't have her in his life. He wouldn't be able to watch over her. Not again. She was trouble. A lot of trouble. She didn't search it out, but it seemed to follow her around.

He pounded up the stairs, disregarding all the alarms that were going off in his head. It was a mistake to follow her. His palm was itching, his cock threatening to take over. She was pushing all his buttons and she had been all damn day. He hadn't missed the way she'd called him sir. She knew exactly what she was doing.

And the entire idea of her being at Sanctum both disturbed and titillated him. What if they could compartmentalize their relationship? What if they could make it work? If he put her under a contract, he could control how much influence she had on his life.

"Laurel!"

She stomped her way back to the office she'd spent six months turning into something warm and inviting. It wasn't that he didn't understand the work she'd put into it. It was just that now all he would be able to see was her on that floor. He'd only be able to see how many different ways someone could get to her.

She held a hand up. That wouldn't have been so bad if she hadn't only had a single finger sticking up. Yes. She was giving him the finger.

He had a couple of things to give to her. His blood started to thrum through his system and his good sense was beginning to seem like a far-off thing. Up ahead he could see the way her hips swayed and how perfectly she walked in those four-inch heels. It made him wonder what else she could do.

She'd almost died. Some asswipe had leveled a gun at her and pulled the trigger and only her quick movements had saved her life. She could be dead. She could be gone, her unique kindness and beauty stopped by a single bullet.

He should have been questioning himself, but it no longer mattered. She'd pushed him past thought and into action. He hadn't had the chance to save her before. She'd been on her own in a place that should have been safe for her. But he could take action now.

She turned at the door and there was a sudden flare of fear in her eyes that sent a thrill through his system. She was finally aware of him. She wasn't looking at him like some sad sack she could push around, but like the predator he'd always hidden from her.

He had to give her one more way out. His cock was threatening to pound out of his slacks, but he still had enough willpower and common sense to give her a shot at coming out of this whole. "If you very politely apologize, I'll walk you to you car and you can leave, Laurel. We can talk about this in the morning like sane adults."

"And if I don't?"

"Don't push me again, Laurel. I've had enough. You push me one more time and you're going to see a side of me you don't want to see." For the second time that day, adrenaline pounded through his system.

Come on, baby. Push me again. Let me take over.

His dick was so close to getting what it wanted. All these months and it had been ruthlessly controlled, tamped down and put on a leash. Hell, since he'd met Laurel he hadn't taken a lover, not even for a night. He didn't want anyone else. He wanted her and if she pushed him one more time, he could chuck his morality for the night and have her. He'd given her every out. She was a smart girl and he'd given her control. All she had to do was make the sensible choice for both of them.

"Fuck you, Mitch."

Decision made. He fell on her like a hungry lion.

* * * *

Laurel's whole body came alive when Mitch's muscular body pressed her against the door. She could feel the wood at her back, but there was more at her front. He was hard, his cock already thick, and he didn't hold it back. It was pressed against her belly, insistently telling her that no matter what happened, nothing was going to be the same after tonight.

"I fucking warned you. I won't stop this time. I won't play the gentleman again," he whispered before his mouth descended on hers.

Thank god. Six months. They'd passed and every night she dreamed about what they could have had if he hadn't played the damn gentleman that night in Hawaii. They'd wasted six months. Six months when she could have felt him against her, when she could have had the heat of his body to warm her own. They could have been sleeping together, sharing a life beyond the confines of this office.

His lips found hers and he was ravenous. He slanted over her mouth again and again, dominating and taking what he wanted. His tongue surged in and she could feel that slow slide in her womb.

Just like that she was wet and ready. Her body felt malleable, as though it knew this man was the one who could mold her and bring her to fruition. Every inch of her body felt primed. Her nipples rasped against the fabric of her bra, her breasts heavy and wanting. Her clothes were suddenly too tight and she wanted nothing more than to throw them off. She didn't need clothes around him.

A sudden vision of what it would be like now that Mitch was finally claiming her stamped itself in her brain. She could hear him commanding her to be naked when they were alone. She would curl up at his feet as they relaxed. It would be the two of them and they wouldn't have to argue. They would be together.

His hands found her backside, squeezing. A low groan ground out of his mouth as he explored her. She could feel herself softening, offering herself up for his slow exploration. This was the man who would finally teach her what all the fuss was about.

Mitch pushed her to be better than she was, to think more clearly about points of law and to challenge herself to greater heights. She'd always known it would be the same in the bedroom. She'd had lovers before, but sex had been something to do, a way to show affection. Sex with Mitch was a force of freaking nature.

He pressed her against the door. His mouth was a marauder, plunging in and taking what he wanted. His hands gripped her hips and suddenly she felt her feet leave the ground. Mitch had a good half a foot on her, but it didn't seem to matter. He simply lifted her to where he wanted her to be.

"Feel that. That's what you fucking do to me," he growled against her mouth.

His cock. His very large cock, from the feel of it, was pressed right against her pussy. She had to gasp when he ground that big erection against her clit.

She intended to give as good as she got. "You can't tell what you do to me because there are way too many clothes between us."

"Tell me, Laurel. Tell me how wet your pussy is." His voice had gone deep, smooth and richer than normal. This was his Dom voice and it made her obey with ease.

"So wet. My pussy is already soft and wet for you, Sir."

"Do you want my cock?"

"I want everything," she answered honestly. She wanted him to take her in every way a man could take a woman. She wanted long nights where they simply explored their boundaries. She'd been fooling herself. Sanctum wouldn't mean anything without Mitchell as her Master. She only wanted to submit to him and only in the bedroom. She wanted to be his partner out of it. He needed her. He needed her to push him past his shell and she needed him for so many things. She needed the safety she'd found with him. No one had ever taken care of her the way he did.

His hips kept moving as he kissed his way across her face. He licked the lobe of her ear. Damn but that felt good. He nipped her before lifting her easily. "Put your legs around me. I don't want to wait. I can't. I need to be inside you. I've waited too fucking long."

She did as he asked because she'd waited too long, too. Months of yearning made her reckless. She wrapped her legs around his waist, forcing her skirt up around her upper thighs. She could already feel the way her panties were damp and clinging. She was going to make a mess of his slacks, but it didn't matter. Her brain couldn't wrap itself around anything but how good he felt as he held her up and opened the door.

He strode through the office she'd worked so hard to turn into something comfortable for him, past her own office where she kept the set of legal books Mitch had bought for her when she'd finished her paralegal certification classes. He'd said anyone who could put up with him while she attended school deserved something. Most women would see them as a simple tool, but the law was the only thing Mitch truly loved, and sharing it with her had been an act of affection on his part.

She could see through him, see to the softer side of the man. Why had it taken him this long to acknowledge that they were good together?

He strode into his office, her weight not holding him back at all. She'd watched him as he played basketball with her brother and their friends, so she knew the strength that lay under his white dress shirts. Always white with black slacks. He had what must be fifteen pairs. The only things that changed were his ties.

He kissed her as he moved toward his desk. Their tongues melded and there was nothing awkward. She'd always found kissing awkward, a little messy. She was never sure what to do with her hands or how to move. She didn't have to with Mitchell. He took over. He moved and she followed as though they'd done this a thousand times before.

Heat flashed through her system. She'd never been so aroused in her life. It was like all the tension of the day, of the last six months, was being crushed under a tidal wave of desire. Her blood thrummed through her system, waking up parts of her body she'd never thought of as sexual. When he touched her back, she shivered all along her spine.

She heard a crash and realized Mitch had shoved everything off the top of his big desk. He set her there, one arm around her at all times. Even in his passion, he was gentle with her, making sure she was safe. Now she could see the advantages to the massive thing as he settled her on it. He didn't stop kissing her for a second. Their mouths moved together, tongues sliding and playing.

His big body was in between her legs, forcing them apart as his hand moved under her skirt. She felt his palm on her thigh, moving up and up to where she needed him to be. Her head fell back as his fingers moved under the waistband of her undies and started to slide over her labia.

"You're so wet," he groaned against her neck.

"I told you, Sir. I've never been this wet before." Only for him. He invaded her every thought, all her dreams. She had no idea why this surly, gloriously masculine misanthrope did it for her, but he did. Chemistry. They had it in spades. Mitch walking into a room could make her temperature spike.

He moved back and she watched as he pulled his soaked fingers from her core and brought them up to his nose. He breathed her in deep. "God, you smell like fucking sunshine, Laurel." He sucked them inside his mouth, licking her essence off. "And you taste even better. I knew you would. I knew you would be the sweetest thing I'd ever tasted."

"Please, Mitch." She knew she was begging, but she couldn't do the whole foreplay thing. She needed him. They'd waited far too long to take their time.

His face turned savage. "Yes, I think it's about fucking time I pleased Mitch."

His hand went to the buckle of his belt and he shoved his slacks and boxers down with a single thrust, his cock jutting out. She caught a brief glimpse of the gorgeous monster before he was kissing her again. His fingers were back on her pussy, but he seemed to be pushing her undies aside...and then he was there.

Oh, she had to force herself to breathe as she felt the broad head of his cock start to push its way inside.

Alarms bells started to go off in her head, but they were a distant thing. She clutched at his arms, feeling the muscles of his big biceps through the fabric. She loved how his daily wardrobe hid the gloriously masculine body underneath. It made her want to unwrap him, to slowly rid him of the garments until he was naked in front of her and there was nothing else between them.

She longed to throw off her clothes, but the moment was coming too fast. It was like life had sped up the minute she'd started to climb those stairs. Anger had fueled her and she'd wanted nothing more in that moment but to piss him off. He pushed her buttons, too. Sometimes she thought they were gasoline and fire. They could fight until they were blue in the face but neither one would leave.

But this, this was what it had all led up to.

"God, Laurel, you're so tight." He gripped her hips and pushed in.

She could barely breathe. "I'm perfectly normal. You're too big. God, don't stop, Mitch."

One of his hands found her hair, tangling in it and pulling her head back. There was the tiniest bite to his hold that had her scalp lighting up with sensation. "Even here you argue with me."

For a second she felt like he was disappointed, but the moment passed as he forced his cock in another inch. He kissed her again and she held on for dear life as he thrust in using small movements. In and out. Gaining ground with each pass. He was so big. She was stretched and super wet, but he still was almost too much for her.

"I'm not going to last. You're too tight. Too long." His breath sawed from his chest. "Gotta make it good for you."

She bit her lip as he held himself still. His hand made its way between their bodies and then she was the one who was whimpering. His finger slid against her clitoris. He rubbed the pearly button while their mouths played together. His tongue slid inside as though trying to make up for the fact that his cock was still. Over and over he rubbed and played and the pressure built inside Laurel until she came, her body bowing, nails digging into his arms as she rode out the pleasure.

He moved his hand to her thigh and drove his cock deep. It was like she'd let him off the leash and he pounded inside her. She looked up and his eyes were closed, his head thrown back as he shoved in one last time and she felt heat streaming from him to her.

She looked up, ready for another kiss, another caress from him. They had all night. It might take forever to get enough of this man.

Mitch stared down at her. Just for a moment, his eyes were soft, as though he was utterly satisfied. That look was quickly replaced with tension and dawning regret as he took a step back, pulling up his slacks. "I can't believe we just did that."

"Mitchell?" She'd felt so sexy a moment before, utterly lost in the moment. But apparently the moment had passed and the Dom had left the building because it was Mitch's frown on that handsome face.

She sat up, her undies shifting back though they were soaked beyond repair at this point.

Soaked because Mitch hadn't used a condom.

Oh, god. They hadn't used a condom.

"Laurel, this was a mistake." He scrubbed a hand through his hair and turned away from her as if he couldn't stand to look at her another moment. "God, what did I do?"

She got up on shaky legs. "You simply did what was inevitable, Mitch. We've been moving toward this for six months."

His hands were fists at his sides. "I've been fighting to avoid this for six months, Laurel. I didn't want this. I didn't want any of this. God, am I ever going to grow the fuck up?"

Tears pricked her eyes and she tried to smooth out her skirt. It was a mess. She was a mess. She could still feel him inside her. Her mind was complete chaos, but her heart was a nasty, aching mess. How could he not have felt what she felt?

"I'm going home."

He finally turned to her, but he wouldn't look her in the eyes. "Yes, I think that's a good idea. We can forget this ever happened. We can go back to the way it was."

Go back to the way it was? Hardly. But she'd learned where arguing with him got her. It got her screwed. What he didn't realize was that she argued and fought with him because she cared about him, wanted the best for him.

Now she wanted to curl into a ball and cry because she'd been wrong. She'd thought if she could get him to make love to her, everything would fall into place.

Stupid. She'd been so stupid.

And she might pay the price. She tried to remember when her last period was.

"Laurel?"

She couldn't look at him. They hadn't even taken off their clothes. She'd thought at the time it was because they'd been too much in the moment, but now she knew he'd never had plans to slow down. She'd been a quick lay for him, a way to burn off the tension of the day.

He'd warned her. He'd told her he wasn't good enough for her. She could see now all the times he'd practically begged her to leave well enough alone. He'd told her he was too old for her, too damaged, and she hadn't listened. Even tonight he'd given her shot after shot of leaving well enough alone, but she had to poke the beast.

She'd learned her lesson.

"I'm fine, Mitch. I just want to get home and take a shower." Her voice sounded hollow even to her own ears. Devoid of emotion, which was a complete joke because she was weeping inside.

Please hold it together. Don't let him see you cry. Don't. Don't make a bigger fool of yourself than you already have.

"Laurel, I didn't use anything."

She was not having this conversation with him. "It's fine. It's not a problem."

For the first time she heard some relief in his voice. "Good. That's good. The last thing we need…"

She was out the door before he could finish that sentence. Yes, she'd been an idiot. There wasn't some soft Mitchell Bradford waiting under the surface. All of that had been spent on his two ex-wives, and all that was left for Laurel was a man who meant it when he said he didn't want another commitment, didn't want to even try to love her.

Or maybe he simply couldn't. He sure as hell had never lied to her about wanting marriage and kids. He'd been plain about that. He'd never lied.

She'd lied to herself.

She grabbed her purse and her computer bag. "I'm going to take tomorrow off."

He was standing in his doorway, his shirt untucked and his eyes grave. "All right."

"I'll call and cancel the glass on my way home."

"Why? I thought it would stop the natural light or something."

She shook her head. "It's your office. You're the boss. I'll cancel it and you do what you like."

"Laurel, why don't we have a drink? I've got some Scotch. We fucked up. We should talk about it. Please, I'll let you handle the glass and stuff. You're better at that than I am. Come and sit with me and we'll talk about it."

He sounded so lost, like a little boy who didn't know what he wanted but he knew he didn't want to be alone.

She forced herself to turn away. "No. I need to go."

He followed her out the door and down the stairs. She didn't argue. He'd always walked her to her car. He wasn't going to change. Mitchell Bradford didn't change and it would do her well to remember that one rule of the universe.

She waited for him to shut off the alarm and then stepped out and into the parking lot. Her Honda was sitting next to his massive SUV.

Even his car could rip hers apart.

"Laurel?"

She unlocked her car and turned to see him standing in front of the building. "What do you want, Mitchell?"

It was the question she should have asked before. She'd gone into her whole relationship with him asking what she wanted and having one answer—him. She'd never asked him what he wanted for the simple fact that she knew. He didn't want her.

He stared at her. "I'm so sorry, Laurel."

She nodded and got into her car. When she looked in the rearview mirror, he was still standing there.

She drove off, determined to never make the same mistake again.

Chapter Three

Two weeks later Mitch stared at her through the big bay windows of The Legal Defense Aid office. Laurel was talking to some kid, probably right out of law school. He was tall and lanky, with a handsome face and stylish clothes. He probably didn't wear the same white shirt and black slacks day in and day out. Laurel smiled at him, her face vibrant. And then she turned to her sisters, obviously introducing them to the man. Lisa smiled and gave Laurel a wink that let Mitch know she liked the new guy.

Laurel was good. She was happy.

"Mitch? Are you going to go in?"

He took a deep breath before turning and facing the one person he didn't want to face. He'd been ducking Will Daley's calls for ten days, ever since he'd gotten back from Chicago. The demise of his relationship with Laurel was almost certainly the end of his friendship with Will, and damn but he would miss the guy. He turned and shook his head. "No. I was just checking in. I won't bother her."

He'd tried to bother her. He'd called and sent her e-mails, and all he'd gotten back was one terse reply.

Thank you for you concern, Mr. Bradford. I'm quite well, but under the circumstances, I think it would be best for both of us if I quit. I'm attaching the resumes of two paralegals who would do quite well in my place. Please know I don't blame you. You were never anything less than honest with me. I was only fooling myself. I beg your forgiveness for quitting in such a cowardly way, but find I can't meet with you again. Also, you don't have to worry about meeting up with me again in a social fashion. I've let Mr. Taggart know I'm no longer interested in his club.

Yours,
LD

An e-mail. He'd gotten an e-mail from her. He had to guess that was better than the divorce papers he'd gotten from his last two women.

"I'm having lunch with my sisters, but I can call and tell them I'm running later than usual if you need to talk. I could buy you a drink." Will gestured to the bar across the street. It looked like exactly the type of seedy place that fit in this part of town. Legal Defense Aid wasn't exactly a money-making venture, so their building wasn't in an upscale neighborhood.

He didn't like to think about Laurel here at night, but he doubted she would care that he was worried. And Will didn't have to worry either. "No need, buddy. I should get back to the office. She looks like she's settling in nicely. Like I said, I won't bother her again."

He turned to go, but Will stuck to his side like glue. "Yes, you said that. Tell me something. Did she finally push you too far and you fired her? What did she do? Go behind your back and change your lunch order? Because she's so good at that."

He'd had two weeks of getting to eat whatever he wanted. Two weeks of no one bugging him about his cholesterol or working too long.

It kind of sucked.

"She quit. She decided I was too surly to deal with." He was surprised she hadn't told her brother, but now that he thought about it, maybe he shouldn't be. She wouldn't want him to know any more than Mitch did. He wasn't about to tell his best friend that Laurel had taken exception to his lack of romantic tendencies.

He definitely wasn't going to tell anyone that he'd shown up on Monday morning and placed a dozen red roses and a box of her favorite Danishes on her desk.

And then waited. And waited. And at ten o'clock, he finally found her letter of resignation in his inbox.

No. He'd go to the grave with that information.

"Did something happen between the two of you?" Will asked. His voice was deceptively soft.

Mitch knew him well enough though. "I told you I didn't think a relationship between Laurel and I would work. I think she finally understood that I was serious and she chose to cut her losses."

And he would go to his grave remembering the feel of her wrapped around him. He would remember that for a moment he'd been bigger than himself, larger than he'd been before he'd taken her. For that one moment he'd been a part of her, and it had been the single most intimate episode of his life.

It had terrified him.

Will put a hand on his back as they made it to Mitch's SUV. "I told you she could be tenacious but once she's done, she's done. So you shouldn't have to worry about her any more."

"I like your sister, Will. I'm going to miss her." He already did. He felt alone without her. He was a man who craved solitude, but over the months Laurel had taught him he wanted a partner in his self-imposed bubble. He wanted her.

He simply shouldn't.

"Laurel is amazing, but she's so young. She's just starting out. I think you made the right choice. Mitch, you've done so much for her. She never would have gone back to school if it hadn't been for you. She's found a real passion and it shows. I don't think she ever would have found out how much she loves legal work without you."

"She would be a good lawyer. Encourage her to give law school a try." He had his keys in hand, ready to make a swift getaway, but he couldn't seem to help himself. "Are they paying her at the new place?"

Will chuckled. "Not much, but she's one of the few paid positions. She's doing a ton of the up-front work so the lawyers who are working pro bono don't have to."

A good paralegal like Laurel could do a lot of legal work all on her own. "That's good. If she ever wants to move back into a more lucrative position I can ask around, maybe find her a job."

"I'll keep that in mind. So where have you been hiding? You going to Sanctum tonight? It's the last weekend before the big reveal. I don't know if you've been working on it lately, but Big Tag has got some crazy shit in the new Sanctum. Did you know he put in a human hamster wheel? I'm a little afraid that's not for subs. I heard him saying something about shoving Adam Miles in it when he pisses Big Tag off."

He was certain the new Sanctum was going to be a mind trip. "I'm actually taking some time off. I'm buried in work over this solar deal."

He was working on the sale of the company Harvey Dixon had taken such exception to. It was one good thing that had come from Laurel quitting. He no longer had to worry about her getting in his line of fire.

Dixon was still in rehab, but weird things had started happening. His tires had been slashed three nights before. He'd called Derek, but there wasn't much he could do. He'd checked in on Dixon and then explained that three other vehicles had been vandalized in the area that very night. Kids?

He was paranoid, but that didn't mean someone wasn't out to get him. At least he no longer had to worry about Laurel.

Except he did. Every single night.

"Is there something I'm not getting here, Mitch?" Will was staring at him suspiciously.

Mitch shook his head and put his best game face on. "Nope. This is a very complex contract and I stand to make an enormous amount of money off it. Once this deal goes through, I might think about retiring, maybe go down to the coast and do some fishing."

Will's eyes had gone wide. "You don't fish."

He shrugged. "Just because I haven't before doesn't mean I won't in the future. This deal should set me up for a good long while as long as I'm not stupid enough to get married again. Hence the fishing."

"I'll believe it when I see it," Will said with a smile. "I hope you'll change your mind. I haven't seen you in weeks. Kai says he hasn't either. At least come to poker night if you don't want to play. Though I have heard there are a couple of new sub trainees."

And that was something he took exception to. "Including your sisters."

Will had the good grace to blush. His face screwed up as he winced. "That was so not my idea. Laurel and Lisa got interested because of Bridget. They have very romantic notions about D/s. I almost had a heart attack when I found out they'd tried another club. Despite the fact that it's weird to see my sisters there, I'm happier having them at Sanctum. Thank god, Lila has a boyfriend and neither of them seem to have any interest in kink at all. Although now it seems Laurel has lost interest, too. She turned down her further training but asked if she could keep working there. I guess she likes babies more than Doms."

But she wouldn't always. He intended to leave Dallas in a few months after this deal was done and then everything would be open to her. Her one night with him would be nothing but a much-regretted mistake that would fade away once she found her soul mate. "I think she'll want to try eventually, but don't let Taggart put her with someone cold like Smith. Talk to Kai. Get involved. She needs a softer hand. Try someone her age."

Will was back to looking suspicious. "For someone who's not interested in my sister, you seem to have thought this through."

He shrugged. There wasn't much else to do. "She was my employee for…well, for longer than most. I've got to get going. I've got a couple of interviews this afternoon."

"You having a hard time replacing her?" Will asked.

"I'll never replace her." That was a stupid thing to say. "You know. I'll never find anyone as willing to argue with me. See you around."

He didn't like the way Will stared at him as he drove away. As though he was a puzzle. Will liked to solve puzzles.

It didn't matter. He had things to do and plans to make. Plans that didn't involve her.

* * * *

"Will's late. It's the doctor thing," Lila said with a frown on her pretty face. "They think they're all gods and we mere mortals should wait at their leisure."

Laurel thought Lila had been a nurse for way too long. "Or he's stuck in traffic."

Laurel kind of wished her brother would get here. She thought she'd seen his car pull up a few minutes before, but he hadn't walked in yet. She'd skipped breakfast and now she was shaky. She was totally ready for her neurologist brother and trauma nurse sister to pay for lunch. Especially since she'd taken a pay cut in order to salvage her pride.

"Where are we going?" Lisa asked as she stepped up, settling her purse on her shoulder. Her little sister was a senior in college, and she'd done it the hard way. She'd been working part time and going to school full time for most of her adult life, and it was all going to pay off in a few months. Baby sis was graduating with an MBA, and she was already in talks with Bridget's sister, Amy, about going to work for Slaten Industries.

"Mexican, please," Laurel said. She was totally willing to beg. "I've been dreaming about enchiladas all day."

"Is that why you didn't eat breakfast this morning?" Lila asked with a judgmental eye.

Yeah, it was awesome to live in the same apartment complex with her two sisters. Lila would show up randomly to make sure she was eating right. They'd had to watch out for each other growing up due to their mom's preference for drugs over parenting, and it seemed her older sister hadn't gotten out of the habit.

"Are you on some weird diet again?" Lisa asked.

"You know how those diets go," Lila said with a sigh. "You starve yourself and then binge later. It's not good for you."

Said the two skinny chicks. She sometimes wondered who her father was. Not because she had a grand desire to meet the man so much as to punch him in the face for passing on his faulty metabolism. Lila and Lisa were graceful and willowy. Will was lean and athletic. Laurel got teased all through school for being on the chunky side.

Maybe that was why Mitch hadn't wanted her. Maybe he'd wanted a slender, graceful sub. She wondered what the two exes looked like. Probably movie stars.

"I'm not on a diet. I just was a little off this morning." A bit nauseous, but that could be anything.

Or you could be pregnant. Because you had sex without a condom. You had crazy, wild, can't-forget-about-it sex without a condom and Mitchell Bradford's sperm are probably as masculine and arrogant and aggressive as the rest of him. Knocked up. You're all kinds of knocked up.

She shoved that thinking to the side because she was an optimist. She wasn't late. Her period was coming sometime this week. She'd already felt crampy and had a nice ache in her back and her boobs were slightly tender. All signs that Mother Nature was sending her a monthly package and her egg had been wilier than that army of sperm Mitch had sent her way.

The nausea this morning could be explained away as nerves about starting a new job. She'd only been here for a week and she got a little nervous about handling cases without having Mitch on call to answer questions. That was all.

She wondered if Mitch had hired either of the paralegals she'd sent his way. Tom and Cindy were both exceptional. And Cindy was married, so Mitch wouldn't have to worry about another employee hitting on him and making things uncomfortable.

Now that she looked back at it, she'd been the one to behave badly and Mitch had to put up with it. Yes, they had chemistry, but he'd been clear about not wanting to act on it. She'd practically sexually harassed the man.

"Are you all right?" Lila asked. "You went pale. Give me your hand."

She didn't have to. Lila moved in, grasping her right hand and feeling for her pulse.

"What's going on?" Will asked, his eyes concerned as he strode in. Her brother was dressed in slacks and a snowy-white dress shirt. He'd likely left his white coat in the car. Sometimes she thought he should wear a Superman shirt under his clothes. Super Doc. That was her big bro.

"Her pulse rate is high," Lila said, her voice the same flat monotone she used in the ER.

"I'm fine." She pulled her arm out of Lila's hand, but then Will was checking her. She rolled her eyes and looked to her youngest sibling. "Have I thanked you for not going into the medical field?"

Lisa grinned. "They would have been bossy either way."

Will let go. "She's fine, though she is paler than normal."

"Complain to my northern European ancestors. Can we please get some food now? We're supposed to be celebrating Lisa passing her classes, not worrying about my health. Which is fine by the way. I'm perfectly normal."

Because it was normal to get pregnant when you have sex while you're ovulating and forget to wear protection of any kind.

She was done. She was stopping by after work and getting a stupid pee on the stick pregnancy test and putting these thoughts out of her head. Worrying about being pregnant was making her insane. Of course, so was worrying about Mitch.

Had he fired Sharon? She should call and see. Had he managed to turn the office into a fortress yet? She would bet he'd blocked off all the natural light and now the only illumination was fluorescent. And he'd likely eaten like crap and stopped recycling.

None of that was her concern. She was off the Mitchell Bradford improvement committee.

"All right, you say you're fine, I'll believe you," Lila said with a nod. "I'm going to run to the bathroom and then I'll be ready to go."

"I'll go with you." Lisa followed their sister.

She was left alone with Will, who was staring at her the same way he had when she'd been fifteen and had snuck out of their trailer to make out with Jimmy Hodges.

"What happened with Mitch?"

She rolled her eyes. She'd been playing the brat with her brother since before she knew the word had more than one meaning. "He was difficult, to say the least. He was absolutely the most annoying boss I've ever worked for."

And weirdly the most thoughtful. He'd been the one to push her to become a paralegal. He'd supported her through all the training. Most bosses would have offered to hire her back when she was done with school, but Mitch had understood she needed the money. He'd let her work part time but never changed her salary and never complained when he had to do things she would have done as the office manager.

And he'd given her those law books for graduation and told her if she wanted to go further, he would support her through law school.

He'd actually been a great boss. He simply couldn't love her.

"I got sick of banging my head against the massive wall that is Mitchell Bradford. I need a job where I don't have to fight the boss every single time I need to change something. Back when I was only his office manager, I had the time to plot and plan my way around him. Now that I'm also his paralegal…was his paralegal, I don't have time to try to make the new copy machine look like the old copy machine because Mitch has issues with change. I had to kick the damn thing in exactly the right place to get it to work, but does the high-and-mighty Mitch see reason? Nope. He liked the copy machine. He brought the stupid copy machine with him from California. He claimed the copy machine had been more faithful than his last wife."

Will winced. "I told you not to get him started on his ex-wives. It's a sore spot for him."

It was more than a sore spot. The two ex-Mrs. Bradfords were very likely the reason Mitch had never been willing to give her a shot. He'd spent his love and affection on women who hadn't returned it and now he wouldn't try again. He would hold on to his bitterness the same way he'd attempted to hold on to that rattrap old copy machine. Of course, she'd managed to get around that. While Mitch had been playing poker with the Taggart brothers one Friday afternoon, she'd simply had a new one brought in and the old one scrapped.

And now he loved the new copy machine.

"Well, I don't have to worry about any of it now. I have a spiffy new job."

"That pays less than half of what your old job did."

She frowned. Where were Lila and Lisa? This was starting to seem very much like a classic Will interrogation. And how did Will know what she was making? "I'm going to get a lot of experience here."

"Will they let you go to law school and continue to pay you? Because I believe that was Mitch's offer. You're telling me he was so difficult that you would walk away from twice the pay and a boss who supports you financially through school for some experience that won't mean anything if you don't go to law school?"

Yep. This was an interrogation. "It wasn't working. It was too hard. Look, Will, you know I had feelings for him."

"Yes, which is exactly why I had to wonder if Mitch had done something he shouldn't."

She was getting weak in the knees. "No. He didn't do anything. I decided it was a good time to start over. I like it here so can we stop talking about this?"

He slanted a suspicious stare her way. "Fine. You don't want to work with Mitch any more. Is there a reason you no longer want your Sanctum membership? Because the last time we discussed it, you were quite adamant about getting training. You jumped through all the hoops, and you've even been spending your weekends watching kids to pay your way. But now, all of the sudden you quit without any better reason than you changed your mind."

"I did." She wasn't sure what else to say. Everyone had been right. She'd been interested in D/s because of Mitch. She didn't want anyone but Mitch. Hopefully in a few months she would be able to get the irritating man out of her head. "I changed my mind."

"Without even meeting the training Dom selected for you? I'm supposed to believe that? You fought me, tried to get around me, and all so you can quit before you start?"

Her head was now extremely light and it made her stomach churn. "I'm keeping my promises. I told Taggart I would continue to work in the nursery, and he's going to pay me now."

Will was frowning at her, but it seemed like that was all he'd done since he'd walked in the door. "Are you all right? Laurel, sit down. You're very pale."

But it was already too late. Her peripheral vision was fading. She heard Will shout as she started toward the floor.

Four hours later she was doing some frowning of her own. "I'm fine. I needed to get something to eat and now I've wasted an entire afternoon, and I don't even want to think about how much that ambulance trip is going to cost me. I could have solved the problem with a five-dollar sandwich but no, Dr. Daley has to subject me to a million and one medical tests."

Will sighed as he moved to her hospital bed. He glanced around the room where Lila and Lisa were sitting. "Has she been this surly the whole time?"

Lisa nodded. "Yep. And don't get her started on the food."

No one would let her have any food until all the vampires had done their worst. Finally, after they'd decided she wasn't dying, she got to have some pudding. Yippee.

"I'm ready to go home, Will. I'm fine. I feel great. I want to go home." She was sick of being bullied by Will and Lila, who were using the whole "we work at this hospital" thing to their advantage.

She was really glad there was that patient confidentiality law in place.

Will held his hands up. "All right. I'll push the nurse to get you out of here as soon as your blood work comes back."

The doctor chose that moment to enter. He was a kid, probably in his first year or two of residency. He had a clipboard in his hand and a big smile on his face. "Dr. Daley, your sister's blood work is all perfectly fine."

"Hey, what happened to confidentiality?" She sat up but took a deep breath. She was fine. Her blood work was fine.

She wasn't pregnant. That was good. That was amazing.

So why did she feel so…lost?

Will patted the ER doc on the back. "Thanks, Barry. I appreciate it. I know I've been a little paranoid, but she's my sister. I've been watching out for her for a very long time."

Barry practically beamed at Will. "Of course, sir. All her blood work is normal. I'm glad to be the bearer of good tidings and, on another note, I'm so excited to be on your service next week. I'm looking forward to a stint in neuro, and you're the best."

She was going to vomit for different reasons now.

Lila was on her feet. "I'd like to see her blood work, please. Something's off with her and it has been for a couple of weeks."

Now that she wasn't hiding anything, she didn't think twice about letting Lila take a look at her chart. She didn't care. She wasn't pregnant. She wasn't carrying Mitchell's baby and it was all over. That was a good thing.

Wasn't it?

Barry turned the chart over. "Of course. At this point, I'm sure she feels a little off. Remind her to eat and to get enough rest. She's healthy. The pregnancy is in its early stages, so she needs to eat and get enough water and rest and she'll be fine."

The room seemed to stop. Everything got very quiet, and slowly all three of her siblings turned her way.

Barry seemed to understand something had gone wrong. His eyes went wide. "Uhm, so no one knew she was pregnant?"

"I thought you said my blood work was normal." She was pregnant. Knocked up. Having his baby. Oh, god. She was having Mitch's baby.

He shrugged and stuttered as he started backing out of the room. "It's perfectly normal for a pregnant woman. I assumed since you're surrounded by medical people that someone would have figured out you're pregnant. I mean, I haven't examined you, but I thought you're probably just a couple of weeks into your first trimester. Right?"

Will's face had turned a nice shade of pink. "I don't have to examine her. I'm pretty sure she's two weeks pregnant. Is that about right, Laurel?"

Lila was combing through her chart. "How can you tell, Will?"

"Because that's when she quit working for Mitch," Will said, every word dropping like a lead pipe.

Lisa was the only one who didn't look grim. "Whoa. You quit working for Mitch because you finally went at it like a couple of rabbits, didn't you? This is some serious drama. We're going to need more pudding cups. Don't they keep popsicles somewhere?"

Will sent their youngest sister a stern glare.

Lisa simply shrugged. "Laurel isn't the only one who had to skip lunch. I might not be eating for two, but I'm still hungry."

"I'm going to get someone to run these results again." Lila shook her head at the chart. "Laurel isn't this foolish. There is no way she's pregnant. I'll call in Dr. Bates."

Will nodded. "She's who I would call. But you're wrong about Laurel. She is that foolish."

"No. She couldn't be." Lila squared off with Will.

Lisa hopped up on Laurel's bed. "I think we're about to get the mom lecture again."

"Laurel wouldn't be so completely irresponsible as to not use birth control. She saw what happened to our mother. She knows how terrible it can be for a child to not even know who her father is," Lila said passionately.

"Oh, I know who the father is," Will shot back. "Don't worry. He'll be in this kid's life. Well, unless I kill him first."

Tears streamed down her face. She had been irresponsible. So irresponsible. She was having a baby and the father didn't want a child. She'd grown up without a father, depending on Will to take care of her when she was younger, and now she was putting her own baby in the same position.

Unwanted. Unloved. A mistake.

Lisa's hand found hers. "Hey, it's going to be okay, Laurel. It's all right."

She shook her head. "No, it's not."

There was a brief knock on the door and Laurel was certain they were about to be asked to keep the noise down. They would have to move this party out of the ER.

She would try to sneak away, try to get back to her tiny apartment that would be terrible for raising a baby in. There was barely enough room for her. Babies required lots of stuff. Babies required love and affection and care, and how was she going to make it work?

The door opened and Mitch Bradford stood there looking like he'd run a couple of miles without bothering to change into sweats. He was still wearing his everyday armor, but his hair was windblown and he had a nice sheen of sweat on his brow. "Laurel, I just got the text from Will. Are you all right?"

Her brother had texted Mitch?

Before she could say a thing, her brother let his fist do the talking. Will reared back and Mitch went flying out of the room.

It looked like the worst day of her life wasn't over yet.

Chapter Four

Mitch hit the nurse's station with a crash, his spine slamming into the edge. It took him a moment to truly register the fact that Will had gone completely insane and was attacking him.

"Someone call security." He heard the nurse's voice behind him.

"No need," Will said. "I can take out the trash myself."

Will came at him, throwing another punch, but this time Mitch was ready. He ducked, narrowly missing getting clocked right across the nose. Will was serious. He wasn't fucking around. He'd obviously found out what had happened with Laurel.

Had Laurel told her brother it was all his fault? He certainly hadn't expected that from her.

"Nothing happened?" Will asked the question in a mocking tone. "Earlier today you told me nothing happened. Want to amend that statement, Counselor?"

Mitch held his ground. If they were going to do this here, then he would take his punishment, but he wasn't going to go out quietly and he wasn't going to stand here and let Will beat the shit out of him. "What happened is between me and Laurel."

"Will, stop it. You are going to break a hand and then where will you be?" The three Daley sisters were standing right outside the door to Laurel's room. The oldest one, Lila, was staring at both of them with a ferocious frown on her face. "Also, none of this helps Laurel."

"I don't care right now," Will shot back and then returned his attention to Mitch. "You promised me she would be safe with you. You promised you would take care of her."

Shit. This was about the incident? He hadn't mentioned that Laurel had been shot at because she'd begged him not to and there hadn't been anything Will could do. He'd been in Chicago at the time. No wonder the man was pissed. "I'm so sorry. I wasn't expecting it, obviously. It never occurred to me that she would be in that kind of danger. I swear if it had, I would have put a guard in front of that door."

Will stopped. "What are you talking about? She didn't need a guard. She needed a fucking condom, asshole."

"Oh, Mitch is talking about when Laurel got shot at two weeks ago," Lisa supplied helpfully.

"What?" Will turned again, this time sending that glare Laurel's way.

Condom? Why was Laurel in the hospital? "I'm perfectly clean. I had a damn checkup a few weeks ago. Call Sanctum. My blood tests are clean."

Laurel looked so young and vulnerable standing there in a hospital gown. It looked like she'd cried off her mascara. His gut clenched. She'd been crying. She clutched at the back of the gown to keep it together. Why was she here? What had happened? In that moment, he no longer cared what she'd said about him. He merely wanted to know she was all right.

"Laurel, I swear I don't have any kind of STD." He kept his distance because it looked like he was the bad guy in this scenario. "My blood tests are clean and I'll be honest, I haven't had sex with anyone in a good long while. Anyone else, obviously. Baby, if you're sick, something's gone wrong, but I swear it's not me. I would never put you at risk."

"You don't have the clap, asshole. You have working sperm," Will said between clenched teeth. "Hence the need for a condom."

The words didn't compute. He stood there like a complete idiot as everyone stared at him.

His best friend waved a hand in front of his face. Ex-best friend. It looked like that was done. He was good at collecting exes. Ex-wives, ex-friends, ex-lovers who promised there wasn't a problem…

"She's on the pill," he said. That's what they were talking about, right? Sperm had been mentioned.

Yes, I am fully functional, buddy, and guess what? We flooded her that night. Is it really any wonder we're here? And you can thank me later.

His dick was still getting him in trouble. Had his dick gotten them all in trouble? Like serious trouble. Like lifetime of being bound together kind of trouble.

Like he couldn't give up Laurel because he'd gotten her pregnant kind of trouble?

All eyes swung Laurel's way and she flushed.

"Did you tell him you were on the pill?" Will asked. He had the pissed-off father-figure thing down.

Father. He was going to be a father. Was he going to be a father? It wasn't like Laurel didn't have a choice in the matter.

"I never said that," Laurel replied and Mitch watched as she steeled herself.

"I asked you about it and you said everything was fine." He'd gone over that night about three hundred times since then.

"It is fine. I'm fine. You don't have to worry." Her chin came up in what he liked to think of as her queenly pose. When she looked at him like that he knew he was in for stubbornness. "Thank you for worrying, but I'll be fine. I'm going to get dressed now. I would appreciate it if the two of you could stop making a scene."

She turned and walked back into her room. Lisa gave him a grin and a wink before turning and following her sister, but Lila remained even after the door had closed behind the other two.

"Well, this is a mess. Will, you're not making this better," Lila said.

"I'm sorry. I lost my head for a minute there," Will admitted.

"You knew she had a thing for him," Lila complained.

Will shrugged. "I did. At the time, I didn't think it would be so bad. I thought Mitch cared about her, too."

"I do. I care about her." Laurel was pregnant. She was carrying his very small, probably-no-more-than-a-couple-of-cells child inside her body right that very moment.

He didn't want kids. He'd never wanted them. It wasn't that he didn't like them. He liked his friends' kids fine, but he would be a shit dad. He hadn't been close to his own but his mother never let up that he was exactly like the bastard. Unreliable. Selfish.

Two failed marriages had proven her right.

"Then what are you going to do?" Lila asked, though a bit more softly now. "Mr. Bradford, I've only met you a couple of times, but I've seen the way you look at my sister. Let me see if I can figure out what happened. Laurel is a stubborn girl and she learned early to fight for what she wants. She decided she wanted you and she pushed you to the point that you gave in. You then did something stupid and caused her to run."

"What did you do that was stupid?" Will asked. "Wait. I want to get back to the shooting thing."

He was stunned. He was actually lucky his freaking knees were still working because the knowledge that Laurel was pregnant—with his baby—was...he wasn't even quite sure what it was. His mind was working overtime, but his mouth seemed to move on its own.

"Derek is sure that it was some kid trying to rob the dentist next door. Apparently he was high and he was looking to get higher. Laurel startled him and he shot at her through the glass in the reception area."

"Oh my god. Why wasn't I told?"

Lila chuckled. "Uhm, because you tend to lose your cool, big brother. Thank you, Randy. I think we've got everything under control. Dr. Daley was a bit upset, but he's calmed down now and he's not going to cause any more trouble with the lawyer who'll probably sue the hell out of him and the hospital we work at."

Mitch turned. Lila was talking to a security guard who looked deeply unhappy he'd been pulled from his nap or something.

"Mitch isn't going to sue us," Will replied.

"No, but if I ever get the chance to punch you, I'll take it."

"Was I right?" Lila asked.

Mitch was totally happy he'd drawn the middle Daley sister. Lisa was an imp who didn't seem to take anything seriously and Lila kind of scared him. And he didn't scare easy. Laurel was stubborn, but she didn't have Lila's grim determination. "About what happened? Yeah. She pushed the hell out of me and things exploded and I was a little freaked out afterward."

"You didn't think you two should talk about it beyond asking briefly if she was on birth control?" Will was right back to pissed off.

Maybe Randy the guard shouldn't have shuffled off so quickly. "She left me, Will. I wanted to talk, but she walked out and she didn't walk back in. I gave her space. Hell, I needed space. I called her on Saturday and again on Sunday. She didn't answer. I walked back in Monday morning like a fucking idiot with flowers and shit and she quit with an e-mail. An e-mail."

She'd decided he was a bad bet and he couldn't blame her.

Was she scared that she'd be stuck with him for the rest of her life?

And so much for going to his grave with the flowers secret. His mouth wouldn't stop.

"Good. Then you and Laurel can work this out." Lila gave him a nod. "I suggest you do that thing you two seem obsessed with doing or she'll walk all over you."

"What thing?" Mitch asked.

Lila gave him a mysterious smile and disappeared into the room.

"She's telling you to top Laurel." Will scrubbed a hand through his hair. "She's probably right. Laurel isn't reasonable when she feels like she's in a corner. You've convinced her you don't want her."

"I never said I don't want her. I simply want better for her." She deserved better than he could give her.

Will stepped in front of him. "You're all she's got now. So man up and be better for her because you've got one shot at this. I get that you've always thought we're so different. You come from money and I don't, but we both had shitty parents who did nothing to get us ready for kids of our own. I had to grow up a long time ago. It's your turn. It's your turn to shove all that shit aside and be more. She needs you to be more."

"I didn't mean to hurt her." And he hadn't really come from money. Sure his father had been wealthy and he'd been given a trust fund on his eighteenth birthday, but his mother had made her money the hard way—by marrying it over and over and over again.

"I know. Why did you lie to me? You said nothing happened."

"I was trying to protect us both, I guess." God, he was going to miss Will. "I didn't want to lose your friendship and I knew Laurel wouldn't want you to know about it. She said everything was fine."

"Lesson number one. When she says she's fine, you're in trouble. There's no such thing as fine. It's like Southern chicks saying bless your heart. What they actually mean is you're an idiot. Fine means something like the same thing except it carries connotations that violence could happen if you don't figure out what's wrong. How bad was it?"

"The sex? It was fantastic." It had been the absolute best sex of his life.

Will groaned. "No, asshole. Never, ever tell me that. Ever. Again." He shuddered. "I was talking about whatever you did to make her run."

He needed to stop being so literal. "I said it was a mistake."

Will winced. "Okay, well, the flowers thing was a good idea. Maybe you can try that again. She also likes those cheese Danishes from the bakery down the street from her place."

"I tried that, too." At least he was on the right track. "Unfortunately, I brought them in with the flowers and..."

"She quit via e-mail. I'm sorry about that, man. It was a cowardly thing to do."

Or she'd stopped caring. This was kind of what he did. He was difficult and after a while, people stopped caring and they disappeared. "I know I let you down, Will. I'm sorry about that."

Will sighed. "You lost your head over a girl and now you're going to do the right thing. I knew you two were combustible the minute you got in the same room together. I thought she would be good for you and vice versa."

What had he been thinking? "How am I good for her?"

"You push her. Laurel sometimes accepts her place far too easily. Did you know she didn't even negotiate her salary at the new place? I have a friend who works there and I had him look into it. She simply accepted the offer and never thought about requesting more. Without you, she never would have gone back to school. She wouldn't have become a paralegal. She stays an office manager, and there's nothing wrong with that, but Laurel needs more."

"She's too smart to get stuck. She should go to law school. She would enjoy it. She needs a job where pay doesn't matter, so get off her back about this one. This type of work is exactly where she should be. Helping people. That's what makes Laurel tick."

"Yes, and you saw that and you made it possible for her to do that, and in a safe environment, and you made sure she didn't lack for money. So get over your damage, as Kai would say. You're good for her."

He leaned against the wall, studying Will. Maybe this wasn't as bad as he'd thought it would be. "Kai would never say that. He would sound like a massive intellectual douchebag. 'Mitchell, your problems stem from a childhood abandonment by your father and verbal abuse and neglect from your maternal influences.'"

Will made a vomiting sound. "I love the dude, but I want to strangle him when he gets going about childhood issues. Doesn't he know manly men don't talk about that shit? We beat each other up and then get a beer. You want a beer, man?"

At least he hadn't lost his best friend. "I would love one, but I think I need to talk to your sister."

"The good news is she came in an ambulance so she doesn't have a car. I'll do you a solid and refuse to give her a ride back. If she gives you any trouble, just pick her up and move her."

He went a little shaky at the thought. "I can't do that. She's pregnant."

Will shook his head. "No. Don't even think that way. She's here today because she didn't eat breakfast and got woozy. She's not a delicate flower. The baby is seriously tiny. So don't let her fool you into thinking she's fragile. Laurel's strong. She'll be fine and the two of you have a lot to talk about. Don't let her shut you out."

The door opened and Laurel emerged, followed by her sisters. She'd changed back into the same clothes she'd been wearing earlier, a sweet-looking floral print skirt, a pink blouse, and flats. Her hair was pulled back and she was looking more like her normal, competent self than before when she'd looked like she needed him.

She did need him. And Will was right. It was time to man up.

"Well, I think the two of you have a lot to talk about," Lila said. "Mitch, weren't you going to say something to Laurel?"

His heart was suddenly pounding because these were waters he'd promised he'd never, ever swim in again. He was about to dive into the deep end of the pool. "Yes. I do have something to say. Laurel, I'll marry you."

Will groaned again. "Buddy, we're going to have to work on your delivery."

Laurel simply turned and walked away.

He went after her because this time, she wasn't getting away from him.

* * * *

I'll marry you.

Laurel walked toward the exit. It didn't matter that she didn't have a ride. She would catch a bus or walk to a train station. She was not going to stay there with Mitch "I'll marry you because I have to" Bradford. He'd said the words with all the enthusiasm of a man on his way to an execution.

Pregnant. She was pregnant and Mitch knew, and now he was ready to do right by the woman he'd apparently soiled. That's how her brother had reacted. For a moment, she'd been transported back in time to where Will was going to fight a duel over her lost honor.

She hadn't lost a damn thing. No. She'd gained a whole other human being and all because she hadn't been able to think straight when Mitch touched her.

That was absolutely no reason to marry the man.

"Laurel!"

She settled her purse on her shoulder and ignored him. There was a train station two blocks over. She knew exactly where it was because she'd come out to this hospital many times to see Will and Lila, though she never would again because neither of those ungrateful wretches had offered her a ride. They were cut off.

Actually, it served her right to have to hoof it. It proved that when a girl screwed up as totally as she had, she was on her own. Or she would be if Mitch would stop pursuing her.

"Laurel!"

She kept walking. Outside, it was a glorious day. It was spring and everything was in bloom. Even her damn womb.

Mitch caught up with her. "Laurel, sweetheart, I'm going to give you a chance to save this. Stop now and come with me. We'll get something to eat and talk about this."

She didn't look his way. "I think I'll take door number two."

"You won't like door number two," he warned.

She was far too stubborn to care.

"All right then. Door number two it is."

Laurel nearly screamed because one minute she'd been walking and the next she was up and in his arms, being cradled against that masculine chest of his. "Hey, you can't do that. Put me down."

"Nope. This is door number two and unfortunately, I'm parked on the other side of the lot." Mitch had turned and was walking right back toward where they'd just left. "What have you had to eat today?"

She was oddly comfortable in his arms. She couldn't remember the last time a man had picked her up and carried her around, her body protected by his. Probably not since she'd been a child and Will had carried her when she'd been hurt or sick. The sweetness of it pierced her. And then she remembered the only reason he was doing it was for the baby. "You should put me down. You're going to throw out your back."

He stopped and stared down at her. "What did you say?"

Oh, that was new. He was cold, arctic cold even as his arms tightened around her. "I said I'm too heavy and you should put me down."

"That's what I thought you said." He started moving again, his eyes back up. "All right. I'm going to give you that one because I've never set rules with you. Here's rule number one. I hear you insult yourself again and there will be punishment. How do you expect to raise a girl who gives a damn about herself if her mother doesn't? How do you expect to raise a boy who respects women if his mother doesn't care about herself? So expect the punishment for those infractions to be harsh."

What was happening? And when the hell did Mitch become the voice of reason? She couldn't come up with one logical argument. He was right. "What are you doing, Mitch?"

"Setting the rules. Now answer my question. When was the last time you ate?"

They were about to walk past the ER doors and toward the west lot.

Naturally her siblings were now outside and they were all watching the show.

"She started a bowl of cereal this morning." Lisa had impeccable hearing. "But it was the diet kind and she didn't eat it because she had morning sickness. At the time I thought it might be a bug, but now we know it's y'all's illicit love child."

She had another shot at getting out of here. Lila would be the weak link. Lisa had obviously become a spy for Team Mitchell and Will was being a jerkface. "Lila, go and get security. Tell them I'm being kidnapped. Mitch, let me down now."

Lila smiled and gave her a friendly wave. "No, honey. I think he's being the sensible one."

"You take care of her." Will's words were for Mitch.

"I intend to. She might not like how I do it though. Can someone pack a bag for her? I'm afraid if I let her inside her apartment, she'll lock me out."

"Damn straight I will."

"I have a key," Lisa said. "I'll do it. Come on, Laurel. Don't look at me that way. He's doing the Dom thing. And isn't this kind of what you wanted? Mitch and a baby? Looks like you get both."

Mitch and a baby. Was that what she'd wanted?

Mitch thanked Lisa and then strode toward his massive, gas-guzzling SUV she'd thought at first was to make up for his penis, and then she'd seen his penis. His penis probably needed the roomy interior of the SUV to feel comfortable.

Mitch and a family were what she had wanted, but she'd been willing to settle for just Mitch. Now it was Mitch who would be settling.

"If I set you down are you going to run?"

And be less mature than she'd already been today? One thing was right. They needed to talk. "No."

He gently set her on her feet and opened the door. "Will you please eat something? I'll take you anywhere you want. We need to figure out how this is going to work."

She'd wanted enchiladas earlier in the day, but now all she could think about was pasta and she knew exactly where to get it. "Take me to Top."

Twenty minutes later, she sighed as Sean Taggart placed a plate of pasta carbonara in front of her. She'd already inhaled a Caesar salad. She might have been nauseous this morning, but she was ravenous now.

"Are you sure I can't get you a glass of wine? The sommelier has this paired with a Chablis that truly complements the creamy texture of the dish," Sean explained. He was dressed in his chef whites. She was much more used to calling him Master Sean and seeing him in leathers, but then Sean Taggart was a Master of more than one thing. He was definitely a master with pasta and sauces.

She was about to turn him down when Mitch decided to take over.

"She can't because she's pregnant."

Why did she suddenly feel like every eye in the place was on her? The crowd was light at this time of day, and it seemed like Mitch had shouted out into an almost silent room.

Sean held out a hand, a smile creasing his handsome face. "Really? That's exciting news. Congratulations, man. I didn't know you two were even seeing each other."

That was just like a man. "We're not seeing each other and how do you know the baby is his? Maybe it's someone else's. And I'm barely pregnant."

"The baby is absolutely, one hundred percent mine, and we're definitely seeing each other now. We're getting married," Mitch declared with ruthless determination.

Sean put a friendly hand on Mitch's shoulder. "Good to hear it, man. Let us know when the wedding is and we'll be happy to cater. Macon's been dying to do a wedding cake. He and Ally got married in Vegas so he didn't do his own. You two enjoy and let me know if I can get you anything else. The dessert this evening is a bread pudding, so you'll want to save room."

She was almost distracted by that. Almost.

"Why did you tell him that?" She leaned over so she could maybe minimize the damage. The servers were looking her way and whispering behind their hands. It wouldn't have been a big deal if it was Ally. She knew Ally, but there were two women she didn't know talking about her "engagement" that wasn't going to happen. "He didn't need to know that."

Mitch looked at her over his porterhouse with truffle mashed potatoes and shrugged. "Everyone's going to find out anyway. And there's no such thing as being barely pregnant. You're either pregnant or you're not."

"Well maybe I would like more than three minutes to process it before we tell the world that we screwed up."

"Did we?"

She sat back, regarding him. He looked tired. Like he wasn't sleeping or he was staying at the office. He did that at times. She would walk in and find him asleep on the couch in his office and she would close the shades and put a blanket over him and try to let him get an hour or two. "What is that supposed to mean, Mitch?"

This was the type of conversation that would typically upset her stomach. Not so now. She couldn't resist the siren call of that creamy sauce or the bacon and pancetta. Even the noodles were perfect.

"It means that I didn't use a condom and you didn't ask me to use one."

She leaned over. "I didn't think. I wasn't thinking, Mitchell."

He cut a piece of steak but didn't eat it. "Do you usually not think?"

"Of course not." How did she put this without sounding pathetic? "Not that there have been many times for me to not think."

"I never have sex without a condom, Laurel. I'll be honest, there hasn't been a lot lately, but that's simply not something I do. I'm always careful. The last thing I want is to get trapped again."

"Well, I guess I should thank you for at least being honest." Maybe she was going to lose her appetite.

He reached across the table and put a hand on hers. It was the first time he'd willingly touched her outside the kiss or that night they'd had sex or when he was trying to kidnap her. Tender. He was trying to be tender with her and it made Laurel stop.

"I wasn't saying you trapped me, Laurel. I was wondering if maybe deep down I wanted to be trapped with you. I was wondering if subconsciously maybe we knew what we were doing and we took the risk anyway because deep down we wondered if it wouldn't be so bad."

She'd wondered the same thing herself. "Maybe we did."

"How many boyfriends have you had?"

"How many girlfriends have you had?"

He shrugged. "Two. But if you're asking about women I've slept with, it's a lot more. I'd ballpark it at thirty."

That was a big number. And only two girlfriends? "You married both of your girlfriends?"

"No. Margot was my college girlfriend. We went to law school together and when we got out, I built my firm from the ground up. My father threw me a bone and got me hooked up with a man named Garrison Cage."

She knew his business story. She'd spent long nights looking him up on the Internet. "The tech guru. That's why they called you the Silicon Counselor."

He'd been a legal consultant to some of the biggest tech firms in the business. He'd made millions before it all fell apart.

"Yeah, I had a partner in the firm. Nolan Pence. We got close in law school. He was kind of my first friend, I guess. I moved around a lot as a kid. I never made close friends. Anyway, he decided he liked both the company and my wife. I'd been stupid because I'd made Margot a partner even though she wasn't practicing at the time. She was mostly fucking Nolan. They had the majority of the firm behind the two of them, so I was asked to leave."

Yes, she knew that part, too. "So who was the other girlfriend if it wasn't your second wife?"

She asked the question with a cautious tone because this was the first conversation they'd had about his personal life. They'd had long lunches talking about the law or sports or politics, but they'd never done this.

They'd had sex and made a baby and they'd never even gone on a date.

"I had a girlfriend when I was a teenager. My mom sent me to boarding school the last couple of years of high school. Best thing that ever happened to me. Her name was Natalie. She went to the girls' school. I guess I was wrong. I guess she was really my first friend. We were together for three years."

"Did you break up when you went to college?"

He shook his head. "She died. Car accident. She was coming home with some friends and a drunk driver killed them all. I found out from the news the next day because all the people who would have told me were dead." He took a quick drink of the Coke he'd ordered. "Those were my two girlfriends. I wouldn't call Joy so much a girlfriend as a hookup gone wrong. I left San Francisco and moved to LA, where I started a new firm, and I met Joy at a Hollywood party. I was drinking a lot back then. I woke up in Vegas married about two weeks later. The marriage lasted three years and then she divorced me and now she's living in our old Hollywood Hills house that I still pay the upkeep for. So that's how I have two girlfriends and two wives but not the same. Now, I've politely answered your question. Could you please answer mine?"

She felt a little battered. He'd spoken in a monotone, but how was she supposed to handle that? The girl he'd loved had died and he'd tried twice more and gotten screwed in every way a man could. And she expected him to try again? The enormity of his losses weighed on her, but she answered him anyway. "I've had three serious boyfriends and that's how many guys I've slept with, too. Well, four now."

Three boyfriends. Not a one of them had cheated on her. There was no grand trauma in her past concerning men. Her high school boyfriend had moved away for college and they'd drifted apart. The guy she'd dated through college had asked her to marry him, but she'd known they were far too similar and broken it off. And she'd split up with her recent boyfriend shortly after she'd met Mitchell Bradford and realized she couldn't feel for the man anything close to what she felt for Mitch.

And now she was wondering if it was all for nothing because Mitch had been through too much. Will had told her once that Mitch was broken. She'd thought she could fix him.

"That's all? That's not a lot, Laurel," he said, his face grim. "I was somewhat wild at certain points in my life."

"I never did anything wild in my life. Well, until that night." Until she'd thrown caution right out the door and made a baby with the man who had fascinated her from the moment she met him.

But now she had to wonder if that meant she loved him. She didn't even know him. Not the real Mitch. She wasn't sure he let anyone know the real him. He was a man who believed in contracts and exchanges.

Marriage was a contract, but not one he put a lot of faith in. But there was another type he did believe in.

"I think we should get married, Laurel."

What if she could get to know him? What if she could find some way inside the puzzle that was Mitch Bradford? It scared her, but her optimism was starting to return. Didn't she owe it to her child? She had to find out where his head really was on this subject.

"I don't have to have the baby, Mitch. There's a simple solution to all of this."

He went white. Like sheet white. "I don't want that. I can't stop you, but I don't want that. I know I've been a shit husband before and if I'd had my way, I wouldn't have had kids. But...Laurel, I don't want that. I don't want to get rid of anything that's a part of you."

And just like that she knew she was going to try and she knew she was going to give her all, and not only for the baby. She was going to try for her, too. She was going to try because the universe was giving her another shot and she was going to take it. "Good because I don't want that either. I'm pregnant and I think I should have the baby, but I don't think that's reason enough to get married."

"I think the baby...our baby might disagree. I grew up without a father."

"So did I. I'm not trying to cut you out, Mitch. If you want to be a part of this baby's life, I think that's great, but have you considered that you could be a part of his or her life and not be a part of mine? You were adamant about not having a relationship with me. I'm the one who pushed it."

"Laurel, I don't think I'm good for you. I'm too old and honestly, I'm tired of the whole marriage thing. I'm not any good at it. But I'm willing to try because I think if we're going to have a baby then we should try to be the best we can be. Can we try?"

Trying was what she'd always wanted to do, but she couldn't end up being another one of his ex-wives.

Maybe there was something else they could try. Something she'd always wanted to try.

"I don't like that look on your face, Laurel."

She smiled because he probably wasn't going to like her plan either.

But she'd definitely gotten her appetite back. She dug in and planned her next step.

Chapter Five

Mitch looked down at the document he'd drafted. It was a contract. He drafted those every day. It was what he did. He wasn't usually the one who signed them though. And he'd never thought he'd be writing this one.

"Is it ready?" Laurel walked in carrying a mug.

"I don't think you're supposed to be drinking coffee. Are pregnant women supposed to drink coffee?" He'd read that somewhere.

Her eyes narrowed.

"Or you could drink whatever you want," he amended. Maybe he should have written a food and drink clause into the contract.

The D/s contract he wasn't completely sure he should sign with her.

Her lips curled up and she sank onto the couch in front of him. "Good. And because you asked, no, this isn't coffee. It's hot tea. I carry some bags in my purse. I have a couple of herbals that help with things like tension and anxiety."

She was anxious? "We don't have to do this tonight. We can go to bed and talk about it again in the morning."

"I'm not anxious about the contract. I'm just tense. It's been a rough day. I have a lot to think about, you know. I need to figure out what I'm going to do about my job. I talked to Lyle. He's the head of the paralegals. He gave me the afternoon off, but he's not going to be happy to find out that I'll need maternity leave so soon. Oh, and I also had to drink tea because you have nothing but sports drinks and beer. And there is nothing in your fridge. What do you eat?"

She always asked him multiple questions at a time. It threw him off. He'd thought on more than one occasion that was her intention.

"Tomorrow, we'll go buy groceries and I'll get rid of the beer."

"Why?"

"It doesn't seem fair that I can drink and you can't. Besides, I lean on it too often at times, and I won't do that when I have a submissive in my home. As for your job, you don't have to have one or you can come back and work for me. I never actually did the paperwork to let you go. Technically, you're still my employee."

"Why didn't you do the paperwork?"

Because he hadn't wanted to let her go. Because it had seemed so permanent. "I'm lazy and Sharon gets confused about using the computer for anything but sending her grandkids e-mails."

"Sharon is still there. I'm impressed."

"Don't be. I fired her twice. She keeps showing back up."

A wide smile crossed her face. "I told her working for you would require tenacity. It's good to know someone listens. I like my new job, Mitch. I like what we do. My only problem is my insurance doesn't kick in for another couple of weeks."

She would never have to worry about money. "We'll pay out of pocket until then."

"Okay." Once he agreed to sign a D/s contract with her, she'd become quite amenable. She hadn't fought him when he'd taken her to his home instead of her own. Lisa was dropping off a bag after she finished up her night class and tomorrow he'd take her to her place after work and figure out what she needed for a long-term stay. "So should we sign the contract? I filled out the list of places you can put stuff in."

Ah, the hard and soft limits questionnaire. "It's called my penis. Let's not call it stuff."

She shrugged. "I thought you played around with vibrators and those glass things. Why glass by the way?"

"Dildos, and the glass is for play. It can be heated up or chilled for the sensation. Don't forget butt plugs, sweetheart. If you sign this, you'll get familiar with those. I like anal sex. I'll want you to try it." It wasn't a hard limit for her. She'd put it down as something she was curious about. "And you're right, you have had a hard day. Take your time and read this contract. It's got everything we talked about in it."

She picked it up. "Anything new in there? You throwing me any curve balls, like I have to greet you at the door each night naked and kiss your feet?"

He liked the naked part. His feet were actually surprisingly sensitive. "No. I did write a specific clause that's catered to our unique position and that goes on past the terms of the original contract."

Her brows rose and she picked up the contract, flipping to the back. She knew him pretty well, it seemed. She knew exactly where he would put it.

"A pregnancy clause? Interesting. You know for a man who said he didn't want kids, you sure want to be there for everything." Her eyes moved over the words, taking them in before she set it back down. Her eyes were soft as she looked at him. "You know I would never lock you out. I agree to all the terms of the clause and I'll sign it, but I want you to know I wouldn't block you even if we didn't have a contract."

The clause stated plainly that he would accompany her to all prenatal visits, all parenting and childbirth classes, and be in the delivery room and welcome at the hospital. It also stated that both parties would work out a child custody agreement no later than a month before the anticipated birth of the Bradford-Daley child in the event the parties were no longer living together.

"Were you going to tell me?" He wondered. He believed her when she said the hospital was the first time she truly knew she was pregnant, but she had to have had a clue.

"Yes. I would have told you. I might have taken a day or two, but trust me, I would have shown up on your doorstep, Mitch. I'm not a 'suffer in silence' kind of girl." Her lips quirked up and so did his dick. She was here. She was sitting on his crappy couch with her shoes off, relaxed and accepting.

If she signed that contract tonight, he was going to have her. He was going to have her every fucking night he could until the day she woke up and realized it was all a mistake.

"Laurel, do you need time to read the rest of the contract? I'm a bit more hardcore than your brother. You should think about this. I need control outside of the bedroom. I'm not picking your clothes or telling you what to eat, but I'll want a nightly routine. I'll want you here with me at night. If you do go out with your girlfriends, I'll want to know where you're going and I'll likely want to drop you off and pick you up. I'll be obnoxious about your safety and god, Laurel, don't ignore phone calls because I will never ignore yours."

She started looking through the bulk of the contract. "And what happens if I'm working or can't answer at that particular time."

"I've set up protocols."

She nodded. "Yes, I can see that."

He was going to lose her. She was going to see all the crap he would put her through and walk away to find one of those "I only want control in the bedroom" Doms.

She picked up a pen and scratched through what seemed to be a paragraph. "I'm not doing that, Mitch. The no talking about our relationship thing is never going to happen, and anyone who tells you they'll honor it is lying. I've got two sisters. I'm going to talk to them."

"I simply think it's best that we keep our relationship private." Maybe he shouldn't have sent her for her paralegal certification. He doubted the sweet office manager would have boldly marked out his clauses.

"Babe, there's no such thing. Maybe if we were having an affair that we intended to keep brief and unemotional we could, but I'm going to give this thing a go. I want to see if we can make it work, and that means I'll talk to my sisters and my friends and you should definitely talk to yours. You don't have to be an island, Mitch."

It was one clause and they were negotiating. "All right. I'll agree to lose that requirement. Do you agree to the communication protocols?"

"Yes, I will text you if I'm going to be out of pocket for more than thirty minutes. I will make every attempt to return your call within an hour and will allow you to track my phone because you're a paranoid weirdo."

"That's five smacks. Did you not read the clause where you're forbidden from calling me a paranoid weirdo?"

She started combing through the contract. "No. I didn't see that."

He chuckled. "I was kidding, Laurel. I can joke, too. I need the comfort of routine, but I'm not so insecure I can't handle your smart mouth. All big decisions that concern both of us have to be discussed. I've got a schedule that we can also discuss and agree upon. If it helps, you can track my phone, too. I'll leave you a list of my passwords."

"I already have those. I was your office manager for six months. I take it when you say decisions that concern both of us, you're talking about me making changes to the house. Because I already want to do that."

She always wanted to change things. "No. I'm not moving on that. This is my house. Maybe if we get married we can discuss certain renovations to rooms that are yours, but I think it's best we have our own spaces."

"You don't want to sleep with me?"

That was not going to happen. "What? No. That's totally in there. We share a bedroom. We sleep together and you can't kick me out without good cause. I was talking about my office and my media room. I like them the way they are. You can have the living room and the kitchen and the guestroom. If we get married. I don't know. We'll have to negotiate again."

Laurel huffed, an irritated sound, and then signed the document. "Fine. Here is your contract. I can see we have a lot of negotiating to do. I want a pretty collar. One I can wear during the day. I'll wear a more pronounced one when we're at Sanctum, but I want pretty and delicate for daywear."

She placed the contract on the table between them. She was demanding a collar. Of course, he'd covered that in the contract. He'd actually stated that she was to wear any collar he deemed fit for her, but shouldn't she like it? He wanted to please her.

"I'll let you pick your day collar. I get to pick your club collar and all your clothes for Sanctum."

"Agreed."

Fuck, he was hard. The idea that she was going to be with him at Sanctum made his cock pulse against his slacks. She would wear his collar, live in his home, let him take care of her.

She would devastate him when she left.

He shoved that thought aside. The truth was he couldn't push her away. They were having a baby and that baby would be a more permanent tie than any contract. He wasn't going to walk out on his kid. He wasn't going to toss money the kid's way and hope Laurel took care of him.

"How much have you learned?" He had to get out of that dangerous headspace. Thoughts like that could send him into dark places, and he wasn't going there with her. She was his responsibility now and he had the paperwork to prove it. He had to be in the moment with her. That was what he would do. He would live in the here and now and not worry about the future or brood over the past. Now was truly all the time they had anyway.

"About D/s? I've been reading a lot. Mostly Bridget's and Serena's and Chris's books, but they're all in the lifestyle."

"Yes, but they write a highly romanticized version of the lifestyle. How much real training have you had?"

"I've been to the classes Eve and Grace teach to new submissives and I've done some work with the married Doms, but nothing serious since someone decided he didn't want me working with Master T."

What the hell had Tag been thinking? The idea of her working with that dangerous Southerner…no. He wasn't going there. He was being in the present. "So most of what you know is intellectual."

"Yes."

"Why don't you show me how the submissives in Bridget's books greet their Doms. I think it would be a nice ritual after being apart for long periods. Something for me to look forward to."

"You would, wouldn't you? You would look forward to me greeting you at the end of the day."

Maybe that made him a pervert, but it was true. It would be the best part of his day. "Yes."

She stood up, setting the contract down beside her mug. She moved from behind the coffee table and sank down to her knees, her head dropping forward. Her knees spread and she placed her palms flat on her thighs. "Welcome home, Sir."

That wouldn't do. "I hardly think that's how Bridget wrote it. I know Will allows her to run wild, but he has his rules, too, and he would never allow Bridget to greet him like that."

Her head came up. "This is exactly how…" She turned a sweet shade of pink. "You're talking about the fact that I'm dressed. You want me to greet you naked. Mitch, you know that might not be possible with a kid."

"The kid is in utero. He doesn't care and can't be embarrassed at this point, so I'll have my naked time with his mom. He's just renting. According to that contract, I own." He owned her body. That gorgeous form was his to please, to hold, to lick and suck and fuck as he liked. He was plain about that in the contract.

He hadn't actually seen her naked. They'd made a baby, but he didn't know what her breasts looked like. It had been so quick, and now he wanted to take his time. They had months before they were going to become parents, before they had to figure everything out. He was going to use that time to memorize her body, to teach her to expect pleasure from him. He wanted her to associate him with long nights in bed spent worshipping her body.

She took a deep breath and seemed to come to some kind of decision.

Before she could rise, he held out a hand.

She looked up at him. "I thought you were a hardcore Dom. Shouldn't I rise gracefully at your command?"

"I'm the Dom who wants to make sure you're safe, Laurel. I'm the Dom who will never watch as you struggle without lending you a hand. I like ritual, but I like being there for you more, so when you get up, I will always be there to help you."

"You know sometimes you're really good at this." She placed her hand in his.

"Remember it because there will also be times I'm really bad at it. Laurel, I'm not very romantic. I forget things. I try to remember, but they slip away and I get caught up in work. I'm going to try to hold up my end of the bargain."

"Can you sum up your end of the bargain for me, counselor? In layman's terms, please."

"To make sure you're safe and happy and taken care of."

"That is a very good deal for me." There was a sheen of tears to her eyes, but he was pretty sure she wasn't sad because she moved toward him, placing her hands on his waist as she looked up at him. "And I'll do the same."

She went on her toes and lightly kissed his cheek before stepping back. Her hands worked the back of her skirt.

He sat back down because this was his time. He was the Dom and his sub was undressing for him. She needed to understand that she had his complete and undivided attention.

Her skirt slipped to the floor and she started on the buttons of her blouse, undoing each with care and precision and possibly the knowledge that she was driving him insane. It was a good insane. Or maybe she was like him. Maybe she wanted to slow down this time and make it last in a way it hadn't before. This time they'd set down the ground rules.

This time it could work.

"Take off the bra," he commanded after she'd divested herself of the blouse and was standing there in her white cotton underwear. It wasn't plain though. She had something on her panties. "Are those flamingos?"

She winced. "I probably would have worn something pretty if I'd realized I was going to get hauled to the hospital and then undress for my Dom. You should know that most of my underwear has cute stuff on it."

Then he would be buying her a whole lot of new underwear. He wasn't a Dom who wanted her to toss out the underwear completely. He liked unwrapping his present, but he wanted her in something that fit her beauty. She should be in silk and satin and lace. He was pretty sure the flamingos were wearing party hats. "Take those off, too. They're distracting."

He hadn't even looked at her breasts. He was too horrified by the underwear.

She stepped out of the offensive panties and he got his first look at

Laurel in her glory. He had to catch his breath because she was even more beautiful than he'd imagined her. She was a fucking fertility goddess with her curvy hips and full breasts. There was a slight curve to her belly that made him wonder what she was going to look like when she was full and ripe with child. His child. "Come here, Laurel."

Her golden brown hair was loose around her shoulders, her eyes slightly suspicious. Did she think he was about to reject her? Was she worried she wasn't pretty enough? Because he thought he'd already shown her how much he wanted her.

"Grip your wrists behind your back," he ordered when she moved close enough.

She took a deep breath and complied, the position causing her breasts to thrust out.

Fuck those were gorgeous. She had full breasts, likely a large *C* cup, maybe even a *D*, with big pink and brown nipples he could suck on for days. "How sensitive are they?"

"They're sensitive, but they don't hurt."

He reached out and let his fingers trace a line from her collarbone to her right nipple. The minute he brushed the top of her breast, the skin underneath flushed, the nipple hardened. Like a flower blooming to his touch.

Because he was sitting down, those pretty nipples were almost at the level of his mouth. He leaned over and placed a very chaste kiss on one and then the other. "Do you know what I'm going to do to you tonight?"

"I'm kinda hoping you're planning on fooling around."

He traced the areole of her nipple with his fingertip, utterly fascinated with her beauty. "Don't be ridiculous. Fooling around is for high school kids. I'm going to make love to you. Properly this time, and with complete control. I acted like an idiot that night."

"You were passionate."

"Passion tends to get us into trouble. I'm going to be thoughtful this time. I'm going to make you scream for me. I'm going to teach you what it means to be my sub. Tell me something and be honest with me. I'll know if you're not honest. I might not be in the courtroom a lot, but I can tell when a witness is lying."

"You're quite good at it," she agreed in a breathless voice.

"Why did you join Sanctum?"

She hesitated and he worried that she wouldn't answer. He filled in the time by moving his hands down to her hips and kissing his way to her belly. He breathed in the sweet scent of her arousal.

Finally, she replied. "To try to get close to you."

"So you were hoping to make me jealous." Her pussy was perfect, but he couldn't truly see it. "Sit down on the coffee table and spread your legs for me."

"Mitch, I don't think that's a good idea."

"I'm going to be patient with you because you're new and we're learning together, so let me make this plain. You have ten seconds to sit on the coffee table, spread your legs, and show me your pussy, or I'll put you over my lap and we'll start with a count of fifteen." He reached around her and grabbed her mug and the contract. Now the coffee table was perfectly clutter free and ready for her. He held a hand out to help her sit down.

Her lips had firmed, her jawline becoming harder than normal. Ah, she was chafing at the confines. He intended to push her a bit harder.

"I wasn't trying to make you jealous." Even as she was arguing, she let him help her down. She placed herself on the coffee table he'd bought because it had a sturdy feel to it. He'd bought nothing for simple beauty, preferring function over form.

Now he had to think that having a naked Laurel totally brought the décor up. He sat back down and couldn't help the smile that threatened. "I was jealous, Laurel. I was blindingly jealous. God, you're lovely. Lean back a little. I want to look at your pussy."

"Mitch, this is bordering on the weird," she began, but did as he asked. "I'm sorry I made you jealous. I won't do it again. I suppose if I'm honest, I was willing to do just about anything to have you see me. Though I wasn't thinking of a gynecological exam at the time."

He waved her off and got down on his knees. He let his hands find the skin at her ankles and started to work his way up those sweet legs that would eventually get propped on his shoulders while he fucked her hard and long. "If your gynecologist does what I'm about to do, let me know because we're going to sue the motherfucker for all he's worth. So tell me what you had hoped would happen when I found you playing with Master T? I suspect I was being set up to find you playing with him. Was I supposed to start a fight?"

"Absolutely not," she began and likely would have continued had he not leaned over and put his nose right up against her pussy. "Oh my god."

It was good to know he could put her off balance. Laurel almost seemed too competent half the time. She would stand there in her prim little outfits and tell him what she thought he should do. It was usually the exact opposite of what he wanted to do. She liked to change things. He liked things to stay the same. It wasn't that he couldn't accept something new. He was definitely liking his new decoration. And he knew damn straight he wouldn't want to let her go. Ever.

He breathed her in, memorizing the spicy, deeply feminine scent of her arousal. And there was no doubt she was aroused. He could see her gorgeous labia. Her pussy was perfectly shaved and a lovely cream coated her pink flesh. He could see the pearl of her clit. It was poking out of its hood, begging for a lick, a suck, some sweet attention. But he had a couple of questions first. "Would you have let him fuck you?"

Her whole body tensed. "My contract didn't even allow nudity until three weeks in. I was kind of hoping you would wake up in three weeks. And no. I wouldn't have slept with him. I was desperate. I only wanted you. I would never have accepted another Master but you, you jerk."

He had been a jerk. He'd overreacted and taken something from her. Yes, she'd put him in a corner, but he wasn't a child. He hadn't had to fight his way out. He should have made the choice. He should have decided to be her Master or to let her go. Now he had no choice. He would be her Master. "I like to think I would have made a proper decision and that would be to take over and make you realize that you need me. I think I can still do that. But if you even look that cowboy's way, we'll have problems, you and I."

He was sure she would have argued on her own behalf. She would have told him that she wouldn't ever play with Master T, but he didn't give her a chance. He would rather let her know what she would be missing if she did.

He licked her, a long, slow drag of his tongue over her pussy. This was what he'd missed. He'd missed her taste and smell. God, he loved her smell and he fucking needed to know how she tasted when he could really take his time to enjoy her. He wasn't sure how he'd lived without that taste on his tongue. He put his hands on her knees, gently pressing out as he very tenderly ate that sweet pussy. He was careful. Despite what Will had said, he was still nervous about hurting her or the baby. He needed to read up. Research was something he was good at. He would read all he could about pregnancy and sex, but for now he simply licked and sucked at her.

She gasped and wiggled, but he had a good firm hold on her. She wasn't trying to get away, but he would bet she also wasn't completely comfortable with having a man spend this much time at her pussy.

"Relax, Laurel. There's nothing for you to do except let me have my way."

"Mitch, I want you."

"And I want you." He sucked one side of her labia as his thumb started circling her clitoris. Not enough to make her come. He didn't want to do that yet.

"Mitch, I want to have sex."

She was taking a deeply Clintonian definition of sex. "We are having sex."

She'd shaved and her skin was baby smooth and god, she was so wet. He delved inside, fucking her with his tongue, gathering all her cream for himself.

"Mitch, I want your cock. I think we should have intercourse. Penetrative intercourse."

He pulled away. "Then you should have found a different lover, Laurel. I told you how this would go." He hated leaving her. He hated the fact that he wasn't going to get what he wanted, but he couldn't let her move him on this. He'd already given in to her. He knew what he needed and if he allowed her to, she would walk all over him.

Again. God, he was a perverse son of a bitch to need control and always be attracted to women who wouldn't give it to him.

"I think I'll go take a shower. Lisa should be here soon. Do you mind waiting for her?"

Her eyes were wide. Her whole body flushed a nice pink and he wanted nothing more than to give her exactly what she wanted, but he'd played that way before and it didn't work out. "You're leaving?"

His dick was protesting, but he knew what he wanted and it wasn't to be pushed around and told what to do. Definitely not during sex. "You should have read the contract more closely, Laurel. I'm in charge in the bedroom, and you obey me there or you use your safe word if you get frightened or find yourself in pain. You weren't scared and what I was doing couldn't have caused you pain, so you were trying to take control. I'm ending the session. I don't play like that and I've explained that to you on numerous occasions. I've never lied to you about what I wanted."

She shook her head. "No, you haven't, and I want to understand what it means to be your submissive. Please, Mitchell. I'm sorry. You can spank me if you like, but I promise I won't try to take control again. I was excited and I wanted you more than I've ever wanted anything. Please forgive me."

"The punishment was clearly laid out in our contract. When you infringe on my bedroom rights, I withdraw and you're to be left to think about your actions." He'd punished many subs this way. So why did it seem so foolish to punish Laurel? Why did something that once seemed like a game now feel so fucking serious?

Things were changing and he didn't like it. The best course of action would be to leave her for an hour or two and get his distance. Then he could return and they would discuss the infraction.

She hopped off the table and stepped up to him. "Mitch, I'm asking you to change that punishment. You're right. I didn't read it as thoroughly as I should have because I wasn't going to let anything stop me from signing, but I can't do this. I can handle a spanking. I can't handle you withholding affection as punishment. You asked me to never ignore your calls because you wouldn't ignore mine. Well, don't play with my heart this way because I won't ever do that to you. This makes me feel very small."

His former subs would have pouted and sulked, and now he realized why he'd chosen the women he had. To those submissives, everything was a game. He'd been careful to pick women who enjoyed the manipulative aspects, who would give him reasons to punish them because they enjoyed the game.

This wasn't a game for Laurel.

He nodded and forced some unnamed emotion down as he reached for her and drew her close. "I don't want you to feel small, baby. You're not small to me. Forgive me. I didn't mean to make you feel that way."

"And I didn't mean to make you feel out of control." She kissed his jaw and then settled herself against him. She didn't seem to be self-conscious in any way. She was like a happy kitten rubbing against him. "I can handle a lot of things, but I can't handle you being cold to me."

He'd been cold for so long. It was all he knew how to be, but he found himself holding her close and then his mouth found hers. How long had it been since he tossed out his rituals and routines and simply let the sex happen? Well, besides what had happened in his office a few weeks before. Tonight wasn't going to end the same way. Tonight he would end up in bed with her, wrapped up with her.

He kissed her, his tongue finding hers and playing. His hands moved across her skin, exploring. She was his for the time being and she was different from the other subs he'd kept. She wasn't after his money or his connections. She wasn't looking for a free ride.

She was carrying his child.

He hated change, but it was here and he was trapped.

He was surprised to find that didn't scare him the way it should have.

Before he really knew what he was doing, he was pressing her back, taking her down to the couch. He kissed her as his hands fumbled at his belt and then the fly of his slacks. His cock sprang free and he wasn't thinking about anything but getting inside her. He shoved his slacks down and made a place for himself at her core.

Her hands tore at his shirt as though she couldn't stand the clothes between them. He ripped the damn thing off himself, hearing the sound of the buttons pinging on the hardwoods as he tossed it away. It didn't matter. He had twenty exactly like it and he wanted to feel her hands on him.

She sighed as she looked up at him. "You're so beautiful."

She was the beautiful one. "Wrap your legs around my waist. The good news is I don't have to fumble around for a condom. That ship sailed."

The smile on her face would have brought him to his knees if he hadn't already been there. "That ship has definitely sailed and there's no getting off it."

But she was smiling. She was stuck with him and she was still smiling. God, he would do a lot to keep that smile on her face.

He slowed down. He was always in a rush to have her. She pushed him past all control, but that smile gave some of it back. He lowered himself down, giving her his weight. Her legs circled his waist and he kissed her, his cock nudging at her.

He groaned as he thrust inside. So tight. God, she had the tightest, hottest pussy. It fit him like a damn glove, like she'd been made to take his cock.

He buried his face in her neck, breathing her in as he slowly forced his way inside her. She was wet, but it was still a deliciously tight fit.

"That feels so good." Her nails ran over his back.

He kissed her neck and let the heat of her body warm his own. "One of these days, I swear I'm going to get out of my clothes, baby."

He pushed in until there was nowhere else to go, until she'd taken every inch of him and he could feel her squeeze him tight. He flexed inside her and was rewarded with a sexy gasp from her.

He thrust in and dragged back out, feeling her all around him. Her legs tightened, arms circling and nails scoring him lightly.

He didn't have sex like this. Somewhere in the back of his head alarm bells were going off. He controlled the sex. He preferred to have his sexual partner tied up or ordered to remain still, to give her body over to him and he would see to their pleasure. But he couldn't do it with

Laurel. He gave over to the primal instinct to mate. He couldn't call it sex. Sex was something he could take or leave, but he wasn't sure he could ever leave this woman, and that was precisely why he'd stayed away from her in the first place.

He was not the man who got lost in freaking passion.

He fucked her hard, not caring to listen to alarm bells or reason. It felt too good to have her around him, to be in the center of her touch, her smell, her heat. He forgot about all the reasons why he shouldn't and let his cock take over. His cock knew exactly what he wanted and he wanted to mark Laurel as his.

Over and over he thrust inside, taking them higher and higher. When she tensed around him and called out his name, he knew this fight was over. The silky muscles of her pussy clamped down and milked his cock. His spine sizzled as he gave up and held himself hard against her, pouring himself into her.

He finally rested, completely spent. Her hands smoothed over his back and there was nothing but the peaceful sound of her breathing, her heart beating as he laid his head on her chest.

He was in deep and he was fairly certain that this time he would drown.

Chapter Six

Laurel looked around the new Sanctum with a sense of wonder. It was big. Three levels. There was a bar, lounge, and gorgeous locker rooms on the first floor. She'd been surprised to discover she'd been given her own locker complete with a nameplate. When she'd opened it, she'd found her favorite toiletries had already been stocked and there were clothes Mitch had picked out for her hanging there.

He was a thoughtful Master. She'd traded the delicate gold chain she wore during the day for a heavier collar. This one was made of leather, but he'd had it custom detailed with green, glossy leaves.

For a Laurel tree.

The second level was the dungeon. She stood there, looking out over Ian Taggart's own version of heaven, and hoped Mitch didn't have a thing for the human hamster wheel. It was a massive thing and someone had lined it with twinkle lights. Serena and Bridget were giggling as they watched a male sub jogging his ass off in the hamster wheel while a big Dom stood watching, threatening to whip his ass if he slowed down.

"Is that Chris?" Chris was her sister-in-law's best friend. Along with Serena, Bridget and Chris were a trio to be reckoned with at Sanctum. Everyone knew that if you gave them a juicy story it would end up in one of their books.

Bridget gave her a spectacular smile. "Yeah, he told Jeremy he needed help getting fit. He kind of threw a hissy fit because Jeremy can eat whatever he wants and still stay gorgeous. Chris got a little bratty and hence the new sub workout."

Chris's legs pumped harder and faster and the twinkle lights changed from white to green.

"That's right. Get it up to green, sub. Five more minutes or I'll have you on a St. Andrew's Cross and you won't be able to sit down for a week. How many calories will that burn, love? Yeah, don't try to talk. Just run." Jeremy winked at her. "That's the last time he tells me I'm a shitty trainer."

"Tag set it up so the lights change the faster you go," Serena explained. "It's kind of the symbol for the new Sanctum. Pretty and functionally torturous. I can't wait to start writing about it."

Bridget pulled Laurel in for a hug. "I'm so glad you're here. I see Mitch was kind with the clothes."

She was wearing a crop top and tiny miniskirt. No shoes for her. He'd explained that while he liked her heels, he was afraid she would trip in them. She hadn't stopped wearing them to work, but he ruled here at Sanctum. "He's afraid a corset would be confining for the baby. I did not even point out that women wore them for many years and they're adjustable. I've found on some things, it's easier to give in. And I really hope we got all the hideously embarrassing questions out of the way with the first doctor's visit."

Mitch had driven her to Dr. Bates's office and waited with her. He'd helped her change into her gown and listened intently while the doctor had searched for the heartbeat. While she'd gotten teary at the sound, he'd been stoic. He'd simply nodded and squeezed her hand as though he'd read somewhere that was what the expectant father did when the expectant mother cried. He'd shown no real emotion, but boy had he had some questions for the doc.

Bridget laughed. "How bad was it? I happen to know your OB. She's very cool and understands the lifestyle, so I'm sure it's nothing she hasn't heard before."

"He asked if anal sex was okay for the baby. I'm not kidding you." It had been horrifying. He'd had a list of questions for Dr. Bates, most of them about sexual things she never thought she would talk to a doctor about.

"What did she say?" Serena asked. "Because when Jake asked she told us as long as it was my ass he was very gently fucking it would likely be all right, but otherwise he might be in trouble."

Dr. Bates seemed to have come from the Big Tag school of bedside manner. "Yes, that seems to be her patent response. Did Mitchell have to go through an entire list of sexual positions and acts?"

"This is a guy's way of caring. He's nervous about it so he has to find some way of taking control," Serena explained. "Pregnancy can be very difficult for the man. Especially a Dom. He can't control it so you have to find ways to make him more comfortable with the situation. Let him pamper you even when it's annoying. Seriously, a foot rub can get boring after three hours, but it soothed Jake to do it. Adam was definitely calmer until we hit the delivery room. That first blood freaked him out. He wasn't prepared for it to be so bloody and painful."

"Hey, ixnay on the ainpay." Bridget frowned Serena's way.

"Oh, because I should tell her that childbirth is a lovely, pain-free, and completely comfortable experience."

"I'm going to take all the drugs," Laurel admitted. "Every one of them. I'm not a Viking woman."

The pain part scared the crap out of her. So did all the things that could happen. Mitch didn't want her to read the childbirth books. He'd told her they would only scare her, but she'd put a couple on her Kindle anyway. One of them had to be ready. He'd asked the doctor a million questions about their sex lives and not one about the actual pregnancy.

Sometimes she wondered if he'd changed his mind about the baby again. Or was it all about his duty to her and responsibility for the child?

She'd noticed that after their first night together, they hadn't spoken of marriage again. She told herself it was good because she didn't want to have that fight, but she had to wonder if she really wanted to be a single mom.

"Do you absolutely have to play tonight? It's hard walking around without looking at things. I'm going to crash into someone's scene," a familiar voice said.

She turned and there was her brother coming up the stairs with Mitchell and Kai. Will's eyes were firmly planted on the ground.

Kai gave her a smile. "He's trying to avoid seeing you half naked."

"She's actually quite covered," Mitch admitted.

He looked utterly delicious. No matter what kind of problems they might have, there was no denying the fact that this man got her motor running like no other. Sanctum was filled with gorgeous men, but Mitch seemed to stand above the rest. He was so masculine, with his broad shoulders and cut chest on display. She loved how petite she felt when he held her. He seemed to like to show off how strong he was by carrying her around.

Will brought his head up, his eyes opening cautiously. He seemed to relax. "All right. I suppose I can handle that. What kind of scene are you two doing tonight?"

Mitch moved to her side, his eyes going to the collar around her neck. She could practically feel the satisfaction pouring off him in waves. He might not want her as a wife, but she could tell he was enjoying keeping a submissive. "I'm doing a ropes demonstration, and no, you will not want to watch. We're up very soon, so you and Bridget should stay on the east side of the dungeon. I hear Weston and his wife are doing an impact play scene."

"I'm going to find a pretty little pain slut and get my freak on," Kai promised. He looked nothing like his normal self. Kai was usually very intellectual looking. Like the professor at college every girl wanted to date. But with his hair down around his shoulders and dressed in leathers and motorcycle boots, the good psychologist looked dangerous. And definitely ready for some fun. Of course, his idea of fun had to do with pain.

"When are you going to play with Kori?" Mitch nodded to a girl across the room.

Kori was standing with her friend, Sarah. The two were pretty women. With curves for days, they looked ready for play in their corsets and teeny tiny thongs.

Kai frowned. "I'm not and I've made that clear. She works for me. I'm not going to play with my employee. I've so recently seen where that leads." He patted Mitch on the shoulder. "I'm going to find a compatible woman and work very hard to not get her pregnant. You look lovely, Laurel."

"I don't think that's a compliment."

Kai took her hand and brought it to his lips, kissing it gallantly. "It was meant to be. I wish you all the best. And know that my door is always open."

Kai strode away.

"If I didn't know he was offering you a counseling session, I might go kick his ass. I think I want to amend our contract. No one gets to kiss you except me. Not any part of you. I didn't like him kissing your hand." Mitch could get the tiniest bit jealous, but he looked so cute standing there staring after his friend like he wasn't sure what to do.

"Somehow, I think he merely meant it as a friendly gesture. Shall we take a look around? I know all the Doms got to see the place being built, but this is my first time."

He took her hand, threading their fingers together. "I suppose that's why you weren't waiting for me outside the locker rooms?"

She winced. He'd been implicit in his instructions, but then Mitch always was. "I wanted to know what I was getting into."

"You knew where I wanted you."

"Yes, Master." She'd actually thought she could run up and take a peek and then get back downstairs. Then she'd caught sight of that damn hamster wheel and gotten off track.

"I like the way that sounds," he said, satisfaction evident on his face.

"Master?" She hadn't called him by his title before. Maybe it would save her. She gave him her more innocent smile. "My Master."

He shook his head. "That's not going to save you, sweet brat. While we're showing people how to form a rope dress, you'll also receive twenty swats."

Will shuddered. "See, I don't need to hear that. Ever."

Bridget sent Laurel an apologetic glance. "Sorry. He'll get used to it."

"No, I won't," Will complained as Bridget led him off.

Serena went to join her husbands and Laurel was left alone with her Dom.

"I didn't like you not being there when I came out. I would have stood there waiting for you had another sub not come out and explained you had already left. Will told me where you would be. Apparently he knows you better than I do."

"Living with a person for eighteen years will do that to you."

"That's another five for sarcasm."

She should have known he would be more rigid in the club. The play parties they'd attended over the last few weeks hadn't seemed as formal. She lowered her head in deference to her Dom. "I'm sorry, Master. I was very eager to see the dungeon and Bridget was walking upstairs. I went with her. I meant to get back down after I took a peek. I understand and accept my punishment."

His hand came out and he gently lifted her chin up so she saw him again. "I don't like not knowing where you are. It worries me."

Her heart melted a little because he really did worry when she wasn't with him. "I'm sorry."

He leaned over and kissed her forehead. "Don't do it again. I want to be with you when you walk this dungeon. Now, we don't have much time. Let's take a walk and then get to our space. Everything's set up for us so we have a few minutes."

He started to lead her around. There was the heavy thud of industrial music playing. It seemed to thump through the entire floor. There were numerous scene spaces. She saw a well-stocked doctor's office. It looked like Mitch's friend Keith was giving his wife a very deep examination using his penis.

"You're blushing." Mitch stopped on the outskirts of the scene. "How are you going to get through our scene if this bothers you?"

She shook her head. "It doesn't bother me at all. They're happy, consenting adults. I have no problem with it. It's very arousing."

His lips quirked up. "You're aroused, are you?"

She was getting more aroused because he was backing her up, his big body invading her space. She found herself against a wall. "Yes."

His hand found her thigh. "I think I'd like to see how aroused you are. Spread your legs for me."

There had been no panties left in her locker and she definitely hadn't been foolish enough to wear the ones she'd entered the building in. She would wear what she wanted outside, but in Sanctum she dressed to please Mitchell. Her Master had tossed out all her old cotton panties and replaced them with gorgeous silk undies, but he'd been plain about not wearing them at all in the club.

She did as he asked. It was her first time in the club. The play parties hadn't truly prepped her for how it would feel. Sanctum was so big. It gave her the sense that any moment anyone could walk by and see her. Her heart raced a little. The club was full tonight. There was a big party for the grand opening with a gorgeous buffet downstairs, but suddenly she wasn't thinking of food. She was thinking of Mitch's hands on her body. His big palms moved up her thighs, taking the miniscule skirt with them. She felt cool air on her most private part.

"I don't want nudity to bother you, Laurel. Certainly not your own. You're gorgeous and you're mine. I'm going to love showing off your body. I'm thinking about showing it off right now. What are you thinking about, baby?"

He slid the skirt to her waist, completely exposing her pussy and backside. Cool air hit her sensitive flesh and she felt the most delicious chill go up her spine.

"You. Nothing else." It was the nice thing about the time they spent playing. She could let go of everything else. There was no reason to worry. This was the place where she could live in the moment. Every other moment of her life she suddenly had to worry about the future, but here she could simply be Master Mitchell's submissive.

His hand moved between her legs. "Let's see what happens when you think of me."

A finger slide through her labia, parting her pussy and gently curving up. His thumb found her clitoris and pressed down and up and then moved in a sensuous circle.

Her whole body responded, softening, preparing.

"Hands above your head," he commanded in that low growl that always got her motor running.

She moved her hands over her head, holding her right wrist with her left. It brought the shirt she was wearing up to the point that the bottoms of her breasts were showing.

He withdrew his hand, much to her dismay. He brought his fingers up, a grin on his face. "I like the way you think about me, Laurel."

He sucked his soaked fingers inside his mouth, obviously savoring the taste of her arousal. When he was done, he crowded her again.

"You're the only man who could ever get me this hot this fast." She wanted him to know this crazy piece of her only seemed to be for him. She couldn't imagine standing here in a crowded room with her legs spread wide for all to see with anyone except him. She'd been perfectly vanilla until she'd met Mitchell Bradford, and she would likely go back into her comfy shell if he left her.

"I intend to keep it that way." It was the closest thing he would say about the future. He tugged her skirt down. "Come with me. It's time to get started."

She followed him through the club, well aware that the ache inside, the desperate wanting, was all part of her Dom's punishment for disobeying him. He'd felt how wet she was and he was going to leave her waiting. It was all part of the scene.

In the weeks they'd been living together, she'd gotten used to Mitch's version of play. He was a man of routine. He liked the discipline of holding to a schedule. While that might sound boring to a lot of people, Laurel loved the fact that the man came home every night at six o'clock on the dot without fail. She knew to be undressed and waiting for him, and had never once been left on her knees waiting.

For a girl who never knew if her mother was going to show up at all, it was comforting.

But she did miss his passion. He'd found the routine of discipline and he no longer deviated. While he'd put aside the use of withdrawal of affection as a punishment, he still wasn't exactly chatty. He would listen to her all day but never said a word about his past or their future.

She walked with him, looking around her at all the happy couples. There were a few women she knew from her training classes. Before subs were ever introduced to Doms, they had to go through classes and pass a psych eval. She waved at a couple of her friends who seemed to be flirting with the new Doms.

They briefly stopped at one of the odder scene spaces. She'd passed the classroom space, with its school desks and chalkboards where professors spanked wayward subs who didn't do their homework. This was like a classroom, but an almost medieval one.

She recognized the "professor" in the scene. Jesse Murdoch was wearing a long, dark robe and standing in front of a series of beakers and cauldrons that had what looked like steam coming out of them.

"Miss Grant, this potion is atrocious and not befitting of a witch of your caliber," Jesse said in a dark tone.

She felt her eyes widen as she realized where the scene was coming from. Phoebe Murdoch stood, her hair flowing and eyes wide. She was wearing a robe too, though hers barely covered her backside and she didn't seem to be wearing anything underneath it.

"I suppose you'll have to punish me, professor. For the good of all the wizarding world," she said as she presented her ass to him.

"I don't think that's what J.K. Rowling intended wands to do," she whispered to Mitch.

He shook his head and continued toward the center of the dungeon and the raised stage. She definitely knew a couple of the people in this crowd, but she couldn't tell what kind of scene was being performed.

That was when she saw the rope that had been placed on a table along with what looked to be a ridiculously large anal plug and some lube.

He was not about to…

"Come on, baby." He started to help her to the stairs.

"This is the main stage."

"Yes, and this is a teaching scene. The new Doms are all expected to attend. We wouldn't want to be late, would we?"

There were a lot of people and they were about to watch Mitch tie her up. What was she doing? She was pregnant. She was going to be a mom. She shouldn't be out here.

"Laurel?"

She realized she was standing there and everyone was watching them. Mitch was going to be angry. He'd planned this whole scene and he wouldn't like her messing it up.

"Laurel?" He stepped back down and stared at her for a moment. His eyes were cold and she felt frozen in place.

He was going to give her an ultimatum now. It was what he did. It was how they seemed to work, or rather how he worked. She'd figured out that she had to adapt to him if she wanted to be with him.

Maybe that wasn't the best way to live.

He stepped up close and she waited for him to tell her to get on the stage or accept whatever punishment he was going to give her, and then she would have to make a choice. God, the moment was here and she wasn't ready for it. She wasn't ready to leave him, but she also wasn't sure she wanted to go on that stage.

His hands sank into her hair, but instead of tugging on it and forcing her to look at him, he pulled her close and settled her against his chest. "Baby, there's nothing to be afraid of. Shhh. If you don't want to do this, you don't have to. We can spend the rest of the night watching scenes and then go down and have a nice dinner. It's going to be all right."

"But you set up the scene." He didn't back down. He plowed through. He did what he said he was going to do.

"And someone can take over." His hand smoothed down her hair. "Laurel, baby, what are you afraid of? I would never hurt you and I certainly won't make you do a scene you're uncomfortable with."

He was making everyone wait. He was holding them up so he could comfort her.

"There are a lot of people here," she admitted. "And I thought about the fact that I'm pregnant and I'm going to be a mom and god, Mitch, what are we going to do when the baby gets here? What are we going to do?"

She wasn't sure why it hit her then and there, but it did. Weeks of holding it together culminated in her shaking and crying and making a complete idiot of herself in front of all the Doms in Sanctum.

Mitch swept her up into his arms. "Alex, could you take over for me?"

Now they would have to go home and talk about why she'd ruined the scene. She wasn't looking forward to going into the locker room alone and having to change back into street clothes. She wasn't looking forward to an awkward discussion.

She held on when she realized he was going up and not down. He was heading to the third floor.

A man was stationed at the top of the stairs. He looked up, his eyes registering surprise. "Master Mitchell? I wasn't expecting you for another hour."

"Sometimes aftercare has to come first, Mike. Is there a room open?"

"You're lucky. I already prepped your room. It's number five, but I gotta warn you. The big boss is in four and he will neither turn the music down nor change it."

Mitch nodded and before she knew it, she could hear the strains of a familiar song as Mitch opened the door and strode in. "Sweet Child o' Mine."

She was having a baby.

She found herself on his lap, sobbing against his shoulder. How had she gone from getting all hot and bothered to weeping openly?

He rocked her, his arms encircling her. "It's going to be all right, Laurel. Baby, it's going to be okay. I'm going to take care of you and the baby. You don't have to cry."

He sounded almost as broken as she felt. She wrapped her arms around him and let go completely.

* * * *

Mitch had never felt so helpless in his whole damn life, and there had been plenty of times when he'd felt helpless. But Laurel sobbing in his arms…he would rather pull his heart straight out of his chest than have her so utterly heartbroken.

She'd seemed happy. She'd wanted to come to Sanctum. She'd been looking forward to it all week. But something had happened to her as she stood in front of that stage. She couldn't be afraid of him or the ropes. He loved to tie her up. Sometimes he practiced as they sat together at night. She would sit in front of him and he would weave the rope into her hair or have her lay across the couch and let him bind her legs before he would ease her to the floor and fuck into her from behind.

It couldn't be the ropes. She'd said something about all the people.

"Baby, were you scared of people looking at you?" He asked the question knowing that women sometimes got weird ideas. Laurel was simply the most beautiful woman in the world, but that didn't mean she believed it. She was so sexy he couldn't be in a room with her and not have his dick get hard. Just thinking about her made him erect, but women often didn't see themselves the way men did.

He'd never actually gotten her naked during a scene before. He'd taken it slowly, tried to allow her to adapt. He was well aware she would still be considered in her training period had he not collared her. She would have been given a training Dom who couldn't undress her or do anything more intimate than hug her or let her sit on his lap. He'd gone much further than that. He'd stroked her pussy in full view of the club, forced her to show herself off.

Had that scared her?

She shook her head. "I'm not scared so much as confused. I don't know what happened, Mitch. I got to the bottom of those stairs and I realized that I was pregnant and I don't know what's going to happen. Am I going to be up there getting tied up when I'm as big as a whale? Or is this temporary and I'll only play while I'm still somewhat small and you won't want to play with me when I'm huge. Maybe you'll want another sub. One who can see her feet. Serena told me by the end of her pregnancy she couldn't see her feet."

Yep. He would rather face a team of lawyers in front of the Supreme Court with a no-win case than have to see her cry. He held her close. He was shitty at the tender stuff, but somehow Laurel seemed to bring it out of him. "You'll only get tied up as long as you want to be, baby. I can't imagine wanting another sub. Even one who can see her feet. I'm not all that into feet anyway. And if you want to see yours, I'll hold a mirror up and you'll be able to see them. Baby, don't cry."

That seemed to make her cry harder.

"Or you can cry. You can cry all you like."

He held her and smoothed a hand over her back as he rocked to the music. There was something both sexy and comforting about the beat.

Until he listened to the lyrics.

Where did they go? From here, where the hell were they supposed to go? Should they simply move through life and play house?

He had to face the fact that he wasn't sure he wanted to get married again. He also had to face the fact that he didn't want to live without Laurel.

He didn't even know what to think about the kid, and didn't that make him the biggest shit of all time?

Somehow, they ended up lying together in the big bed as she slowly calmed. He cuddled her close, almost dreading the moment when they would have to talk again because he had no idea what to say. When he was with her, everything felt right, but she was utterly correct. Things were going to change. They would have to.

She sniffled and laid her head on his chest. "I'm sorry I ruined the evening."

The song started up again and he laid a hand on her head. "You didn't ruin anything, Laurel. We're fine. You're just emotional. Don't you have hormones and stuff?"

She nodded against his chest. "Lots."

They would ebb and flow and eventually go away. He simply had to hold on to her through the rough stuff.

And what about when the kid comes? That's about the roughest stuff possible. No way you can control a kid. You don't even know how to be a dad, and we all know what kind of a husband you make.

His arms wrapped around her almost as though rebelling against the logic of his brain. She was his. He didn't have to give her up now. Not even for her own good. "You'll see. We'll be fine. And you're going to be gorgeous when you're really big… I mean further along."

Her face was red but her lips had turned up when she looked at him. "I'm going to be big, Mitch. Really big. I'm supposed to gain at least thirty pounds, but when I'm not nauseous I'm hungry, so I might gain more. Unfortunately, this baby doesn't get kale cravings. He wants ice cream. Or she. Either way, this tiny thing obviously has a sweet tooth."

Well, Laurel certainly did. "The good news is I heard Macon Miles made a massive cake for tonight. The midnight buffet isn't far away, but if you need something now, we can make it happen. Pregnant ladies get perks."

Or he would steal some if he had to. He would do anything to keep a smile on her face.

"Mitch, do you honestly think you'll still want to play with me? I don't see a bunch of pregnant women running around here. I think I'm the only one."

Was that what she was worried about? She'd been in the nursery for most of her time as a trainee, so she'd only seen the moms coming back after they had babies. "Laurel, it's been a freaking baby boom around here. You feel alone because you haven't seen it. Charlotte Taggart was playing up until a couple of weeks before she gave birth. They modified everything for her, but she and Big Tag weren't going to give that part of their life up. From what I hear, Serena and Avery played long into their pregnancies, and so did Sean's wife, Grace. And you won't be alone. I happen to know Keith and Ashley are trying to get pregnant, and so are Jesse and Phoebe. Although they'll probably name their baby after Harry Potter, so I'm praying for that kid. And you know one of these days Will's going to give in and convince Bridget to have a kid."

He feared for a world where Bridget Daley had pregnancy hormones running through her veins.

But he didn't want Laurel to feel alone.

"So no one's going to think it's weird or irresponsible?"

"To play with the father of your baby?" He'd almost slipped and said husband.

She shrugged as though it didn't matter when it so obviously did.

"Just to play. Maybe I should only think about the baby."

"Laurel, you don't have to give up your sexuality because you're pregnant. No one here would ever want you to do that. You're beautiful and nothing makes me prouder than to show you off, but if you're uncomfortable, then we'll play privately."

"Do you mean that?"

He would miss coming here, miss the camaraderie. "Yes. My place is with you."

At least he knew that much.

"You love this place."

"But I need to stay with you." There was something else, something he couldn't even think. *I love you more.* "I need to look out for you and the baby. If I can't do that here, then I'll do it where I can. But Laurel, you don't stop being a woman because you become a mom. I've seen it happen, though more on the other side. My mom didn't stop being a woman. Ever. She wasn't much of a mom, but even I know you're different. You can be both because I know you'll never neglect your child. You'll find a balance."

He hoped they would both find it. Somehow, he couldn't see himself being a father and if he couldn't manage it, then he wouldn't be able to keep Laurel. Unlike his mother, she would choose her child's needs. Even if it meant giving up the child's father.

She buried her head in the curve of his neck. "I can't believe I did that. I burst into tears. How am I ever going to walk back out there?"

"Why wouldn't you walk back out there?"

"Because of how embarrassed I'll be."

Now that the storm had passed, it seemed like a good time to take control again. "What would you be embarrassed about? Because everyone here knows you're pregnant. And almost all subs cry at some point. It's expected. No one will think less of you. Now tell me what happened. What really made you cry?"

She sat up and her eyes slid away from his. "It was the thought that I'll be a mom soon and…it's not like I'm thin now. Everyone would see me. You would see me."

What the hell did that mean? It was definitely time to take charge. He sat up beside her. "Laurel, I've seen you naked many times. I see you naked every single night, so you're going to have to explain how my seeing you naked could possibly cause you to cry."

"You haven't seen how your friends might react. Maybe they have prettier subs." She frowned. "I know it sounds stupid, but I'm trying to be honest with you. I might be all right now, but everything is going to change. I'll gain weight, and even afterward I'll have stretch marks and I'll breast feed so my boobs will likely sag, and it's really hard because you keep telling me to live in the moment, but I can't."

"Laurel, I'll still want you." He wasn't sure she would want him. He wasn't sure she wouldn't figure out exactly how many men there were out there with whole hearts and easy tempers.

"How can you know that?"

"I know." It was the one thing he was certain of. "If you're worried about the future, you know what to do." He was also certain that marriage would be best—even if he found the entire idea unsettling. "I've already asked you to marry me. We can get on a flight to Vegas and be married tomorrow."

She stared at him, her eyes wary. "Is that what you want?"

"I think that would be best for our baby."

Her eyes turned down and she seemed to shake something off. When she looked back up there was a smile on her face, though a hint of sadness permeated her being. "I think our baby is going to be fine. And you're right. Living in the moment is for the best. Marriage isn't a promise of permanency. Let's make a pact. Whatever happens, we'll respect each other and be friends."

He didn't want to be her friend. And he didn't want to be her ex. He didn't want to only see her or hear from her when she needed money or wanted to take him back to court. "We'll always be friends."

It was why he hadn't wanted to get involved with her in the first place. Laurel had become essential to him. She was the bright spot in his days, the reason he wanted to get up in the mornings. He truly would have stayed in the background. He would have watched her date and find a good man and get married. He would have watched over her and counted himself lucky to have her in his life.

Friends stayed. Friends stuck it out.

He was almost certain they could never be friends again.

"Sweet Child o' Mine" started up again and there was a banging against the wall. Rhythmic and loud.

Laurel laughed suddenly, her whole face lighting up.

At least it proved a point. He gestured to the wall. "Proof positive that there is sex after children. And hey, we've only got one in there. We're better off than Big Tag and Charlotte, but they seem to have found a way around it."

She stood up and walked over to the closet. He watched her

cautiously, unsure of where she was going. She opened the door and he heard her rummage around inside. When she turned, she had a length of rope in her hand. "Mitch, I know I screwed up the demo."

"You didn't screw it up. You had an emotional reaction. It's fine. Alex can handle it."

"Maybe we could at least show off your skills. Maybe you could make me a dress for the after party."

His dick jumped at the thought. "Come here."

She stepped toward him, offering him the rope. "Do you think that's a good idea? I love the patterns you can make. They're beautiful."

"You're beautiful, but we have something we need to take care of first." He patted his lap. They wouldn't be able to do this for much longer. When she started to show she wouldn't be able to lie on her belly, but he wanted her across his lap while it was still safe. He usually disciplined submissives on spanking benches or in some fashion where he had the most control and the least amount of intimacy. He tended to use crops or paddles. Canes if the submissive was amenable.

But he wanted Laurel over his lap, wanted her dependent on him, needed to feel her squirm and writhe under his hand.

"I thought you didn't care that I ruined the scene."

"This isn't about the scene. You disobeyed my direct command that you wait for me outside the locker room. You're not allowed to run around the dungeon without me."

"Bridget was up there without Will."

"That's Will's problem. Not mine. You're my sub and we have our own rules. So let's get the punishment over and I'll make your top. I won't do a complete dress because I want you to be able to move." He would have to go easy. Though right now there was absolutely no sign that Laurel was carrying a child, he wouldn't bind her tightly. He would form diamond patterns around her torso, force her breasts out, but he would bind her in deference to her comfort. And if she simply couldn't stand it, he would run the ropes over her clothes.

She couldn't know how much he was bending for her. She couldn't imagine how rigid he'd been before. If she ever knew how much power she had, it would all be over. It was better to let her think this was the normal way his relationships went.

"You haven't punished me before."

"You haven't misbehaved before."

A sweet grin lit her face. "You have no idea how unlike me that is." She took a deep breath. "Okay. I did the crime. I can do the time. It's twenty-five, right?"

"Yes. Twenty-five. Take off your clothes. Punishment requires nudity. That's a new rule, too." He went to the closet. The room had been prepped for him and had everything he'd requested, including the item he found waiting with a nice bottle of lubricant. "And you'll take a plug in addition to your dress. That's not punishment though. That's preparation."

"I can handle a plug, Master. You've been making me wear one every night."

"You haven't been spanked while wearing a plug. I believe you'll find the experience stimulating."

When he turned, her eyes had gone wide. "That's a much bigger plug than normal, Mitch."

"Master here, Laurel. I don't require formality anywhere but the club. And yes, it's large, but I fully intend to take your lovely ass very soon, and this will make things so much easier." He brought the prepped plug and lubricant back to the bed and sat down, his cock already straining.

This was what he needed to banish the unsettling feelings he had about the future. He needed to play with her, to reassure himself that at least for now she belonged to him.

It was all he could really ask for. She belonged to him now.

"Yes, Master." She drew the shirt over her head and he let go of his cares.

She was all that mattered now.

Chapter Seven

Laurel pushed the skirt off her hips and let Mitch help her lie over his lap. Vulnerable. She was so vulnerable in this position. The room had gone quiet, the music ending. She heard a low chuckle and then a door opening and closing. The Taggarts, it seemed, were satisfied. They would be going downstairs to host the party that was soon to come.

The party she would be attending wearing nothing but Mitch's rope over her chest and likely the skirt.

Unless he chose otherwise. She'd promised herself she would give Mitch the rest of the night. He'd already given her so much. She wasn't foolish. She knew his reputation. All of his D/s relationships had been in California, but he'd played with many subs here and they'd all said the same thing. Mitchell Bradford didn't bend. He was uncompromising as a Dom. If she'd been asked what Master Mitch would do if his submissive threatened to ruin a scene he'd prepared for, she would have told anyone that he would simply find another sub for the scene and then punish his own sub.

But he hadn't even hesitated. He'd been tender and kind and so sweet she'd forgiven him for not being able to say he wanted to marry her.

The man had been screwed over so many times before, he wasn't sure what he wanted. He needed time and she intended to give it to him. She also intended to give him her submission for the rest of the evening, even if it meant taking that damn hung-like-a-horse plug.

After all, Mitchell was that.

The leather of his pants was smooth against her belly. His cock was not. It was a hard ridge that proved the man wanted her despite her crazy emotional swings. She relaxed as he smoothed a hand over her back and down to the cheeks of her ass. He'd certainly touched her there before, but she always loved how he paused as though he was taking in the sight. He cupped her, his fingers tracing the seam before he parted her.

She forced herself to relax. He'd been plugging her for days and she'd learned there was nothing truly painful about the experience. Just some pressure and a feeling of being full. She shivered as he placed the lubed tip to her asshole.

"You are so beautiful."

She held on to his ankle as he pressed the plug in. All that training was paying off because the tip eased in with very little prompting. She didn't clench, merely gave over because in this her Master would have his way. Somehow it was easier when she could see how he gave in to her. It was inconsequential things like where to eat. He didn't love Mediterranean food, but he took her to her favorite place and didn't complain. He preferred rock, but turned the station to country when he drove her someplace.

Tonight had given her great hope despite his refusal to speak long-term future with her. Mitch had held her and rocked her and been kind even though he didn't understand. He was educable. That was all she could ask for.

She breathed out as he slid the plug in, forcing her to open. A low groan came from the back of her throat as he stretched her wider than he ever had before. So much pressure, but she'd come to think of it as erotic now. Her big strong Master was playing with her. Her body was his toy in these moments and he was right. She didn't want to give this up. She shouldn't have to simply because she gave birth. She would still be a woman. She would still need to play with him.

She understood why Big Tag had spent so much time and effort and money on this club. For him and his wife, Sanctum was a place where they could simply be a couple, where they could love each other the way they needed to.

"See, you took that beautifully and you're not going to have any trouble taking me." One big hand was on her back while the other caressed the bare flesh of her ass. "Please count for me."

He didn't give her time to brace herself. One second he was asking for a count and the next his hand came down on her. The sound cracked through the air and it took a moment for the pain to register. She gasped as it flared through her.

"I asked for a count, Laurel."

"I hate you."

The bastard chuckled. "That is not a count and give it a minute. I know what I'm doing. I need a count before I can continue."

"Good." He could shove his count up his ass.

"Laurel, if I don't get a count, I'll add another swat for every ten seconds it takes you to give me what I requested. Or you can use your safe word."

After one smack? It had hurt, but now there was a pleasant heat in her backside. She could try a few more. "One."

His hand came down again and she bit back a shout.

"Two."

Again. Pain flashed and then heat. It seemed to sink into her skin. She gave him his count and he continued. She could feel the plug. Every time he slapped her ass, the plug sent a shiver up her spine, odd at first and then electric. Like lightning was flashing through her system. Her body was getting pleasantly warm and she could feel her pussy softening.

"I'm not hearing a safe word from you." His voice was deep. It wasn't his Master voice. Nope. That gravely, low sound was Mitch's sex voice. He was hot and ready, and if that cock under her belly was any indication, more than a bit desperate.

"You won't, Master. You're right. I'm getting used to it. That was twelve. I believe you owe me another thirteen."

"How do you do this to me?" He gave her a hard smack, though she knew he could hit her harder. He was measured and careful, giving her only what was required to heat her skin and give her a flare that turned to a sensual tingle. She counted and he smacked again, this one making the plug vibrate. "All I want to do is fuck you, Laurel. I want to tie you up and fuck your ass. I need it. I don't need anything."

Or anyone. She was sure his childhood and two failed marriages had taught him not to need anyone, but she was going to change that. "Please, Master. Please let me serve you."

Fourteen through twenty-two came like a firestorm. As soon as the number slipped from her mouth, he spanked her again, never letting up. She gritted her teeth, giving him what he wanted because she trusted him. She counted it out.

"Twenty-three." Smack. "Twenty-four." Smack. "Twenty-five."

His hand rested on her and she could hear him breathing. Shaky. He sounded a bit shaky, as though he was trying to get back into control.

Laurel breathed in, allowing the pain to shift deep inside. She could feel how wet she was, but she wanted more from him. If she pushed even a little, he would break and fuck her hard and quick. She would love it and he would chastise himself for losing control.

"Master, please can you tie me? I want to feel your ropes around me."

He helped her up and had the rope in his hands before she could say another thing. She could see the relief stamped on his face. He needed the control, needed it so badly.

Something about her made him lose it and that was great at times. She loved their passion, but this was part of the man, too. He needed to be patient and slow. He needed to rise above his instincts.

She could give him both.

The room was quiet as he worked, wrapping the rope and tying it off. It wasn't super tight and she suspected that was for her comfort. She found an odd peace as she submitted to him. As he wound the rope around her, working it in diamond patterns, she relaxed. Her whole body was humming. Her blood thumped through her system and she was aroused by the feel of his hands on her skin, but there was no hurry.

She loved this quiet time when they didn't have to talk, when they could simply be together. Peace and passion. They could have both if they tried.

"Did you hate the spanking? I haven't had to discipline you before this evening." They were the first words he'd spoken in fifteen minutes. His hands expertly tied two pieces of jute together before he began a row that would end at her hips.

She could feel where the knots were. The way he'd tied her, they rubbed against her skin, but not in an unpleasant way. It was like everywhere the knots sat was another place he touched her. "I didn't dislike it and you know it. I suspect you can tell how aroused it got me."

He breathed in. "I love the way you smell when you want me. And I love how your whole body blushes when I talk about how good you smell."

It was something none of her previous lovers would have dared to mention, but then nothing was out of bounds sexually as far as Mitch was concerned. He might have a million hangups in real life, but once the clothes came off, he didn't shy away from anything. "Like I said, I didn't mind the spanking. And I like this. I like how the rope feels."

He moved to her back, getting to one knee to finish off the pattern. "You look beautiful. I want you to come downstairs with me. Exactly like this. You can put your skirt on, but I want your breasts out. You look like every Dom's wet dream. I want to walk around the party and know they're all looking at my submissive. They're all jealous because my sub is so fucking gorgeous."

And just like that all her inhibitions melted away. The giving was a two-way street. While she truly believed she had something to give to her Dom, he definitely gave back. He gave her the confidence that came from knowing she was the center of his world. "Yes, Master."

She felt him lean over, his lips touching the small of her back and sending shivers up her spine.

"That's what I like to hear. Yes, Master. Do you know how long I dreamed about hearing those words from your lips, Laurel?"

"No. I thought I was more of a nightmare for you."

"Never. I dreamed about you the first day we met." He moved to her front and finished his pattern. "There. You look perfect. Are your breasts all right? Do they hurt at all?"

They ached, but not from the pregnancy. If she gave him any hint she was uncomfortable, he would cut her out in a heartbeat and ruin all his pretty work. He'd wrapped the pattern around her breasts in a way that thrust them up, making them the centerpiece of his artwork. "They're fine. I feel good though I do have a place where I ache."

Her pussy ached. She needed to be filled.

"Is that right?" Mitch asked. He stood up and his hands went to the waist of his leathers. He worked the ties quickly and his cock sprung free.

She nodded. It was completely right. She needed him.

He shoved out of his leathers and she couldn't help but stare, but she was well aware they were in a club, and Mitch could be very formal in a club. "Master, may I touch you?"

He towered over her and took her hand. "Never ask me that again. You can always touch me, always speak to me. It doesn't matter where we are. You're mine and that means I'm yours. I will always want you to touch me, Laurel."

She had to frown because that wasn't the truth as she'd been told. She placed her hands on his chest, loving how warm and smooth the skin was, how the muscles were hard while his skin was soft. "I heard you believed in high protocol. When I asked around, trying to find out what it would mean to be your submissive, I was told you didn't allow subs to touch you without permission. I was told your subs had to ask for permission to speak in a club."

He was still under her touch, allowing her to explore for a moment. "My other relationships have been more hardcore. I wanted my version of a pure D/s relationship with them, and for me that included certain protocols." When she touched his cock, he winced. "None of that, baby. I'll come in your hand and I don't want to do that. Get on the bed. On your knees."

She had to clench around the plug to move on the bed. It dipped behind her as he joined her. "So I don't know what it's really like to be your submissive?"

His hands caressed her hips and she felt his cock lined up at her pussy. "No. This isn't what it's like to be my sub. This is what it's like to be my Laurel."

He pushed his way in.

Full. She was so full. She could feel him everywhere. The ropes hugged her, the texture caressing her skin. The plug was so big. Mitch had to force his cock inside. Every inch was a delicious fight.

Mitch gripped her hips, thrusting inside. "Do you have any idea how perfect you are for me?"

She'd kind of thought he hadn't figured that out yet, but she would take it. She tilted her hips up, willing him to give her more. "I know you're perfect for me. Master, you feel so good."

He thrust in and pulled back out, taking his time and making her absolutely insane. "You like getting what you want, don't you, brat?"

He said the word with such affection she couldn't argue with him. She was being the tiniest bit bratty. She was moving against him, trying to find the perfect angle that would send her flying. "You know I do."

He pulled out, leaving her empty. "Unfortunately, tonight's not only about you, baby. I'm going to need you to hold on."

"Damn it."

A hard smack hit her ass, sending electric sparks through her. "That's one protocol I'm not giving up. No cursing in the club. I don't curse at you. I treat you with respect."

"I wasn't disrespecting you. I was merely expressing my deepest regret at your choices."

He chuckled. "Oh, I bet you are, baby. I bet you regret what I'm about to do, too. But you won't for long."

She gasped as he pulled the plug out. Empty. She'd been full and now she was so empty. He moved behind her and she heard the sounds of him opening the lubricant and pouring it on. She didn't feel it, so she guessed he was preparing his cock. In her mind, she could see her beautiful Master stroking that thick erection of his. His hand would move from the plum-shaped head to the thick stalk, all the way down almost to his balls. He would already be slick with her arousal, but he would need more for what he was about to do.

She braced as she felt the head of his cock at her asshole.

"Relax, baby. You can take me. We've been prepping for this. You can handle me." He pressed inside, using little strokes to open her up.

So much pressure. He was bigger than the plug, but there was something so intimate about it. This was something she'd never shared with anyone, but then even the acts she'd performed before seemed new with Mitchell.

She wanted him to be her last lover, her only Master, her only husband. When they were together like this, it felt so close to being true.

"I want you to flatten out your back." The words came out of his mouth in a low growl, his hands tightening on her hips. "Take a deep breath and then move against me."

He was right there. He was stretching her and she wasn't sure how much of him she could take. The pressure was crazy but not painful. It was an odd feeling, almost an anticipation of pain that never quite showed its face. She could handle this, she decided. She could handle him.

Deep breath in. She moved like a cat stretching, lengthening her spine, lifting her backside. And he slid inside, filling her to the point that she was gasping for air, the sensation so foreign and complex. One of Mitch's hands slid around and found her clitoris.

Everywhere. He was everywhere. Despite the fact that he was behind her, she felt surrounded by him. All those knots he'd tied were like a hundred hands caressing her. She wanted more, wanted him to tie her up from head to toe and then make love to her. She could be completely under his control and safe. He would worship her with his ropes and then with his cock, and she wouldn't have to do a thing except feel utterly adored by the man of her dreams.

"God, you feel so good. You can't know how good it feels to fuck you. I want you to come back to work for me, baby. I'll call you in when I want you. I'll fuck you on my desk, on your desk, in the break room, in the fucking lobby. There won't be a single inch of that office I don't fuck you in."

She couldn't breathe. He was holding himself still and she was trying to adjust. No amount of taking the plug could prepare her for the feel of hot flesh inside her, burning inside and making her want to move, to see what else he could give her. "I don't think that would be conducive to performance."

He rubbed her clit in rhythmic circles. "It would for me. I'd have you sit at my feet and when I finish what I need to, I'd have you suck my dick long and hard. A treat for staying on task because I never stay on task any more. I'm always thinking about you, always wondering what you're doing and where you are and if you're safe and happy."

That finger circling her made her forget all about the fact that she was stretched to overflowing. Her pussy was humming with his rhythm. "I'm safe, Master. I'm careful."

He started to move, tiny thrusts and retreats, as though his hips couldn't stay still. "I know you are, baby. When I'm not thinking about your safety, I'm daydreaming about fucking you. You're always there. Always in my head."

He dragged back, a long stroke from inside, and her body lit with sensation. She couldn't help it. She tried to stop the moan that came from her throat but it filled the room.

"Yes," he said as he filled her again. "Yes, that's what I want. I want you to crave my cock. I want you to take me anytime, anywhere. I want you addicted to this because I sure as hell am."

He fucked into her again, but this time was easier and she breathed into the sensation. His finger moved on her clit and she felt lit up from within. He pressed down hard and she went over the edge.

It seemed to let him off the leash. He stroked in and out, faster and faster. The heat, the pressure, the pleasure, all swamped her senses as she came again, this time harder than the last. It seemed to never end and then she felt him come. His movements lost their rhythm as he fucked her hard and then held himself against her, giving her everything he had.

He fell on her, cradling her and pulling her into the side of his body as he shifted on the bed. "Never think you aren't the most beautiful creature in the world."

In that moment, she could almost believe him.

Chapter Eight

"It's a dog and an orangutan. I don't see why that makes her cry. Really cry. She was sobbing over a commercial about animals that would eat each other in the wild. I make one comment about the fact that the tiger and the bear would totally go at it for dominance and she tells me I'm the world's worst human being and won't talk to me for thirty minutes. How am I supposed to respond to that? I can't punish her. She's already crying." Mitch sat back in his office and looked at Liam O'Donnell, Kai Ferguson, and Ian Taggart. Though to be honest, he was pretty sure Big Tag was asleep. Oh, he was sitting upright, but his eyes were behind mirrored aviators and his breathing was perfectly even. It had been six weeks since Laurel had moved in with him, since she'd become his submissive, and every night seemed like a new whirl on the roller coaster.

Since the night in the club, they'd found a happy rhythm to their lives, but every now and then he felt like he was stepping into a minefield.

Kai shook his head. "This is why signing a contract with her at this stage is a horrible idea. It's too much change for you and for her as well. This is a good time to take a step back and reassess both of your needs."

Li groaned. "There's no stepping back now, Kai. You want to make this some sort of an intellectual thing, but you can't. Laurel's pregnant. There's no way she's going to be logical, not with all those hormones running through her system. Do you want to know how to handle her, Bradford?"

Kai leaned forward. "The way to handle her is to treat her like a partner. You two got into this because you weren't thinking. You didn't have a solid contract in place when you started your sexual relationship and it looks like you're treating the one you have now with indifference. This isn't the way to start a relationship, much less one that I know she hopes is going to end in marriage."

"Says the perpetually single sadist," Li cracked back. "Love ain't got nothing to do with logic."

Li was right about Kai. And Mitch was beginning to think there was nothing logical or rational about his sub at this point in her life. Laurel seemed to be running on pure emotion and he had no idea how to handle that. "I'm going with Irish on this one, Kai. How do I handle Laurel?"

"Agree with everything she says. She thinks bears and tigers can be best friends, so do you. Absolutely, my love. Let's go buy two. Trust me, by the time you get around to finding that exotic pet shop she's moved on to worrying about something else. Avery cried pretty much every single day of her first three months. And then there were three lovely months where we fucked like rabbits, and I hid for the last three. That's pregnancy in a nutshell."

"Which is why this is a horrible time to begin a relationship," Kai pointed out. "Laurel isn't capable of thinking properly when she's so emotional and has a ton of stress on her. And starting a D/s relationship is even more risky. I applaud you for taking responsibility for the child, but you might take a step back and concentrate on becoming a father and then later, after the baby is born, then you can work on your relationship with Laurel."

That sent Li into a fit of laughter. "Oh, yeah, you'll have so much time for that after the baby's born. You got no idea what you're talking about, Kai. I know you've got some fancy degree and all, but you have zero idea how the whole marriage and parenting thing works. There's no logic to you. Look at the big guy there. His wife gave birth and the poor sap ain't had a decent night's sleep since. Do you honestly believe he's capable of logic?"

Kai rolled his eyes. "Big Tag is only capable of sarcasm and sitting perfectly upright while he naps. That's actually impressive, but not my point. Look, Mitch, you asked my opinion."

"No. I really didn't. I asked if you were ready to sign the paperwork on the office space and I got a lecture on how I'm screwing up with Laurel. And you know, aside from the whole crying at commercials thing, we're doing pretty good." Better than good. They'd had one fight in the six weeks they'd been together and apparently that was more about her hormones than his being a truly evil person who liked neither animals nor friendship. Her words, not his. After he'd gotten her some mint chocolate chip ice cream and rubbed her feet and watched some horrid show about doctors saving lives in between screwing each other in tiny rooms—she'd cried during that, too—she'd settled down and been the loving, affectionate sub he was crazy about.

They'd found a nice routine, one he'd come to crave. They had breakfast together every morning. He was used to grabbing something on his way into the office, but Laurel preferred to cook. He was getting used to egg white omelets and steel cut oatmeal, but he'd put his foot down when she'd tried to buy turkey bacon. Bacon came from pigs and no one was going to tell him otherwise. After breakfast, they went to work. She came to his office or he went to hers for lunch when they could. And she was always waiting for him when he came home. He would open the door and enter the living room and his gorgeous sub would be waiting there for him on her knees. Most of the time he had her right then and there, but a few nights had come that he could tell how tired she was, and he'd scooped her up and cuddled on the couch with her and ordered takeout so she wouldn't have to cook.

It was the times when he felt almost compelled to change the routine that scared him the most.

Li shook his head. "Kai's being pissy because his house exploded and there's no good place at the new Sanctum for him to live."

"I am not pissy," Kai shot back. "I'm annoyed because the place I lived and worked at exploded in a fiery hell ball and took everything with it, including most of my patient notes. I'm having to reestablish everything and I can't do that without office space. I'm tired of working out of McKay-Taggart. Do you have any idea how not peaceful that office is?"

Li shrugged. "Big Tag wouldn't let him put in a waterfall or some shit."

"It's a reflection pool and it's very peaceful and calming for my patients, all of whom have been through hell. I also would like to make myself clear on how wrong it is to bring the entire club in on one of your missions, Tag. Look what happened the last time and you were hiding Jesse and Phoebe at Sanctum. The club blew up. Letting Tennessee Smith work an op at Sanctum is going to cause trouble. But is Tag listening to me? No. He's asleep. That dude can sleep through anything."

At least Mitch could solve one issue. "Well, I got the paperwork for your new office so you can add all kinds of reflecting pools and stuff and still be close to the club. The building next door came up for sale. It's industrial, so you'll have to do some renovations."

The building next door had already been quietly purchased by Big Tag and his brother-in-law, Simon Weston. They'd come to Mitch with the plan to sell to Kai for a fraction of the price. What Kai didn't know was his loan had also been secured via Weston's relatives, the Malones. A whole bunch of very wealthy people were backing Kai's efforts to help soldiers with PTSD reintegrate into the civilian world. They weren't telling Kai, who was on a "stand on his own feet" kick after the club exploded.

"I'll take it. I need some quiet and I can't get it in that office. I swear I don't know how Eve does it. I can't have sessions because someone is always knocking on my door. And damn but there are a lot of babies up there now. Cute little things but…there is one hallway you don't want to walk down."

"He's right about that. The babies can make quite a stink when they want to," Li explained. "Now, do you want to know what I found out about your case or not? I came down here to give you a report. These two latched on. Kai wanted to nag you and Tag wants lunch at Top. I'm not going to wake him up until someone can shove a forkful of food in his mouth."

"How are you going to get him to Top if you don't wake him up?"

"Oh, he'll sleep walk for ya. You gotta point him in the right direction and he walks fine. And that's why you have to work all this out with your girl before the baby gets here." He pointed to Taggart, who didn't move an inch. "Because this is what you'll be like after. Ain't that right, Tag?"

Taggart made some kind of huffing sound and then went still again.

He didn't even think about what would happen after the baby got here. He tried not to think past the now. Making plans would only screw up a good thing. He passed Kai the documents and all the information on the building he was going to buy. While Kai went over his paperwork, Mitch turned back to Liam.

"Okay, can you tell me what's going on?"

"I've had surveillance on both the Dixon brothers for the last six weeks."

That didn't sound right. "I told you I was only interested in what Harvey Dixon did when he got out of rehab."

Li shook his head. "You did, but I changed up the plan. Look, I have more experience at these things than you do. There's always a bloody twist. So I've been watching both brothers and I did a thorough assessment of Dixon Technologies. The name sounds impressive, and in some ways it is. Harvey was the idea man while Patrick handled the money and the actual business operations. The company itself and the patents they hold are worth roughly three million dollars, but it turns out Patrick is a brilliant investor. He diversified the company a few years ago and now they have assets in excess of nine million. The trouble is there are three siblings involved. Patrick has a twin. Her name is Frances Dixon, and apparently she tends to side with Harvey against Patrick."

"Good for them. None of this explains why I'm getting my ass kicked regularly." The phone calls had started two weeks before. He got robocalls at all hours of the night. They began at precisely ten p.m. and went on until six a.m. He'd turned off his phone after the first few and then changed his number.

"Adam traced the calls back to a computer, but it was at a public library. Someone got on the system and upgraded the thing, so to speak. That's why you only got the calls late a night. They were set up to turn on after the library closed and everyone was gone. Obviously this is something a man of Harvey Dixon's brilliance can do, but it's also something most hackers can handle. I've also used surveillance footage and found the kid who's been vandalizing the building and your car. His name's Austin Hunt. Seventeen. Juvie record about a mile long. I took everything to Brighton and he sent his men out to bring the bugger in for questioning, but the kid's in the wind."

He looked down at the picture Liam placed in front of him. He was a kid, but he was a kid who had fired a gun at Laurel. "So you think Dixon hired this kid."

"I think one of the Dixons hired this kid. The question is which one."

"The real question I have is why any of them would bug me. I'm just the damn lawyer. I'm representing a company that made it to market first. I'm not responsible for the invention. If I drop the case, someone else will pick it up. They can't stop this from happening."

Liam sat back. "No, at the end of the day, there's nothing any of them can do, so I have to either come up with a logical reason for this to be happening or accept that Patrick Dixon is telling the truth and this is all Harvey. Harvey could be paying the kid. According to Derek, Austin Hunt is known for hiring himself out. He's already worked for a couple of area drug dealers and his father had mob ties."

But Liam was suspicious, and everyone who knew the McKay-Taggart boys knew Liam O'Donnell was the one with an almost sixth sense when it came to crime. "You want to dig deeper?"

"I do. I know you want this to be cut and dry, but I don't think it is. I think there's more here and I need to find some kind of money trail.

Whether it leads from Harvey Dixon to Austin Hunt or somewhere else, my every instinct is telling me to find the money. It's buried deep, but it's here. In the meantime, you've got the new security system both here and at the house. If it escalates, we'll put someone on you twenty-four seven."

"How is the guard on Laurel doing?" He wanted to forbid her to work at all, but he was smart enough to know that wouldn't fly. However, he'd also known the moment she moved into his house that she would become a target. He'd set her up with an air horn and a bottle of pepper spray, and a bodyguard for the hours he wasn't with her.

She didn't know about the bodyguard. He pretty much hoped she never found out about the bodyguard.

"I've put Remy Guidry on her. He's one of the five professional bodyguards Tag recently hired. Adam and Jake used to do all our close cover, but that's not possible anymore. With the corporate accounts we've recently signed, we've got a lot of bodyguard work."

"Is he any good?" He didn't like the idea of the new guy watching over his sub.

"He's former Navy SEAL. He's patient and very thorough. Talks like a douchebag though."

"He talks like he's from New Orleans, which he is," Kai shot back. "Remy's solid, Mitch. He'll take care of Laurel. He will not take care of you when Laurel finds out you put a six-foot, five-inch Cajun bodyguard on her ass twenty-four seven."

"Hey, if nothing goes wrong then she never has to know." He'd already gone over this line of thinking about a hundred times. "And if it does go wrong, she'll be happy to be alive."

"Keep thinking that, buddy." Kai handed him back the signed paperwork. "Can I get a copy of the file you've got on Hunt? I can take a look at it. I'm sure Eve already has, but fresh eyes are always good. Harvey Dixon, too, if you have it."

"Absolutely. There are also some interviews with business magazines and a couple of stories about the family. Anything you find could be helpful," Li explained. "Could I have a moment alone with Mitch?"

Kai's eyes narrowed. "Sure. Is this a client thing?"

Li nodded. "We do have confidentiality clauses. He might not have a problem talking about this in front of you, but I have to give him a chance to keep it private."

"Kai's cool. He knows pretty much everything. I don't think I have anything to hide." Mitch couldn't imagine what Liam was about to say.

"All right then. While I was looking into the Dixons and trying to see if they had any ties to you we didn't know about, Adam found out that someone is definitely looking for you and it ain't Harvey Dixon."

Maybe it would have been better to ship Kai out. "Are you talking about a man named Flynn Adler?"

Kai sat up. Mitch could guess why. He'd heard the name Adler in connection with Mitch but never Flynn. "Isn't your father's name Adler? John Adler?"

"Flynn is my half brother. I have two. Flynn is Dad's son by his second wife. He's a couple of years younger than me. Chase is in high school, I think."

"You think?" Kai asked. "You have two brothers and you never mentioned them?"

Yep, this was why he'd never brought them up in conversation. "They're my half brothers and I've never spoken to them. They're my father's legitimate children. Liam, I don't have anything to do with my father. He gave me money to start my firm. I didn't want to take it. Margot insisted on taking the money and my father's contacts. The minute I could, I paid the man back so I didn't feel pressure to talk to him. He doesn't want anything to do with me. He never has. Guilt made him loan me that money."

"From what I can tell, it wasn't a loan. Did you know there's a trust in your name? It was started with the exact amount of money he loaned you," Liam explained.

He wasn't even going to ask how O'Donnell had found out about that. There was a reason McKay-Taggart was considered one of the best firms in the world. As for the trust, he wouldn't touch it. "It doesn't matter. I don't need his money. Like I said, it's guilt money. I think he feels it more as he gets older. Now he's sending Flynn after me. I don't read his e-mails and I don't take his calls. As far as I'm concerned, the Adler family doesn't exist."

Li nodded. "All right then. I had to ask. He's been calling you since before the Dixon problems?"

"Yes. The two events are mutually exclusive. Flynn will give up after a while. It's not a problem, but do get back to me about Dixon."

Liam stood. "That's all I have then. I'll keep in touch. Kai, can you bring the car around?"

Kai stared at Mitch for a moment and then sighed. "I don't guess you want to talk about the fact that you have a whole family you've never mentioned?"

"I don't. That's the whole point. I don't have a family." Beyond

Laurel and the baby. They were going to be his family. He had to make sure he made things right for them.

"All right. I'll pull up in front of the building." Kai walked out.

Li followed him. "I'm going to watch for him and then I'll come back up to get the big guy to the car. Don't let him fall over or anything."

And he was left with a very still Ian Taggart.

"What the hell would you do, Tag? What would you do if your dad was still alive and wanted to talk to you?" Big Tag's father had walked out on him and his brother, Sean. He'd married again and had two children Tag hadn't met until the year before, and naturally Tag had welcomed them with open arms and sarcasm. Now they worked together, though Mitch was fairly certain Taggart was closer to Theo than Case.

Should he talk to Flynn? He didn't want to. He didn't want to get dragged into their lives. He'd wanted it so desperately at one point and now he wanted to forget the Adlers existed.

What would Laurel say? Why did it truly matter what Laurel would say? It didn't affect her in any way. She wasn't involved and he meant to keep it that way. She never needed to know they existed as far as he was concerned. So why was he wondering what she would think?

"How did you know you wanted to get married?" He kind of liked sleeping Tag. It was like he had a buddy, but one who didn't talk. "How did you know you were in love?"

He didn't like the word. It was imprecise, but Laurel was very soft hearted. She would want to hear it. She would want to say it to him and hear it back. He was coming to the point that he would have to use it.

"Charlie told me." Big Tag stretched and pulled off his sunglasses.

"Sorry. I didn't mean to wake you up."

Tag put a hand over his mouth to cover a yawn. "Hey, I woke up to a whiny manheart question and not the sound of two warrior princesses trying to out wail each other. I'm counting it as a win."

"Okay. I feel better about my life."

"Yeah, you can for the next seven and a half months or so and then you're up shit creek, buddy. You going to marry Laurel?"

"I already asked her." He hadn't really asked her though. He'd told her he would and in an almost grudging fashion. Not the most romantic of proposals. But what could she expect? If she'd wanted romance, she should have found someone else. "I suppose you knew it was the right time to marry Charlotte because she told you to."

"Bingo. If I'd had my way we would have simply signed a contract and I would have kept her as my submissive. I would have put a collar around her throat and shown her off at clubs and been very happy."

"That doesn't sound so bad." It actually sounded kind of perfect. He'd tried marriage. Maybe he and Laurel could try a long-term contract. Once a year they would review and renew it.

"You didn't let me finish. I would have been very happy until she decided she wanted more."

"Why does there have to be more? I've tried this twice, Tag, and it doesn't work for me. Still, I'm willing to give it a try for the kid's sake."

"Does she know that's why you're willing to try?"

He shrugged. "I might have mentioned it. I try to be honest with her."

Tag frowned, his mouth turning down. "That's where you're going wrong. Totally wrong. Honesty is horrible. No wonder she won't marry you. Hey, but that's a good thing because you don't want to get married."

"You didn't want to get married either."

A mysterious smile crooked up the sides of Tag's face. "Didn't I? I don't remember. I'll have to ask Charlie. Well, the good news is Laurel's got a whole family around her and once the inevitable happens, she and the kid will be fine."

This whole conversation was making him antsy. She didn't need her brother or her sisters to take care of her. She had him. "She'll be fine because I'll make sure she's fine. One way or another."

Tag gave him a thumbs-up. "Sounds like you know what you're doing then. No need to worry that you don't have legal ties to her or the kid. I'm sure it will all work out on its own. That's the great thing about relationships. They happen on their own with no work or compromise at all. I'm going to go and eat whatever Sean made. He said it was..." Tag yawned again, looking a whole lot like a sleepy lion. "I don't remember. Meat. It better be meat. I want to put meat in my face before I go back to the office. I've got a meeting with some bigwig computer dude to nap through this afternoon. You'll be fine. Hey, you're totally used to breakups and stuff."

What the fuck was that supposed to mean?

Before he could ask, Liam was rushing into the room. "Mitchell, we need to get over to Laurel's. It seems there's been a break-in at her apartment. I got a call from Derek. Lisa was going over to check on the place and found the door open. She called the police and Derek is on his way."

Thank god Laurel was at work. He rushed out, ready to hurt someone.

* * * *

"Laurel Daley?"

Laurel looked up from her computer. "Yes?"

She had to stop and do a double take because for a moment, she thought she was looking at Mitchell. It took a few blinks to realize this man was younger, a bit less broad than her Master. He was also far better dressed, a thing she intended to address eventually with Mitch. She had to go slow with her Dom, introduce things gradually. She was going to sneak in a couple of pairs of navy-colored slacks. He wouldn't even realize he was wearing them and when he did, she would point out that he'd been wearing them for weeks and the world hadn't ended.

But none of that mattered because she was looking at someone who absolutely had to be related to her Master.

The gorgeous man in front of her was dressed casually in an open-throated black shirt and khakis. His hair was stylishly long, brushing the tops of his muscled shoulders. "My name is Flynn Adler. I'm so happy to meet you, Laurel. I've read an awful lot about you."

That forced her attention away from the fact that he looked like Mitch. She immediately went on full alert and thought about how she should handle this. She didn't know this man, but he knew her.

"I'm afraid you're going to have to explain what that means." She put as much chill as she could into her voice. She was well aware of the situation with Harvey Dixon. If he was now sending someone to intimidate her, she wasn't about to give him what he wanted.

But how the hell had Dixon found someone who looked so much like Mitchell? That couldn't be a coincidence.

The man in front of her frowned. "The private investigator told me you're living with Mitch."

Now she was nervous. Luckily, it wasn't quite lunchtime. The office was still full of people. It gave her some measure of comfort. "Private investigator?"

"I'm sorry. I'm...well, I never expected that Mitch wouldn't tell you about us. He's never mentioned me or Chase?"

She didn't recognize either name. "Who's Chase? For that matter, who are you?"

"I'm Flynn Adler." He placed careful emphasis on his last name, as though it should mean something to her. When she said nothing, he continued. "Of the California Adlers. I'm Mitchell's brother."

Her stomach dropped. Brother? He had a brother and he'd never once mentioned him? Mitchell knew all about her family. She told him everything. She thought he'd always been quiet because all he had was his mother, and they weren't close. Now she found out he had a brother? Only one? "And Chase?"

"He's the youngest. Mitch is first. He's eight years older than me. Chase is significantly younger. He's a junior in high school. Mitch really never told you about us?"

She shook her head. What else hadn't he told her? How did he hide a whole family? And why? Did she mean so little to him that he didn't bother to mention his brothers? "Did he mention you to me?"

Flynn huffed. "Uhm, no. He doesn't talk to me, Laurel. I found out about you through the private investigator. I'm so sorry to invade your privacy this way. I had no other choice. I thought it would be better to talk to you. You're obviously important to my brother."

"I don't know about that. Our relationship is fairly casual." It hadn't felt that way. It felt serious, but she had to question the fact that he'd hidden this part of his life from her. Was he never going to tell her their baby had two uncles?

"I thought you were living with him."

"We're not engaged or anything. Not really looking to do it." Mitch had made himself plain. He would marry her, but he didn't want to. He would do it for the sake of the baby. "I'm not sure how much I can help you. I can give you Mitch's office address."

He held a hand up. "No. I have it. I've tried to contact him about a hundred times over the last twenty years. I've called and e-mailed and sent letters. I'm worried that if I show up at his office unannounced, he'll call the cops. If I show up announced, he'll probably lock the doors and leave me outside. So I thought I would come and talk to you."

"Why won't he talk to you?"

"I have to think it's more about our father than me. I've only met Mitch once. I was a kid. He didn't say more than two or three sentences to me. He was really only interested in talking to Dad about the money to start his firm. Once he had that and Dad had introduced him to some important clients, he dropped us. Well, Dad. He never was interested in me. I sent him a note when Chase was born. Nothing. Not even a card."

Mitch had told her Margot, his first wife, had been the one to go to his father. He hadn't wanted to. Now it seemed like there was more to the story. If her baby had more family, she wanted to know about it.

Sometimes Mitch could be very stubborn. He could let really good things pass him by because he was afraid of the change they would bring to his life. She'd spent weeks thinking about him, weeks trying to dig under the surface and find the real man she knew was buried underneath his pride.

His pride would keep him from his family unless she did something. His pride might keep their baby from knowing his or her relatives, and she couldn't allow that to happen. "Maybe we should talk. How about an early lunch? There's a sandwich place next door. It's not great, but if you stick to deli staples, you'll be okay. Don't try the special."

He smiled. It was what Mitch would smile like if he ever relaxed and let himself be truly happy. "I promise."

Ten minutes later she sat across from Flynn Adler, a chicken sandwich loaded with veggies and cup of tortilla soup on her side. He'd gone for the all-meat special. Another way he was an awful lot like his brother. He was courting heart disease and apparently loved cholesterol. Still, she wasn't allowed to nag no matter how much she wanted to.

Discussing the Master's diet was off limits. So naturally she'd taken to cooking breakfast every morning and dinner every night. She'd gotten a cookbook that taught her how to sneak vegetables into staple meals. It was meant for kids, but worked on Mitch, too.

Sometimes she felt like she had to sneak in her love or Mitch would reject it.

"So why are you here?" She took a sip of her water. It was hard not to see Mitch in his brother.

"I'm here because Dad is dying and he needs to see Mitch. I gave up trying to get to know Mitch years ago. I get it. He doesn't want anything to do with me or Chase. I wouldn't be here for me. I'm here for my dad."

"Your dad, who walked away from Mitch? Who didn't have anything to do with him for most of his childhood?" She knew enough of the story to defend Mitch a bit.

When he raised that singular brow and his jawline got hard, he really looked like Mitch, the Dom. "There are always two sides to a story, and you would do well to remember that. I'll admit that my father was married to his first wife when he had an affair with Mitch's mother. I don't know everything."

"Mitch grew up without him. Isn't that all you need to know?"

"Did you know Dad settled a bunch of money on Nora Bradford? Do you know what she did with it? She moved them out of San

Francisco and as far away from Dad as she could get. Once she ran through the money Dad meant for Mitch, she went through a string of lovers and wouldn't allow Dad to see his son without sending a hefty check. After a while, it got too hard to keep up with where Nora had taken him. She moved about ten times before Mitch got to high school."

Chaos. It would have been so chaotic for a child to constantly be on the move. Always the new kid. Always having to adapt to his mother's new man. Never having a family to call his own. His mother, from what she could tell, was always more interested in herself than Mitch. She didn't call him unless she wanted something, usually money.

What had it been like to be Mitch growing up? She'd had a rough childhood. Her mother had been in and out of jail, in and out of rehab, but they'd owned their trailer and somehow Will had always found a way to keep them together and fed. She'd always had Will and Lila and Lisa. They'd given her support and love and stability.

Mitch, it seemed, had none of those things.

"He could have fought for custody. It sounds like he would have won."

"I didn't say my father was perfect. He went through a divorce and married my mother. And then another divorce. I suppose he lost track of Mitchell, lost the will to fight. Like I said, he's not perfect."

She couldn't imagine having a child in the world and not fighting to be his mother. "What does he want with Mitchell now?"

Flynn leaned forward, his eyes on her as though he could will her to believe him. "Laurel, he's dying. He was recently diagnosed with stage four cancer. The doctors have given him maybe a month to live. Six weeks, tops. He wants to make things right with Mitch. He needs this. It's his dying wish."

"And you've written to Mitch?" How could Mitch know his father was dying and not talk about it? She talked about her mother often. He'd even driven her and Lisa halfway across the state the prior weekend to visit their mom in prison. He'd made sure her mother had everything she needed.

But not once had he mentioned his own father was dying.

"Multiple times. I've sent e-mails, letters, left voice mail messages. He changed his number, naturally, and now I can't find it."

He'd changed it for a different reason, but Flynn didn't need to know that. She wasn't sure how much to tell him. "He hasn't talked to me about it. Mitch can be stubborn. I know he feels your father abandoned him."

Flynn's hands were fists as he moved them off the table. "Then Mitch should confront him about it. All my dad wants is to see him. I don't think it will matter if Mitch needs to yell and scream and let it all out as long as he gives our father a few minutes of his time so he can say what he needs to say."

"Mitch would never yell." He never lost control that way. Except the first couple of times they'd made love. When they made love now, he was very controlled. He brought her an enormous amount of pleasure, but it felt like there was a distance between them. He was thoughtful and she knew she should be grateful for it, but she missed the passion they'd had those first two times.

Mitch wouldn't yell. Not at his father. Not at her. Maybe it was a good thing or maybe he simply didn't care enough to yell.

"He needs to. My father would take it. He knows he hurt Mitch, but how can he ever have any chance to make it right if Mitch won't talk to him?"

"I'm not sure Mitch believes in second chances." It was another thing that frightened her. They were happy for now, but when the pressure hit and she couldn't play the perfect submissive, when she had to be a woman with all her flaws, how would he handle it?

He always said the reason he hadn't wanted a relationship with her was because she deserved better. What if he'd just been kind by saying that? What if the real reason had been he simply hadn't wanted her?

Flynn sat back, his sandwich untouched. "Then there's not a lot I can do. I'm sorry I wasted your time."

He started to push his chair back, like he was leaving. She couldn't let that happen. Flynn had ties to Mitch, knowledge she needed. Flynn was his brother. He couldn't walk away with nothing. She reached out a hand and put it over his.

"Please don't go. I know Mitch won't talk to you or your dad, but I will. I lied to you. Mitch and I are serious. Maybe not about getting married, but we've got a commitment between us and you should know I'm pregnant."

Flynn sat back, a smile covering his handsome face. "That's great, Laurel. It's about damn time, as my dad would say. Mitch isn't getting any younger. When's the wedding? Or are you waiting until after the baby's born? I know that's a popular thing to do. Damn, Dad's going to be happy to hear that. He doesn't have any grandkids."

Why did she always blush when she had to answer the wedding question? It was the twenty-first century. Plenty of people had babies without getting married. She'd grown up in a household where her mother had never married and had four kids. Not that she wanted to follow in her mom's footsteps, but still. "We don't have plans to marry at this point. I'm afraid this baby wasn't planned, though I'm very happy about the pregnancy."

Was she? She wanted the baby. She knew that, but it was hard to be happy about it when Mitch didn't want to talk about baby things. Every time she brought up things like nurseries or baby names, he shifted the conversation to something different, saying they had plenty of time to discuss it. They needed to live in the now and let the future work itself out.

She was getting sick of living in the now.

"That's great. I know you don't know me very well, but I would love to know my niece or nephew."

She sat up straight. Maybe it was time someone knew Flynn Adler. "I would like that, too. Are you married?"

He shook his head. "No. I run the family company. I don't have time to date. We're moving into a couple of new and exciting areas. I always wanted to run R&D, but I was needed in management. Chase is a better programmer anyway. He's incredible. I'm worried he won't make it out of high school. He's had some trouble with drugs. It scares the hell out of me."

Flynn seemed like a man who had the weight of the world on his shoulders. He reminded her a little of her brother. There had been a time when Will had to juggle school and work and being a dad because they didn't have one. "Where is your mother in all this?"

"She's in Monaco with her second husband, who happens to be younger than me. Chase's mom died of breast cancer a few years back. We're all that's left. I seem to be failing at raising a teenage boy. I don't know how to get through to him. I can't make him understand that life isn't high school."

He was alone. "Would it help at all if I talked to your father? I can't promise you that Mitch will, but I can at least tell him about the baby and how well Mitch is doing professionally."

Flynn had his cell phone out in a heartbeat. "I can't tell you how much that would help." He punched in a few numbers. "Hey, Dad. Guess who I'm talking to?"

A few minutes later she took the phone and had a long talk with the grandfather of her child.

Chapter Nine

Mitchell looked around the small apartment and thanked god Laurel hadn't been here. Someone had kicked in her door and then taken a knife to the place. Her furniture was slashed all to hell, pictures broken, all her dishes smashed.

Lisa walked in, her eyes red. She'd been the one to call the police, and then Derek Brighton had immediately contacted Li. It had been a good thing to let Derek know McKay-Taggart was on the case. Otherwise, it might have been hours before he would have been notified.

Lisa walked right up to him and threw her arms around his waist, crying. "Who would do this, Mitch? Who would try to hurt her like this?"

The good news was he was totally getting used to dealing with crying Daley women. He was sure at one point in time he would have hesitated, but now he simply hugged her back. She was Laurel's sister and he was Laurel's…damn. Well, he was Laurel's Dom and it was his job to comfort her sister and that was that.

How would they view him after a while? He knew the whole Daley family thought they were only months away from a wedding. Would Lisa seek comfort from him if he knew he and her sister were never going to get married?

He pushed the thoughts aside because only one thing mattered now and that was dealing with the problem in front of him. The police were busy, taking pictures, looking for fingerprints.

"This isn't about her. It's about me," he explained to Lisa. "And I'm going to fix it."

She stepped back. "It's about you?"

"Someone doesn't want me working on the contract I'm writing at the moment."

Her jaw firmed and a stubborn light hit her eyes. "Well, screw them. You can't back down."

The Daley women were a bit stubborn too, he'd learned. Oh, they could be sneaky, but they tended to get their way. He wasn't an idiot. He knew the mashed potatoes Laurel served hadn't had a damn potato in them. He suspected cauliflower was the culprit. But she'd looked so excited about it, he'd played along.

He'd specifically requested she stop nagging him about his diet. Not requested. Ordered. And he hadn't even thought about punishing her for lying. He'd smiled like an idiot and eaten every semi-nasty bite, and then found out that Laurel's version of brownies contained something that wasn't sugar, but also wasn't half bad, and he hadn't disciplined her for that either.

"I'm not going to back down. I'm making a lot of money on this contract and I'll need it. Besides, me backing down only sends the problem along to someone else. I'd rather catch this guy and make him pay." He nodded as Derek stepped out of the kitchen with Liam.

"Mitchell, we haven't been able to get hold of Laurel," Derek said. "We were hoping you would know where she is."

She'd texted him and told him she was going to lunch with a friend at the deli close to work. "Her phone was dying. Something's wrong with her battery. It's being replaced this afternoon. She texted me she would be out of pocket for an hour or so right before Liam and Kai showed up. Where are Kai and the big guy?"

"Kai took Tag to lunch. I can't let him go into a meeting hungry. He tends to eat the clients. Derek will give me a ride back to the office," Li explained. "Lisa called it in. She has a unit at the end of the hall. She was coming back from a class and noticed the door was open."

"It was kicked in," Lisa said, sniffling. "I looked past the door but that was all I needed to do. I was too afraid to go inside. I tried to call my sister but it went to voice mail. When I called Will, he told me to call Derek directly and here we are."

"You did the right thing." He worried Laurel wouldn't have. She would have marched in and tried to confront whoever was in her apartment. And why did she still have this place anyway? She was paying rent on a place she didn't live in. Why would she need to do that? They should have packed the place up and moved her stuff to storage.

Derek gestured back to the techs he had working the scene. "We've already got a couple of prints. We need Laurel's and whoever else would normally be here so we can exclude them. This place only has security cameras at the gates. If someone jumped the fence, it's likely we don't have them on camera, but we're going to look."

Which meant they likely wouldn't get much. "I want to know where Harvey Dixon was while this was going on."

"I'm already on it."

He looked around at the mess that had been made. Laurel had brought most of her clothes with her. She'd brought books and some pictures, but she'd left her dishes because he'd had his and there wasn't a ton of room for more. Now he wondered if she'd spent time selecting the pattern. They weren't in one piece anymore but there was color to her dishes. His were a plain white chosen for utility. Laurel would have picked something she thought was pretty or had reminded her of something that made her happy.

Why hadn't he offered to bring her things into his home? Was he still thinking of it as his home? Not theirs?

When he thought about it, the house he'd bought when he moved to Dallas didn't fit Laurel. He'd given the realtor a set of parameters and when he'd found one that met his needs, he'd purchased it. Good neighborhood. Close to work. No big yard upkeep.

Laurel would have liked a yard. He didn't have anywhere to sit in the back and when she'd brought it up, he'd told her no because it would be hot soon and no one sat outside in the Texas heat. He'd told her it was silly to spend good money on outdoor furniture they wouldn't use for more than a few months of the year.

And she'd simply sighed and gone in to cook dinner.

Why had he done that? Why was it bothering him now?

Because she's going to leave you. Because she's going to find someone who'll move heaven and earth to get her a damn patio set so she can sit outside and have her coffee even if it's only a couple of days out of the year. Because she'll find someone who can make her happy.

"Are you sure this wasn't random, Mas...Lieutenant Brighton?" Lisa winced. "Sorry, Sir."

Derek put a hand on her shoulder. "It's fine though I notice he's just Mitch to you. No formalities for him?"

She blushed. "He's family. You put a baby up in my sister, you're family. I don't call my brother by a title either. Ever. It's not going to happen no matter who spanks me."

Liam chuckled, but Mitch was thinking it was nice that she didn't even think to follow club rules with him. Because he was family.

"And I think the note left in her bedroom is solid proof that this wasn't random." Derek pointed to the door in the back. "If you're careful, I'll let you come back and see it. Try not to touch anything. Mitch, I'll need your prints, too."

But he wouldn't. "I've never been here before. Lisa brought her a bag for the first week and when we decided she would stay with me, she came after work and picked up the stuff she wanted. I was stuck on a call about a liability claim against a company I represent."

"You've never been here?" Derek asked, stopping in the doorway. "She's lived here for three years."

He'd never been to her apartment because he'd known what would happen if he came here. It had happened anyway. He'd pushed her away back then and now he had to wonder if he wasn't doing the same thing now. He was crazy about her, but he still kept his distance. He still placed that very significant mileage between them.

Did he want it? Did it make him feel safe because she couldn't quite touch his essential self?

He followed Derek. "No. I brought her to my place when I could. She worked for me. Our relationship was kept to the office until recently."

"But she's pregnant. At least that's what I heard."

"Yes, our son or daughter was conceived on my desk." He nodded as he realized certain truths. "I probably should keep that desk. It's kind of historical."

His child—maybe his only kid—had been conceived on that desk. Would it be his only? How much better would his life had been if he'd had brothers or sisters to depend on? What if he hadn't been alone in the world?

How could he get her pregnant again and quickly, so she would need him even more?

God, he was such a shit.

Liam was chuckling. "It's good to keep that handy. Avery and I have a couch very much like that, brother."

Derek laughed and entered the bedroom.

He heard Lisa gasp and felt her move closer to him.

When he saw the far wall, he pretty much wanted to kill someone.

Someone had spray-painted the wall over her bed.

Bradford's whore

Oh, someone was going to die.

Lisa gasped and then he heard a low growl from behind him.

"Son of a bitch." Will stepped into the room, his eyes wide and an angry look on his face. "Tell me you're taking care of this, Mitch."

"I'm doing everything I can. I've got O'Donnell on the case." He hesitated mentioning the bodyguard. As sweet as Lisa was, she would absolutely go straight to her sister and tell her everything, and then he would have one very stubborn Laurel to deal with. He tried her phone again. She should be back from lunch by now.

It went straight to voice mail.

"Maybe it's time we thought about getting her out of the line of fire," Will said. "She can come and stay with me and Bridget."

"No." He wasn't giving her up. "I told you, she's safe at the house. My place is far more secure than your building. I've got the rest of it handled. There's a reason he's going after soft targets like this place."

Will stared at him as though he could see through him. He finally nodded. "All right, but the minute he gets anywhere close, she needs to be out of this."

"The contract is finalized next week. A few more days and it's all over. He'll have to find another target for his irrational rage."

"Will, we've got an eye on all of this," Li explained. "And Derek is taking another look, too."

Will nodded and seemed to calm a bit. "I tried Laurel, but I can't get hold of her. I'm going to run over to her office."

Derek smiled and asked Lisa to join him so he could take her statement, leaving him alone with Will and Li.

Li leaned in, making sure Lisa couldn't hear them. "Mitch put a bodyguard on Laurel a couple of weeks back."

Will let out a long breath, obviously relieved. "Thank god. Does she know about the apartment?"

Mitch dialed her again and it went to voice mail. "No. I think you're right. I think we should go and talk to her. Let me check in and make sure she's all right." He punched in a number and a Cajun accent came over the line.

"This is Guidry."

"Do you have eyes on Laurel?"

"That's my job. Though you should know that keeping my eyes on that pretty *chère* ain't no job at all."

Maybe she needed a new bodyguard. He had to hope all of Tag's new employees weren't such flirty assholes. "So she's back at work?"

"Nah, she's taking an extra long lunch today. Must have something to do with her male friend. You said this was a protection job. You didn't tell me she was cheating on you. Do you want pictures or something?"

His blood seemed to chill. "What are you talking about?"

The line went quiet for a moment. "So this wasn't about the fact that she's getting cozy with someone else?"

His blood started to thump through his system. This was a place he'd been in before. It wasn't the first time he'd stood there like an idiot while some professional investigator gave him the rundown of all the ways the woman he was committed to had given her body to someone else. A vision of Laurel in bed with some nameless man assaulted him. The man would be younger, kinder, more giving, he was sure. The new man would be all the things Laurel needed. All the things Laurel had given up when she'd gotten pregnant by Mitch. "Where is she?"

Guidry's voice came over the line. "No, slow down. I was joking around. I was surprised that she was spending so much time with someone I haven't seen before. She usually follows a routine. She eats lunch at her desk or in the break room. Maybe this is completely innocent."

But she hadn't mentioned that she was having lunch with a man. She'd texted him, as they'd agreed, to let him know her phone wasn't working, but now he had to wonder. Was it truly not working or did she merely want to be alone with someone? She hadn't mentioned any male friends. Laurel loved to talk about work. He knew the names of everyone there. She was friendly with some of the male workers. Maybe that was all it was.

"Is it one of her coworkers? I know she's friends with a Jeremy." That was all. Jeremy was young and good looking, but Laurel told him they were only friends. He forced himself to calm down. He was being an irrational freak. He trusted Laurel.

"No, I've documented all the coworkers. This is a new guy."

"Where is she?" He would go and see for himself. Maybe she was interviewing a client. She took her work seriously and she was a compassionate woman. It didn't mean she was cheating on him.

"She's at the deli next to work. It's not like she's in a motel."

"How long has she been there?"

"An hour and fifteen minutes. Look, Bradford, I really was joking. I was ribbing you. She's been eating and talking." There was another pause over the line. "That's all."

That little pause made him think. There was something else. Something Guidry wasn't telling him. "What else? Damn it, Guidry. You work for me. I'm the one paying the bills, and I want to know what else she's done with him."

A long sigh came over the line. "She hugged him for a while and she seems pretty affectionate with him for a man she just met, that's all. At one point, she held his hand for a little while as they talked. But from what I can tell, she's an affectionate girl."

She was affectionate with her family. She wasn't with anyone else but her lover. No. God, this couldn't be happening to him again.

Not with Laurel. Please not with Laurel.

He felt a piece of himself go cold. If Laurel was cheating, he had to go cold. If Laurel was sleeping with someone else, he might never warm up again.

"Call me if she leaves and get photos. I want to know who this man is and I want the information soon. I don't care who you have to get on it. Find out who he is and how long she's been seeing him." He hung up.

"What the hell is going on, Mitch?" Will followed him as he started out of the apartment and toward his car.

He didn't want to have this conversation now. He needed to get there. He needed to see for himself that Laurel was exactly like all the rest. She was looking out for her best prospect, and he'd always known it wouldn't end up being him.

"It's between me and your sister." The last thing he needed was Will coming with him.

"I don't like the look on your face. You need to calm down." Will kept following him.

Mitch made it to his car. He wasn't about to tote her brother around. He was sure Will would make a hundred excuses for her. He had to see it for himself and then he could figure out what to do.

He got in and immediately locked the door, started up the car and backed out. Will stared at him, shaking his head. He immediately got on his phone, very likely trying to warn Laurel that hell was coming her way. Poor Laurel. She'd left her phone behind so he couldn't interrupt her date, and now that action was going to come back to haunt her.

He drove toward her work like a man possessed.

* * * *

Laurel sniffled as she hung up and passed the phone back to Flynn. "He seemed happy."

Flynn slid the phone in his pocket. "I'm sure he was. You have no idea how much not having Mitch in his life has haunted my father. I think he made a choice at one point. He decided it was too hard to deal with Mitch's mother and Dad gave up. He would send money, but not fight her on seeing him. He thought after Mitch turned eighteen they could start over again."

She could have told him that would never have worked. Mitch was far too stubborn to allow that to happen. Though he didn't talk about his father, she knew Mitch had to be angry with him. How could he not be?

She'd been angry with her mom. Her mother had battled addiction throughout Laurel's childhood, but at the time all Laurel had been able to see was the fact that her mother consistently chose drugs over her children. Now she could look back with more mature eyes and see how hard her mother had it. Nothing was ever cut and dried. There were always two sides to a story and rarely was any one person perfectly good or perfectly evil. Most people tried. Her mother had come from an abusive family and despite her struggles, she'd never gone back, never exposed her kids to her fist-wielding father, though Laurel was sure at some points it would have been easier for her to have gone home. She'd come to peace with her mother, and it had been freeing to not have all that rage in her heart. She wasn't sure how she could go into being a mom without it.

Mitch needed to see his dad. He needed to come to terms with his father before it was too late.

"I'm sure Mitch was stubborn. I'm surprised he took the money your father offered."

"That was all Margot."

He'd met Mitch's ex? "Did you know her?"

Flynn frowned. "Yeah. When I met her I'd recently started college. I was pretty excited to meet Mitch since I'd heard about him all my life. Margot was an interesting woman."

There was something about the way he said "interesting." "I know she cheated on him with his business partner."

Flynn's eyes wouldn't quite meet hers. "I would suspect that was just the tip of the iceberg."

"What happened? Did she hit on you?"

"My father. I walked in once and she was all over Dad. He turned her down, but she was always looking for the best bargain. I remember that's pretty much exactly what she said. She asked why would she go for the imitation when she could have the real thing. Dad tried to talk to Mitch about it but he wouldn't hear anything he had to say. There was a huge fight and a few years later, Margot had Mitch's firm and Mitch pretty much spent everything he had left to pay Dad back. When he started up the second time, he didn't engage my father at all. I never met his second wife."

Mitch had a lot of reasons to distrust relationships. From what she'd managed to uncover, his second wife had cheated on him, too. "His mother had a lot of relationships."

"Oh, yes. From what I understand she went from wealthy man to wealthy man. It didn't matter if they were married or single. If they could take care of her, she was okay with it. She's been married five times, but there were many more men. She moved often. I'm sure that had an effect on Mitch."

He held on to things that didn't matter because he found them comforting. All those places he'd lived and likely not a one of them had been a home. He couldn't trust the ground underneath his feet. It was constantly changing.

She could see him as a child. Alone. Confused. Afraid.

That would not happen to her baby. And it wouldn't happen to Mitch again either. Not if she had any say in it.

The door to the deli opened and she gasped in surprise. Mitch stood there, his face a bright red as he looked over the customers, his eyes finally falling on her. His jaw hardened and a nasty light hit his eyes.

She hadn't had enough time. She needed more. She'd already told herself she could take a few days and figure out how to broach the subject of his father with him. It looked like her time had completely run out. There was nothing to do but brazen through. She smiled his way. "Mitchell, we're over here."

Flynn began to turn, but it was too little too late. Mitch crossed the space between them in a few long strides and had a hand on Flynn's shirt, hauling him up. "You think you can fuck around with my woman?"

"Mitch!" She was horrified. She watched as Mitch's fist came out and connected with Flynn's face with an audible crack. She stood up and tried to move between them. Flynn was stepping back, his hand on his jaw. He stepped between her and Mitch, placing himself between them.

Mitch didn't take it well. As she tried to move around him, Mitch reached out, dragging her to his side. There was a wild look in his eyes as he looked down at her. "You will get in the car and wait for me there while I deal with your boyfriend. Don't even think about walking away from me, Laurel. You won't like what happens if you walk away from me."

"I don't think I like what's happening right now," a new voice said.

She looked through tear-filled eyes at the man who had come to stand behind her. He was roughly six foot three, with dark hair he'd pulled back in a queue at the back of his neck. He was dressed in jeans and a black T-shirt that showed off broad shoulders and a chest to die for. He stepped between her and Mitch. "You might be paying me, boss, but you're paying me to protect her, and in my mind that means I protect her from everyone—including you. You need to take a couple of minutes and get your head right before you talk to the lady again."

"What the hell was that for?" Flynn stared at his brother.

Laurel was still trying to process what the guy with the slow Cajun accent had said. He was being paid by Mitch?

"She's taken, asshole. And she probably didn't bother to tell you, but she's pregnant." Mitch stepped toward Flynn, looking like a bull about to charge.

The guy, who was apparently supposed to protect her, gently grasped her elbow and pulled her back from the brothers. "Yes, she's pregnant, and that's a damn good reason to be civil around her, Bradford."

Flynn stopped and stared at Mitch for a minute. "You don't even know who I am. You have no fucking idea who I am."

Mitch didn't know what his brother looked like? She tried to step around the bodyguard she hadn't even known she had, but he was apparently serious about his job.

"Not on my life, *chère*. Those men aren't going to listen to you. Bradford's got his panties in a wad, and the best thing for you to do is let him have his hissy fit."

"I'm not having a hissy fit and you're fired, Guidry. And why the fuck would I..." Mitch stared for a moment. "Flynn?"

She tried to shove around Guidry. "Yes, it's your brother, Mitch. Not that you told me you have one." She frowned at the bodyguard, who still wasn't letting her through. "He said you were fired."

"Ain't no one firing me but the big guy. When Taggart says I can go home, I will. Though I still probably wouldn't. I don't like the look in that man's eyes." Guidry kept his gaze on Mitch, though she was fairly certain she still wouldn't get around the man. "Since this is a family matter, why don't you take this someplace less public, gentlemen? I think all the testosterone is making it difficult for the other patrons to enjoy their lunch."

Mitch turned around. "You're right. Laurel, get in the car. We'll discuss this at home."

She looked back and saw that Flynn's face had fallen. "I think you should talk to Flynn."

Mitch pointed toward the door. "I think you should remember our contract. You don't tell me what to do, baby. You follow orders. Get in the car. I won't ask again and punishment for disobeying me won't be pleasant."

"Punishment?" Flynn stepped up.

God save her from over-dramatic men. "I'm fine. He has never and will never hurt me."

"There's a first time for everything," Mitch said in a low growl.

His panties really were in a wad. What had gotten him to stalk in here like an angry bear? Had he thought she was cheating on him with his brother and a chicken salad sandwich? "I'm not going anywhere until I'm sure you're not going to kill your brother, and you can also explain the Cajun dude who seems to think he's supposed to protect me. How long has that been going on?"

She was pleased with her calm tone of voice. It was obvious none of the men were going to remain calm, so she had to.

Mitch turned and she watched as he visibly forced himself to chill. He reached for her and then stopped, his eyes closing as he took a deep breath and seemed to mentally count. When they opened again, his blue eyes were icy cold. "Laurel, we'll discuss this at home. For now, the police need to talk to you. Someone broke into your apartment and trashed the place. This is Remy Guidry. I hired him because someone nearly killed you and I wanted to ensure your safety. He's watched you when I couldn't. As for my brother, he's none of your business and the fact that you would talk to him behind my back makes me question your loyalty—another thing we'll discuss this evening. Don't be surprised if I ask for that collar back."

The room seemed to still, everything around her moving to the background until there was only Mitch and his cold stare. "Are you serious?"

He was cold as ice as he stared down at her. "You've read the contract. You know what I require and you defy me at every turn. You sneak in your wants and your desires and I give in. This is what happens. You aren't capable of being my sub and I knew it the minute I met you."

Anger flared through her system and before she could think about it, her hands went to the gold necklace around her throat. They'd selected it together, spending the day at NorthPark Mall, trying on pretty jewelry. He wanted it back? She could give it to him. "Well, I'm sorry I proved you right, Mitchell. We don't have to talk at all."

It seemed they had nothing to talk about. She tossed the necklace at him. He could use it on the next idiot, and there would absolutely be a next one. He was too gorgeous, too sexy, to not have another woman dangling for him. Likely, as soon as they realized he was available.

She turned and walked out the door, tears clouding her vision. This was what she got for her trouble. The minute she didn't do what he wanted, he dumped her.

Except that wasn't exactly what had happened. And she did try to get her way on things he was unreasonable about.

It didn't matter now. And apparently she had to go and talk to the police.

Mitch was on her heels the minute she stepped outside. "Laurel."

Guidry moved in beside her. "I'll drive you to your apartment, and that's not a suggestion. Just because Bradford wants to act like a jealous asshole doesn't mean you're out of danger, darlin'."

God, she wanted to tell them all to go to hell. She wanted everyone to go away and let her mourn. How could she have a relationship with a man who shoved her away the minute things got tough? He didn't even recognize his brother? Would he even bother to call and check on the baby now that they were through? Sure, he'd written it into their contract, but seeing how he avoided his father and brothers, she couldn't know that he'd want anything to do with their baby now.

Mitch was used to walking away.

"Hey, I didn't say I was through talking to you, Laurel. I'll drive you to the police station and then I'll drive you home. We have a few things to work out," Mitch insisted.

She stopped on the sidewalk and looked back. Flynn had stepped out of the deli and he looked positively heartbroken.

That was what she would likely look like in a few months. When Mitch decided he was done with a person, he was done with them.

She should have listened. He'd told her he was bad for her. He'd said it in plain English. He'd tried to stay away.

In the end, she had to be sensible. Someone was out to hurt Mitch, and right now, they thought they could use her to those ends. It might take a few weeks for Dixon to realize there was no place in Mitch's heart for anything, much less her.

"Remy can drive me and I'll be a good client. I understand why he's here and I'll cooperate with him until we're sure it's safe. I'll pick up my things from your place later tonight."

"What do you mean?" Mitch asked. For the first time the chill was replaced with an almost expectant wariness.

He'd really thought she would fall in line? "You say I'm not your sub. So I'll find a place to stay until my apartment is safe. I'll call my brother. His building is secure. I think you should talk to your brother."

"He isn't my brother," Mitch returned, his tone savage. "And don't think this is over, Laurel. Are you forgetting you have something of mine?"

Her hand went to her stomach. "This is a baby and not a piece of property, and don't you dare try to use our baby against me. Go to hell, Mitch."

She turned and started back down the street. This time, he didn't follow her.

"My truck is close. You should probably go in and let them know you won't be coming back this afternoon. I'll call in and let my boss know what's going on. If you're not with Mitch, then I need to stay close to you," Guidry explained.

The last thing she needed was another man watching out for her, but she wasn't about to let her stubbornness get her baby killed. She nodded, walked into the building and explained about her apartment. She was the world's worst employee, but her boss seemed to understand. She grabbed her phone, which had finally charged back up.

They were supposed to get a new battery today. Well, Mitch was. He was going to order a new one and then take her out to dinner. She sniffled as she looked down at the phone. He'd called several times and left her texts about getting in touch with him the minute she could.

Why would the man seem so panicked about a woman he could throw away like a used tissue?

Maybe she was the drama queen.

"I'm parked out back," Guidry explained.

"Of course you are. I might have noticed I was being followed if you'd parked out front." She understood the need, but was irritated Mitch hadn't told her.

But then Mitch wasn't the most reasonable of men.

And pretty much every woman he'd ever cared about had cheated on him.

She turned suddenly and was pleased to see the big strong Cajun stop and look the slightest bit off-kilter. "What did you tell Mitch that had him in a jealous rage?"

To his credit, the Cajun boy didn't flinch. Still, it seemed like he was the honest type. "I told him you were having lunch with another man and you seemed cozy. You hugged him. You seemed close. You aren't openly affectionate with other men. I've been watching you for weeks and the only men you've touched past a handshake are Mitch and your brother. In my defense, I was unaware Mitch had any family at all. Had I known you were spending time with his brother, I likely wouldn't have mentioned the physical affection. That being said, it doesn't seem like Mitch appreciated you spending time with his brother."

"Well, that doesn't matter now, does it?" She settled her purse over her shoulder and started out the back door.

Guidry escorted her to his massive truck and helped her up. "I'll bring you back after we deal with the police. I'll follow you back to Bradford's place and let you pick up your things. You're being more reasonable about this than I thought you would."

She was barely hanging on. She wanted to wail and cry and feel incredibly sorry for herself because she was going to be alone.

She would be alone without Mitch. Or would she? Why should she live the rest of her life alone because Mitchell Bradford was an asshat? She didn't have to be alone. She'd wasted the last year of her life on him and she was going to have a child by him, but that didn't mean she had to be alone.

"I'm always reasonable," she said in a quiet voice. She folded her hands on her lap.

"You're not being very reasonable right now." He turned out of the parking lot and toward the freeway.

"What is that supposed to mean?"

He shrugged as he maneuvered through the streets. "I'm surprised you gave up so quickly."

She didn't like the sound of that. She hadn't given up. He'd told her she wasn't good enough to be his submissive. And he'd never lied to her about wanting to get married. If she wasn't his wife or his sub, she wasn't anything to him. He'd proven that utterly. "It doesn't matter anymore. He made himself plain."

"Did he?"

"Are you always this chatty with your clients?" How the hell had she gotten here? She was moving toward the police department to talk about the break-in at her apartment. Mitch had let her go pretty easily.

But didn't he do that with everything? He let people go all the time. Things were harder for him. If she was an old concert T-shirt, he would hoard the hell out of her.

Objects were the only things Mitch could count on, so he tried to keep them. He simply didn't think he could count on her. His head had immediately gone to cheating. She didn't deserve that.

But wasn't it kind of inevitable?

"We don't have to talk."

"He was horribly rude to me."

"Yes. Men in pain are usually horrible. That boy's got a thorn in his paw and it's not coming out by itself." He was quiet for a moment as he sped up to get on the freeway. "You two seemed pretty happy."

"It was an illusion." He'd always been waiting for her to screw up so he could get her out of his life. He'd been waiting to do it from the moment he'd heard she was pregnant. This was what he wanted, wasn't it?

"If you say so. I'm saying as an outside party, you seemed pretty happy, and since you two have a baby on the way, maybe it's a little hasty to throw in the towel. Or the collar, as it seems. Men will say a lot of things they don't mean when they're hurting, and finding out the woman they love is seeing another man behind his back would hurt a lot. I've looked into Bradford some and he's the kind of man who hasn't had a lot of support in his life."

He'd had no support. None. She'd been surrounded by family. Yes, they'd been children, but she'd learned to lean on them, to trust and love her brother and sisters.

Mitch had learned that everyone left.

He wasn't completely ignorant when it came to love. But she'd learned long ago that there was a difference between being ignorant and being dumb. Ignorance was merely an absence of education.

Mitch was a smart man. Could he be taught? Did he even want to be?

She was well aware that tears flowed down her cheeks, but she wasn't capable of stopping them. Remy Guidry wanted to be her bodyguard? Well, he had to deal with her emotional state, too. And if he wanted to listen, then maybe she should talk. She'd kept quiet about so many things because she didn't want her family to worry, didn't want Mitch to look bad in front of them. Guidry seemed to know everything, so she could lay it all out there. And it didn't matter because it was over.

Yes, she was seeking counseling from her ridiculously attractive bodyguard. "I'm worried there's nothing for me to do. I can't go back and erase the things that happened to him. I can't right the past for him."

"No, you can't, but you can make him believe in the future."

She'd been trying. How could she make him believe in a future when he was so tied up in the past? He kept things forever. Stupid things like old T-shirts and stacks of comic books he never read or looked through any more. "How do I do that?"

"Oh, that's simple, *chère*. You be you. Don't have to be any more than that. I'm going to ask you a question and it's going to seem silly, but I want you to think about it. Let's say you got this dog and he keeps coming around your house. He's growling and barking every time you come outside. Now, most people would be scared. Most people would know that tangling with a nasty piece of dog is gonna get them bit. But there's a few people in this world who look at that dog and see something else. There's a few people who see deeper. Even though they've never been a mangy dog themselves, they seem to understand what it would feel like. So I'm going to ask you, how would you handle that dog?"

She cried pretty freely in that moment because the minute he'd given her the scenario, she'd known what she would do. "I would feed him. I would put out a dish and then wait. I wouldn't push him the first couple of times. I would put the dish out and then walk away. After he got used to that, I would stand in the door until he learned it was all right for me to watch him."

"You sound like you've done this before."

She nodded. "We had this dog when I was a kid. He was the bane of the trailer park. He was quick though. Believe me, some of the residents tried to shoot him because they said he was too far gone. He'd been abused and they told me once a dog got mean, he couldn't come back."

One side of his mouth tugged up and he smiled at her. "You didn't think so, though, did you?"

"I don't know why, but he spent a lot of time outside our trailer. I guess there was a warm place or something. He would scare the crap out of us when we would go to school. I was afraid Will was going to do something to him. Not because my brother's mean or anything. He just took his responsibilities very seriously. So I saved some of my dinner one night and I brought it out to the dog. I did it the night after and so on. He stopped growling at us. He wouldn't come in the house, but he didn't bark at us anymore. And then one day I opened the door to go to school and he was waiting for me. We had that dog until he died of old age."

"Mitch is growling and barking at you because it's the only thing he knows to do. I promise you that man is telling himself it's all for the best because you would have kicked him in the end. No one will think less of you for moving on to an easier man, *chère*. But he'll be alone because I think you're his one shot at finding something good. You walk away and he won't ever try again. That's something for you to think about."

She watched the streets go by and wondered if she would think about anything else.

Chapter Ten

"Wow. You are really bad at that."

Mitch stared at the spot where he'd last seen Laurel and only vaguely thought about punching his brother in his movie star, good-looking face. But that would require him to turn around, and he might never be able to do that again. He might spend the rest of his life watching this spot and praying for her to show up again.

Guidry nodded his way as though letting Mitch know he would handle things from now on and then he, too, disappeared into the building where Laurel worked.

She was gone.

Suck it up. You knew it would happen eventually. It's better that it happen now before you got too deep.

He was already too deep. God, she was gone and he felt something open deep inside him. A wound that was never fucking going to heal.

"Aren't you going after her?"

Flynn. Laurel was gone, but Flynn was still here. His younger brother. The one dear old dad wanted. It was so fucking good to have a place to throw his hate. He turned and was slightly pleased that Flynn took a step back. He would bet Flynn had never had to defend himself because no one was around to help him. Flynn would have been given the best of everything while Mitch hadn't even gotten fucking scraps. "I would rather deal with you, Adler. You want to explain why you're here fucking around with my submissive?"

Flynn's eyes narrowed. "Submissive?"

Oh this was going to be fun. He was sure Flynn was perfectly vanilla and would be so horrified at big brother's perversions. "Yes. You were flirting with my sub, Adler. When I talked about punishing her I meant pulling her skirt up and smacking her ass because it makes her hot. I've tied her up six ways to Sunday and I didn't leave her untouched, if you know what I mean. You couldn't handle her even if I allowed it, which I won't. Go back to California, you little prick."

Flynn's face went red, but he took a step forward, his fists clenched at his sides. "Yeah, I guess it doesn't surprise me to find out you're an abusive piece of shit."

Like he hadn't heard that before. He turned and started walking to his SUV. He had work to do. He would find a way to get her back. Oh, he'd do it in a nasty way, but she was going to be back in his home, in his bed before she could play around with someone else.

"Mitch." Flynn was suddenly beside him, jogging to keep up. "Mitch, I said that in anger. I'm sorry. I'm not a complete idiot. I watch TV and stuff. I know some people have relationships like that. Hell, I even knew you went to clubs. It was just surprising to hear you say it like that. Which I'm sure was why you did it. You seem to want me to think the worst of you."

Mitch turned. Flynn didn't seem to understand him at all. "I don't care what you think. That's why I avoid you. I don't care about you or Dad or anyone at all, so get the fuck out of my state. Why do you think I left California? It damn sure wasn't to get closer to you. Go back to your cushy life and leave me alone."

Flynn had cost him everything. If the jackass had stayed away, Laurel would have been sitting at her desk and he would be the one taking her to the police station. He would be the one holding her hand and promising her everything would be fine. He would be the one she turned to.

He crossed the street and stalked toward his car, all the while thinking about how he was going to keep her. He was stupid. He knew he'd been a major asshole, but she was in the wrong, too. She knew he didn't talk about his past unless he specifically brought it up, and she'd sat right down with one of the biggest pieces of his past and had lunch. She'd known damn well he wouldn't have approved and she'd done it anyway.

Likely because she thought she could help in some way. Because Flynn had given her some kind of sad story and Laurel had bought it hook, line, and sinker.

He was about to get into his car when something struck the windshield. A rock. He turned and Flynn had another one in his hand.

"What the fuck is wrong with you?"

Flynn threw that one, too. He let that sucker fly and it cracked against the windshield. "Me? What the fuck is wrong with you? You think my life is so cushy? Dad is dying, you asshole. He's dying and the only thing he wants is to spend a few minutes with you. I have no idea why since it's obvious to me you aren't worth talking to, but does he listen to me? Fuck no. I've spent the last five years of my life taking care of him, but he wants you. And I won't even go into what's happening with Chase. I'm going to lose him. Do you even care? You've got a little brother and he's going to die because I can't convince him life doesn't suck. Because for him...for him it does. So I'm going to be alone and miserable very soon, and I'll still be happier than you are because at least I'll have tried."

He wanted to pick up one of those rocks, shove it right back at Flynn, get in his car and leave. This wasn't his problem. Laurel was his problem. Laurel was all that mattered now.

He'd screwed up with her so badly she would likely never come back, so it didn't matter.

It didn't matter that Laurel would want him to have some small piece of empathy for the brother who hadn't asked to be born either. It didn't matter that Laurel would think more of him if he would put aside his pride for two seconds and talk to the man he hated for no good reason except the circumstances of his birth.

Flynn hadn't asked for any of this. He hadn't had a choice in parent or birth order, but he was making a choice by seeking out Mitch.

And Mitch had to make a choice, too, and it didn't matter what Laurel would want because Laurel was gone.

So he was going to smash his brother's face in and that would make him feel better.

For a second the sun caught Flynn, illuminating his features, and Mitch realized he'd seen that face in the mirror. He'd seen the starkness, the emptiness. He'd seen the hopelessness reflected there before he put on his mask for the day.

Damn it.

"How bad is he?"

Flynn's head came up. "Dad has stage four pancreatic cancer. He doesn't have long. I don't know what to do. He asked me to reach out. He wants to talk to you before he dies."

"I don't want to talk to him."

"Please. You don't have to talk. Please just listen. What do I have to do? If you want me to beg, I will."

"Why would I want you to beg?"

Flynn shrugged. "Maybe you would like seeing me on my knees. Maybe it would make you feel better."

To see the chosen child beg and squirm and plead? "No, it won't make me feel better, Flynn. Let me think about it. Can I have a day or two?"

"Yeah." Flynn suddenly looked younger than he had before, his eyes wide. "Of course. Take the time you need, but know he doesn't have a lot of it."

"What did you mean about..." He'd been about to pretend he didn't know his youngest brother's name. He did it out of habit. He did it to show the world he didn't give a damn. "Chase? How old is he anyway?"

Flynn stepped forward, his shoulders sagging a bit. "He'll be seventeen soon. If he makes it."

Don't ask. Don't. Stay the fuck out of it. He didn't want to go into this. He liked his life the way it was. Except he didn't. He only liked it because Laurel had been with him, and now she was gone. "Why do you say that?"

"He got mixed up in drugs. He says his overdose was an accident, but I found out he's being bullied by this kid at school. I tried to get Dad to pull him out and let him go to the public school, but they have a problem with violence there. I don't know what to do."

"It's only one kid?"

"It's a group, but you know how these gangs work. One asshole runs the crowd and the crowd runs the school. They outed him. Publically. One of them found out Chase likes boys and catfished him."

"I don't know what that means."

"It's where you make up a false presence on the Internet. He claimed to be another gay kid and they started an online relationship. Once Chase was sure the kid loved him, the group posted every embarrassing moment online."

"Huh. Go after the parents. Go after them hard. Threaten to take them for every dollar they have and I bet the little shit will fall in line."

"They don't want to talk about it. They said it was all kid stuff and Chase should be stronger."

"Did you threaten to sue them and take it all public so their darling baby boy can't show his face at college? I don't know where you've been but most places don't take kindly to bullying anymore. The tide turned a while back. No one takes the side of the mean kid, and threatening to haul them all into court might give Chase some peace. He needs to stand up for himself. A lawsuit could give him that."

"Our lawyers don't do those types of suits. I don't know if I could even convince Chase to consider it. He thinks it's all going to go away. Or he tells me that and then I find him barely breathing. I take him to the hospital and find out he's been buying pills at school."

"Nice. We can sue the school, too." He kind of wanted to. He was sure the school had brushed off the fishing thing as nothing. To them it would be something to work out between the kids. They would likely say that working it out among themselves would prepare them for adulthood, but adults who acted like assholes got fired or shot. There were consequences for adults. "I can talk to him. I can be persuasive when I want to be. It sucks to be a kid."

If anyone did something like that to his kid, they might not get the courtesy of a lawsuit.

"It sucks to be human sometimes."

Maybe Flynn didn't have it so great. "I'm sorry about punching you."

Flynn touched his jaw gingerly. "For a lawyer, you know how to throw a hook."

"I've found beating the shit out of my friends makes me feel better. In the ring, of course, and with rules. A couple of the guys I hang out with work out this way. You should try it sometime. Don't tell your girlfriend though. They get weird about it." It made perfect sense to him. You put on gloves and took out your aggressions and everyone was bruised and happy, but he'd learned to never mention it.

"Like I have time for a girlfriend." Flynn sobered a little. "I'm sorry about yours, man. That was some kind of argument. You should know nothing was going on between me and Laurel. She's a very nice lady and it's obvious she cares about you. Why did you freak out on her like that?"

"I don't know."

"She's not Margot."

"I know that."

"Do you? If I'd been through what you have, I don't know that I would truly understand that Laurel's different."

"I know she's not Margot." But he'd gone to the worst place he could. It had taken him a couple of minutes, but he'd finally arrived at the most improper conclusion he could have about Laurel. He'd basically called her a tramp when she'd only been having lunch with Flynn.

And then he'd questioned her loyalty.

He pulled his phone out. No calls. She hadn't called or texted. Not that he expected her to. She likely wouldn't ever speak to him again unless he forced her to.

Maybe it would be better this way. He wasn't cut out to be a father or a husband. He wasn't ready for any of it. He definitely wasn't ready for her. He'd hurt her and he would do it again if she stayed with him.

What the hell should he do?

How could he let her go? How could he keep her? This was everything he'd feared from the moment he'd met her. He'd known it wouldn't—couldn't—work. He'd known there was no way and now there was a baby involved.

Did he even deserve to be a dad? He had no idea how to be one. Would it be better to let Laurel find someone ready for the job?

"Are you going after her? I think you should. I think you should find her and apologize," Flynn said.

"And after that?" He'd tried to live in the moment but the truth was the future was almost here. Oh, it might be a few months away, but it would catch up to him. It would get him in the end. "No. I need to figure a few things out."

Lonely. He was going to be so fucking lonely without her.

"Like how to sue her so she comes back to you?"

Mitch frowned. When he put it like that it sounded really bad. "We do have legal things to work out."

Despite the thoughts playing in his head, he knew he couldn't do it. He couldn't walk away. Not from her. Not from their kid.

Flynn leaned against the car. "Let's go and get a beer, which I will buy since I kind of damaged your car."

"I damaged your nose." When he thought about it they were kind of even.

"True. You can buy the second round and we can talk about less litigious ways to get your girlfriend back. I might not have a girl right now, but I'm pretty good with them."

"I've ignored you for years. Why would you help me?"

Flynn sighed and put a hand on his back. "Because you don't know this yet, but that's what brothers do."

He wanted to go after her. He wanted to stay away from her.

He wanted…fuck, he just wanted.

He nodded and got into the car because maybe it was past time to confront all his fears. It seemed he had nothing left to lose.

* * * *

Mitch pulled up to the driveway but couldn't manage to hit the button on the key fob that would raise the garage door. He didn't want to see the empty spot where her car should be. It was funny the things a man got used to. He was used to opening the garage door and seeing her piece of crap nestled in there. He'd fully intended to replace said piece of crap with a car that had all the up-to-date safety features as soon as Laurel would have the conversation with him. She'd been all independent and hadn't budged on it.

Would it have been different if he'd been smart enough to convince her he wanted to marry her in the beginning? Would she have taken the car and his crap for a little while longer?

He turned the engine off and got out. A few hours with his brother had been somewhat illuminating. Flynn didn't seem to have Mitch's "the world is half full of assholes" philosophy of life. He seemed to think if Mitch got on his knees and begged for Laurel's forgiveness, she might think about it.

He'd never gotten to his knees before. Not for any woman. Not for anything.

He needed time. He needed to think about what was best for all of them. Perhaps that meant taking a step back. He was going to write her a very polite note requesting that she keep him up to date on any and all developments with the baby and asking that she honor their contract and allow him to escort her to appointments having to do with their child. He would concentrate on the baby.

Perhaps at some time in the future he and Laurel could be friends again.

He sighed as he noticed a big truck in front of the house. He would have to talk to the neighbors because it was utterly ridiculous that they had guests park in front of his house when they had a massive circular drive.

Hell, he couldn't even work up the will to argue anymore. He was about to put his key in the front door when it opened and Remy Guidry stood in the doorway, a frown on his face.

"You are in the doghouse. Dinner's been ready for damn near thirty minutes and it's cold. You should probably come up with a good excuse right damn now." The big Cajun shook his head. "That woman makes a fine roast. If you're stupid enough to lose her, give me a call. I'll take her."

Mitch stared at him as Remy walked through the doorway and toward the lawn. "What?"

The Cajun kept walking, his keys in his hand. "I'll pick her up at eight tomorrow. The good news is now we're out in the open and I can stay close to her. Night, Bradford."

Laurel was here? Laurel was here.

He could hear the sounds of soft country playing through the house. He'd hated it at first, but now it seemed like the sweetest thing he'd ever heard. He locked the door behind him and set the alarm. He dropped his briefcase and walked through the living room. Slowly. Like this was a dream and he wasn't sure he wanted to wake up.

"Laurel?"

She was standing at the sink, rinsing off one of his boring dinner plates that had no personality or color to them. She was the color in his home, in his life. She looked up. "Hello, Mitchell. Are you hungry? I made dinner."

"Why?"

She set the plate in the dishwasher and dried her hands. "Because we eat dinner at night."

There wasn't a lot of expression on her face. God, she looked tired. He'd done that to her. But still, he needed to understand. He didn't understand her at all. "Why are you here, Laurel?"

"Do you want me to leave? I can call Remy back."

He moved around the bar, almost wanting to block her path. "No. I don't want that. But I thought you left me."

"I can't leave, Mitch. We don't get to throw everything away. I don't know if we can go back to what we were before, but I think being apart is a mistake. So I think we should sit down and have dinner, and later, we'll go to bed and maybe you can make love to me because I had a shitty day."

He stepped up and dragged her into his arms, pressing his lips to hers. He took her mouth in a long, hungry, grateful kiss. She wasn't leaving. She was here with him.

It was enough.

"Maybe dinner can wait," he said against her lips, his hands moving to her blouse.

She sighed against him. "Definitely."

* * * *

Deep in the night, Laurel looked down at her sleeping...what did she call him now? They still had a contract but it felt broken despite the way they'd ended the evening. They'd avoided all talk about the future like it was a land mine waiting to explode in their faces, and she wasn't sure what to do about that.

She loved him. She simply wasn't sure love was enough in their case.

When he kissed her, when he put his hands on her like he would die if he didn't, it felt like love. The D/s sex they had was over-the-top insane with pleasure and she craved it, but there was no doubt she also needed those times when Mitchell lost control and had to have her without any protocol or rules between them.

That was when she felt like he adored her.

She'd thought a lot about what Remy had told her today. She'd thought about that dog she'd coaxed into the trailer finally. It had taken weeks and weeks. Will had forbidden her to get anywhere near that dog. Come to think of it, Will hadn't been spectacularly excited when he'd realized she was interested in Mitch. It seemed like her brother recognized the destruction capability that lived in both beasts, but she'd seen something else. She'd seen a chance to give something to a creature that had obviously been broken.

The world could break a spirit, but that didn't mean it had to stay that way.

She looked over at him. Why was this man precious to her? Why couldn't it have been someone simpler? Someone happy and whole? Why did he move her?

At the end, it was a mystery and she wouldn't solve it. There were some things that simply were. If it didn't work out between her and Mitch, she would miss him forever. She would move on because she wasn't the type to lie down and fade, but she would always love him.

Why hadn't she told him?

It seemed like the last wall she had, the very last defense.

"You can't sleep?" Mitch's voice rumbled as he turned over. Even with the lights out, she could see the hard line of his jaw, watch as his hand came out to touch her shoulder.

"I'm fine." She wasn't sure what to say.

He sat up. "That means you're not fine. I know that much."

She had to laugh at that. "No, I didn't mean it that way. Physically I'm good. I'm a bit restless, that's all."

He pulled her into his arms, resting against the back of the bed. His warmth surrounded her as he stroked her hair. "Because we're not settled. Laurel, I'm worried you want something I can't give you. Nothing is ever settled. I learned that a long time ago. We can be good one minute and broken the next. There's no guarantee."

And that was precisely why he refused to talk about the future. He didn't believe in it. He didn't trust it.

"I know." It wouldn't do any good to lecture him about it. She felt him sigh.

"I'm sorry about today. Baby, I'm sorry I reacted the way I did. I did the one thing I promised I wouldn't do."

Yes, he had. She sat up and looked at him, an idea in her head. Sometimes ideas got lost in the muddle of communication. People didn't always use the right words to make someone truly understand. Words got filtered through the drain of a person's history, giving them weight or lightness that others wouldn't place on the definition. "You withdrew affection. You promised you wouldn't do that, Mitch."

"I know. I'm very sorry, Laurel. If it means anything to you, they were just words."

And so was the rest of it, but words could drag a man down. A couple could drown in words if they weren't speaking the same language. "Affection is something that can go away."

"No. I don't think so," he argued in a low rumble. "Not this kind. I can't imagine a time when I won't feel this way for you."

Marriage was a hard word for Mitch. Love was a word he didn't even understand. So she would find the ones that would get to him.

"Even when I walked away, I adored you, Mitchell Bradford."

He hauled her close again, his arms so tight around her. "I adore you, Laurel. I don't know why you're still here with me. It scares me, to tell you the truth. I don't trust it."

But he could. He wanted to. He simply needed time, patience. "You don't have to right now. Just know that when we fight, I'm going to be here when it's time for you to come home. I promise."

She let her head rest against his chest, listening to the strong beat of his heart.

"I'll go with Flynn."

He held her tight when she tried to get up. She eased back down, understanding he needed her in his arms. She hadn't expected him to give in on that. Not at all. She'd expected to have to tell Flynn to go home alone. "Why?"

"Does it matter?"

Did it? "Not really. I'm happy. I think it will be good for you. I know it's going to be hard, but I'll be waiting at home for you. You simply have to let your father talk and then you say whatever you need to. I don't want you to have regrets after he's gone."

"I won't. I wouldn't. I'm not doing it because I need closure, Laurel. I'm doing it because I want to make you happy. Tell me this will make you happy."

Mitchell Bradford was a man who took his responsibilities seriously. He followed the letter of their contract and tried to hold her to hers. He was unbending about certain things and didn't lie about them. He'd told her flat out that discussing the past was out of bounds, that she had no place there.

And now he was facing it because he wanted to make her happy.

"Yes. Yes, Mitch. You make me happy, but this will make me even happier."

"Then it's good. I'll go. And Laurel, I think while I'm gone, I want you to talk to a decorator. We should pick one of the rooms for a nursery. It's still a long time away, but we should start making plans and stuff. Babies need lots of things, I think. God knows Tag's kids do. Last time I was at his place, there was baby stuff everywhere. I think we should clean out my office."

His office? His office was a train wreck of things he kept. He loved his office. "Mitch, I can use the guest room."

"Too small. And it's not close. I want the baby close to us. We can get rid of the stuff. Well, I'd like to keep some of the comics. They're worth money, but no more than a box or two."

"Mitch, you love that stuff." She thought it was junk, but it was important to him.

"I want to love the baby more. I need to. I need to not need those things, Laurel. I need for us to be enough."

She held him in the quiet of the night and for the first time, felt real hope for them.

Chapter Eleven

He had exactly forty-five minutes to get to the airport. He glanced down at his watch. He wasn't more than fifteen minutes away, but in Dallas, one always had to allow for some traffic. "Are you sure you're going to be all right?"

"I'm good, babe. Lisa is spending a couple of days with me and Remy assures me he won't let us out of his sight. I'm actually interested in seeing how Lisa takes to the big guy. She's always had a thing for that sexy Cajun accent."

"You think it's sexy?"

"Absolutely not, Master. I think it's terrible and it makes my ears bleed."

He grinned. Such a brat. "See that it continues to. I'm going to miss you while I'm gone. Why did I talk you into going back to school?"

He'd tried to convince her to come with him, but she was in the middle of saving some tenants from their evil landlord or something. That was his Laurel.

"I believe at the time you hoped I would find someone younger and less broody to turn my attentions to."

He'd been an idiot. "I'm sure that wasn't it at all. You stay safe and I'll call you after we land."

"Bye."

He hung up as Sharon looked in from the doorway. "Mr. Bradford, you have a very insistent man in reception. He does not have an appointment."

He hit *send* on his laptop. The contracts were in place and all negotiations were finalized. He'd just billed one very lucky company a couple of thousand hours. Damn, he was looking forward to that check. He might expand. Maybe it was time to think about taking on a couple of associates. He would keep the core clients for himself, but he could use some help around here, and Laurel was far too happy making the world a better place to ever come and help him sue people for cash. Lots of cash. Heaping wads of lovely cash that he was going to need because babies cost money.

Babies. He'd started to think about babies. Not just the singular. Laurel had a big family. She would want one for her kid. After the long talk with his brother and spending a few days with him while he got ready for the trip, he'd kind of turned around on the sibling thing. Flynn was cool and he seemed to truly care about Chase. He'd been on the phone with Chase, too. They'd talked about handling his problems. Mitch had told him about some of the things that happened to him in school. They'd agreed that Chase should come out to Dallas and spend some time getting to know Mitch during the summer.

After their father…

He wasn't thinking about that now. He would have to later on today, but not now.

"Flynn is going to be here to pick me up any minute now. I've got to be at the airport very soon, so it's going to have to wait."

Sharon shook her head, that brown helmet of hair not wavering at all. It was solidly sprayed down. "I'll tell him." She turned. "Mr. Dixon, he cannot see you now and you're going to have to leave. As soon as the boss goes, I'm heading out of here. My grandson has a baseball game and he forgot his favorite bat. I have to get it to him."

Dixon? What was Patrick Dixon doing here?

He took a step back when he realized the man charging into his office wasn't Patrick. This was a big man, much bigger than his slender, intellectual-looking brother. He was messy, his eyes red, as though he'd gone days without sleep.

Harvey Dixon.

"Sharon, call the police and then get out of here."

Harvey Dixon shook his head. "No, you don't have to do that. Or maybe you should. He's not going to stop. He's going to keep going until one of us is dead. Are you Mitchell Bradford?"

He wished he was someone else. Someone who carried a gun. That might come in handy right now. Hopefully someone from McKay-Taggart was currently watching his security feed and would be on hand soon.

"That depends. You still planning on murdering me?" He didn't see a gun in the man's hand. Both hands were empty, but that didn't mean he couldn't pull one lickety-split. "You should know I sent off the contracts. They'll be signed in a few minutes and filed with the court system. There's nothing you can do."

"Contracts? For what?"

Great. He was delusional, too. Maybe he should keep him talking until the cops got here. "Why don't you sit down, Mr. Dixon, and we can have a talk."

Or the minute the fucker sat down, he could clock him with his umbrella. Except it was sitting in the stand out in reception because Laurel had put it out there along with a pretty coat stand she'd found.

Laurel's OCD problems were going to be the death of him. If she'd simply let him toss things wherever he liked, there would be an umbrella on the floor right now. If he lived he was so going to spank her pretty ass.

Harvey—who needed a shave—shook his head. "No. I think we should go somewhere else to talk. He could be behind me. By now he knows I got out."

"Out?"

"Of the prison he locked me in while he was setting me up."

"I thought you were in rehab."

"I have never touched a drug in my life. Never. My brother made it look like I did and he somehow convinced Frances I was in danger. This is all about the company. Mr. Bradford, I never meant you harm."

What the hell was going on? "I was told you were trying to kill me because I'm the lawyer pushing through the sale of a certain solar energy technology you feel like you pioneered."

"I toyed with it in the past. I will admit that, but I haven't touched solar in a few years. This isn't about solar. This is about money. I've come up with a device to measure domestic power consumption. It's an inexpensive device that measures energy pull."

Mitch wasn't following. "Energy pull?"

Harvey paced, his boots dragging the floor. "Homes waste incredible amounts of energy from appliances that bleed it. A refrigerator that doesn't work properly, a laptop that pulls energy even though it's fully charged and off but plugged in. My device could help people figure out what needs fixing and what to unplug completely when it's not in use. People simply pay their energy bills without discovering where they're wasting the most. And they could fix that problem with one machine that reads the electrical currents. They wouldn't even have to walk through testing devices and plugs. I can do it all from one fuse box."

"That sounds great." As a person who'd made a lot of money on start-ups, he would look into that. One of his clients was Keith Langston, an angel investor. He'd taken some of Sanctum's wealthy members and formed an investment pool for promising new technologies. Keith was known for having an almost preternatural ability to find start-ups that would pay off. This was one of those ideas he would float by Keith. "It should make Dixon Technologies a fortune."

"My brother wants the fortune for himself."

Shit. "Patrick wants to sell the idea to an energy company, doesn't he?"

Now that he looked back, he could remember the way Patrick Dixon had sweated the day he'd come in, how his hands had been shaky. At the time, Mitchell had chalked it up to Patrick being upset about what his brother was doing. What if he'd been nervous about selling his brother out?

Harvey nodded. "I didn't know until he had me committed. He hired a police officer on the take to set me up and force me into rehab. He thought he could wrest the company away from me. All it would take was Frances and him forcibly buying me out. Our father put it in our bylaws in case one of us was incapacitated or doing something wrong."

"Frances is your sister. Why didn't she get you out of there?"

"Patrick has her believing I've gone crazy with rage about the solar project. I've been secretive the last two years because I knew Patrick would want to make as much money as possible off this tech. I want to help people. It's all I've ever wanted to do. I want to share this, keep the cost down. Patrick would never let me do that. Somehow, he found the plans and he started talking to an energy company. They're going to bury it. The only reason I'm still alive is he doesn't know where I hid the specs."

"Why would he send people after me? Someone's been making my life very difficult. There's been a campaign of harassment against me and the woman in my life. What's the purpose of that?"

"Our father always taught Patrick to have a contingency plan. If I'm convicted of a violent crime, they split my piece of the company and Patrick can still make his deal. It could be worth millions. It could take much longer to make that kind of money if we take the product to market. Development and retail takes money and time. He wants the money now."

The door opened and Flynn walked through. "Ready to go?"

His brother looked particularly dapper this morning. He'd spent the last few nights in their guest room, getting to know both Mitch and Laurel, and one of the things Mitch had discovered was his brother's penchant for wearing clothes that weren't selected for their utility. Maybe they could shop while they were in San Francisco. Laurel would probably be shocked if he showed up in a non-black suit. Or was it navy he was wearing today? He must be getting old. He never bought navy suits. Were his eyes going?

"Give me a couple of seconds, Flynn." He saw an opportunity. If Harvey was telling him the truth and he wasn't a big old crazy pants who had gotten out of the asylum, then Mitch could help him get his company back, and it looked like old Harvey would be needing a lawyer in his near future. "I'm going to put in a call to Lieutenant Brighton and we'll get this cleared up."

Flynn sighed. "This is a lawyer thing, isn't it? I can already see billable hours lighting up your eyes."

Harvey's eyes widened. "Lawyer. Yes." He reached into his pants, but the pockets were empty.

Flynn seemed to understand. He pulled out his wallet and handed Harvey a bill.

Harvey smiled and slapped a five-dollar bill on Mitch's desk. "There you go. That's a retainer. Now you're my lawyer, right?"

For five dollars? Someone had been watching way too much TV. "That is five dollars. That will retain approximately thirty seconds of my time."

Flynn frowned. "Mitchell."

Mitch shrugged. "I did not go to law school for five dollars, and I've got a baby on the way. Those little suckers are expensive."

"Five dollars now and a promise to let you handle Dixon Technologies contracts and sales in the future. I'm firing every single person who sided with Patrick."

A firm of that size and with those types of ideas would be worth thousands of billable hours…visions of college funds danced through his head. He took the five dollars. "You've got yourself a lawyer. Now let's get some cops here because this is going to get so messy."

Lawyers liked messy. Messy took time. Messy made money.

He wondered briefly how many lawyers actually represented the men who had harassed them. And Harvey better be telling the truth because he damn straight wasn't repping the man who had sent someone to shoot

Laurel. He would shove that five dollars so far up Harvey's asshole it would come out his nose.

"I wouldn't dial that number if I were you," a new voice said.

He looked up and his day went to complete hell. Sharon walked in, her eyes wide, tears running down them. Patrick Dixon was behind her, a gun pointed at the back of her head.

"I'm so sorry, Mr. Bradford. This one didn't have an appointment either," she said.

Nope. He really needed some new security to keep the riffraff away. It looked like they were going to have a Dixon family reunion, and he hoped it didn't turn deadly.

* * * *

"See, I told you he would still be here." Laurel rushed up the steps to the building, Remy following behind her. She had a bag in her hand. Chocolate chip cookies from Mitch's favorite bakery and his earbuds. He'd left them behind this morning. He could buy more, but this particular pair were the ones that fit the best. He always complained that he must have a weird ear canal because most didn't fit.

He wouldn't be comfortable without them. She wanted to make sure he had everything he needed. He didn't particularly like to travel. He was doing it for her, so she was going to go out of her way to make it nice for him.

But she'd wanted to surprise him and get in one last good-bye kiss, hence the subterfuge.

"You're lucky he's on a private plane because the rest of the world has to go through security, and that means getting to the airport two hours ahead of the flight," Remy complained.

Remy, it seemed, wasn't looking forward to a whole weekend of watching two women. He'd seemed awfully flirty until he'd seen the lineup of movies she'd chosen for her sister's sleepover. He wasn't a big fan of the romantic comedy. From what she could tell, Mitch's sudden trip had also screwed up a date Remy had planned, though it had taken him a few minutes to remember the woman's name.

Candy. She was fairly certain Remy had met her at a strip club. Her bodyguard didn't have particularly good taste in women.

"Security isn't so hard to get through. You just have to avoid mornings and weekends."

Remy opened the door for her. "Yeah, it might not be hard for the curvy little white girl who looks like she shits sunshine. Try looking like me and having a metal plate in your head. See how those TSA officers treat you then."

She laughed as she started up the stairs. "I do not look like I shit sunshine. I'm very tough."

"You keep on believing that, *chère*." They had made it to the fourth floor when he stopped. "I've got a call from the office. I'll be right here."

That was all for the best since she intended to have an impromptu make-out session with her man. She'd already given him something to remember her by. She'd woken up in the early morning light with Mitch's hands on her body, his mouth covering her skin with kisses. He'd made slow, lazy, languid love to her. And then he'd taken her to the shower and washed her off, holding her like he never wanted to let her go.

It didn't matter that she could still feel him. She wanted one more kiss before he left.

She walked through the door, happy that he'd gone with the windows. Even when they hadn't been speaking, he'd given over to her wants. The building was still filled with gorgeous natural light.

Sharon wasn't at her desk, but that wasn't shocking. Her purse was still here and that was. She usually took Friday afternoons off for whatever baseball/soccer/school play was going on that day. Sure enough, there was a little slugger baseball bat sitting behind her vacant chair.

She smoothed down her skirt and started back toward Mitch's office. She loved what she was doing now. Because they were a nonprofit, she was allowed to do far more than a paralegal at a big firm would be allowed to do. She loved the feeling that she was making her city a better place to live, but she missed getting to see Mitch all the time. She even missed their silly battles over decorating and what to cater in for lunch. She kind of missed her old office.

"And what exactly do you think to gain by this play?"

She stopped outside of Mitch's office. It sounded like he had a client in there. His voice was hard, like this was a nasty, come-to-Jesus meeting. He had some clients who required a firm hand. Some people thought lawyers were like genies unleashed from their bottles—capable of granting them anything they wished. Mitch tended to put those clients in their places, and very quickly.

"It isn't my fault," a low voice said. "I didn't mean for it to turn out like this. Harvey was supposed to tell me where he hid the designs. He was supposed to give up the designs or go to jail. And Frances was supposed to vote with me."

Who was Frances? He'd mentioned a Harvey? He couldn't be talking about Harvey Dixon. Her heart threatened to stop as she eased to one side and saw through the half-open door that Patrick Dixon was in Mitch's office. He had a gun in his hand and Sharon as a human shield in front of him.

"This should have all been over, but that prick went to Frances when I couldn't pay him anymore," Patrick was saying.

"Austin? The man you hired to kill my girlfriend?" Mitch's voice was practically arctic.

"He wasn't going to kill her. He was supposed to scare her and you into filing police reports against Harvey. Austin was going to confess he'd been hired. He was going to serve some time in juvie and then get out and I would have given him a job," Patrick whined.

"But the little fucker got greedy," Mitch surmised.

She couldn't see him, but from the sound of his voice, he was likely at his desk.

"What did you do to Frances?" The man she had to figure was Harvey Dixon took a step toward his brother.

"Move again and I kill her." Patrick tightened his hold on Sharon, who whimpered.

Poor Sharon. She just wanted to be around her grandkids. What was she going to do? She took a step back, still able to hear everything that was going on.

"I don't know where Frances is. She called me and said she was going to get you out of the facility. She's being detained by my man on the inside. I'll have to get rid of her now, too, and all because you're such a selfish shit, Harvey. All of these people have to die because you won't save your family."

Her family was in there. Her heart raced. She moved to the reception area and pulled out her phone, dialing 911. As quietly as she could, she explained the situation. She could still hear Mitch talking in the background.

"So you think the police are going to believe that Harvey came in here and killed all of us because he was upset that a company I represent stole his solar storage idea?" Mitch sounded so calm, so patient.

The operator told her to get out of the building as quickly as she could. The police were on their way.

She hung up, but she couldn't leave. Where the hell was her bodyguard?

"It will work. I have several people who are more than willing to state that Harvey is insane," Patrick promised. "He's pissed off a whole lot of people in his time."

"What did you do? Did you get in with that bookie again?" Harvey asked.

"Are you even considering all the problems that are going to come up?" Mitch completely ignored the family argument. "First of all, you're not wearing gloves. How are the police going to believe Harvey did this when his prints aren't on the gun?"

The baseball bat. It was sitting right there. She picked it up and took a deep breath because she was so going to get spanked for what she was about to do.

The cops wouldn't come in quietly. She hadn't thought about that. Maybe all those sirens would scare Patrick Dixon into letting everyone go, or maybe they would make him desperate and he would start shooting. She couldn't take that chance.

She took the bat in hand and moved back into the hall. There he was. Patrick was standing with his back to the door. He hadn't closed it all the way. There was plenty of room for her to move into the office and clock the son of a bitch.

"I'll figure out a way to make it work." Patrick screamed suddenly. "You stay back!"

"Flynn, get behind me now," Mitch said, his voice a low growl.

"I'm not hiding behind you," Flynn insisted.

"Me, big brother. You, little brother. Remember that in the future and don't argue with me. You wanted me for a brother. Well, we follow the rules of the pack in this family. Get the fuck behind me now," Mitch ordered. "Anything happens to me and you…"

"Take care of Laurel," Flynn promised.

Oh, he was so not going to like the fact that she was breaking the rules of the pack. She would bet his rules included not putting herself and their baby in danger, but she couldn't let him die. She couldn't live in a world where there was no Mitchell Bradford to growl at her and get irritated when she changed things, and make love to her like she was the last woman on earth.

He couldn't die when he was finally learning what family meant.

She would show him what it meant.

She swung the bat back as she strode through the door and let that sucker go. There was a horrible crack as the bat met Patrick Dixon's skull, and she felt the reverberation all the way up her arms and through her chest.

He dropped to the ground, blood welling from his skull.

The whole world seemed to stop.

"Laurel?" Mitch was standing behind his desk, his eyes wide.

"What the hell?" Remy strode in, his gun in hand as sirens started to blare. He kicked the gun away from Patrick Dixon's still body. "I got a call from Liam that Austin Hunt had been spotted trying to follow Patrick Dixon into the building. I caught him downstairs with an arsenal strapped to his body. He's tied up and out of the way."

"Yeah, well, tell Li he was right," Mitch said as he strode around the desk. "There's always a twist. Meet Harvey Dixon. He's my newest client and not responsible for anything but being brilliant. Make sure Patrick doesn't get back up. Sharon, take next week off. Be with your grandchildren. And I'll get you a new bat."

Sharon shook her head. "Oh, no. I think this one is lucky now. Well, after I get the blood off it. And I'm so glad you mentioned it. I was hoping to take a couple of weeks off. My daughter recently bought a new RV. Grand Canyon here I come."

Mitch frowned at her. "Shouldn't you be more freaked out?"

The older woman kicked Patrick's body. "Mad is more like it. And I've worked for lawyers for a very long time, Mr. Bradford. You people tend to piss off the world. This isn't my first rodeo. I think I'll make a pot of coffee for the nice police officers on their way up."

Mitch took Laurel's hand and led her out. He didn't even look at her. He simply dragged her away from the scene of the crime.

He didn't stop until he got to her old office. He pulled her inside and locked the door.

She held her breath and prayed he wasn't too angry.

* * * *

Mitch could feel his heart beating in his chest as he looked at her. When he'd realized she was coming through the door with that bat in her hand, he'd wanted to die. Anything could have gone wrong. The gun could have gone off. She could have not hit Patrick hard enough.

She could have died.

"Mitch, I know you're mad at me."

Mad didn't cover it. He was overwhelmed. His body was a riot of emotion and he wasn't sure where to start. He'd been proud because his girl didn't hesitate. He'd been horrified that she was in danger. He'd been so fucking helpless.

But one thing had played out in his head and that was the fact that they weren't done. God, they couldn't be done.

She sank to her knees in front of him. "I know I upset you, Master. I know I scared you and I'm willing to take anything you have to give me."

She hadn't left him the day she should have. She hadn't walked away because he'd fucked up and lost his temper. He'd woken up the next morning and realized that he could get this situation back in hand. He could steer her toward the relationship he was comfortable with. He could go back to being her Master. Hell, if he played his cards right, he could probably train the waywardness out of her. He could likely manipulate her so she was comfortable accepting his dictates. She wouldn't try to sneak things in or go behind his back because she thought she was helping him.

She was proving it right now. She was kneeling before him, her head bowed.

She would be his submissive for the rest of her life, if he wanted.

God, he just wanted her to be his Laurel.

He dropped to his knees and wrapped his arms around her and said the words he'd sworn he would never, never say. "Please don't leave me. Don't ever leave me."

He was five again, clinging to a mother who cared more about parties than a child. When she'd turned him away, he'd stopped asking, stopped hoping, stopped wishing. He couldn't do that anymore. He couldn't live in that world because if he did, he forced Laurel and their baby to live there, too. He had to find a way out.

He had to find a way to believe. He knew only one real thing he believed in and that was her. If he held on to her, if he followed her lead in the things he didn't understand, maybe, just maybe he could be a better man. He could be better for her, better for their children.

Laurel's arms came out, holding him tightly to her. They were on the floor, their bodies pressed together as though they were trying to meld into one. "I won't. I promise. Mitchell, for as long as you want me, I promise I won't leave you. I'll be here."

He tangled his hands in her hair, desperate to be surrounded by her. She was his everything. How had he ever thought he could leave this woman alone? She'd been made for him. "Don't you ever do that again. Don't ever put yourself in danger. I swear to god, Laurel, you nearly gave me a heart attack."

"I can't promise you." Tears shone in her eyes. "I won't ever let someone hurt you when I can help it. You'll simply have to punish me."

"No punishment, baby." He would do the same for her, and he wouldn't change her in any way. He loved her exactly the way she was. "But you will have to calm me down. I'm going to do something I wanted to do from the moment I hired you."

"Are you going to take me rough and hard on my desk?" She was grinning up at him. "Even though the cops are probably storming up the stairs as we speak?"

Yes, that had always been on his mind, and he was definitely going to do that. Since the moment she'd walked through his doors, he wanted to have the right to come into her office and demand she take him. But there was something else. Something he should have done all along because it had been inevitable.

"I'm going to tell you I love you." He framed her perfect face in his hands. She'd become the most precious thing in the world to him. She was the reason he breathed. "I love you, Laurel. Be my wife."

"Yes." She pressed her lips to his. "Yes, Mitchell."

He got to his feet and hauled her up and into his arms. He hadn't changed a thing about her office since the moment she'd walked out. It was neat as a pin and clean, so he felt zero guilt in setting his fiancée on top of the desk and running his hand up her skirt. His mouth found hers and he kissed her. His bride. He was going to kiss her for the rest of his life.

He heard the Dallas police enter and start asking questions, but it didn't matter.

His life started now.

Epilogue

Six months later

Mitch stared down at the baby boy in his arms and wondered how he'd managed to get so lucky.

"He's very wrinkly." Chase stood beside him, looking down at the little boy they'd named John William Bradford.

After his father and Laurel's brother. "He's only a few hours old. The whole birth thing can take a lot out of a baby."

His son yawned, and it was the single cutest thing Mitch had ever seen. His tiny mouth opened and his whole body wriggled before he settled back down and blinked his eyes up at Mitch.

Blue. Like his. Like his father's.

"He looks a little like Dad," Chase said. His brother was living in Dallas. He'd decided to finish school here after their father had died. Flynn had packed them both up and moved to the Dallas office where he was running things remotely. He'd said they needed a new start, but Mitch had a suspicion that after John Adler had peacefully passed, they'd both wanted to be near family. Near him and Laurel and their new nephew.

"He does." Mitch had spent time with his dad. It had been easier than he thought it would. Somehow, loving Laurel had opened up possibilities he hadn't expected. He'd walked into his father's hospital room and there wasn't a monster there. He hadn't seen the man who neglected him. He'd seen a man who wished life had gone differently. He'd seen the man he could have been without Laurel.

His father had asked for forgiveness and when Mitch had given it, a great weight had left him. He wouldn't trade the three weeks he'd spent with his father for anything. Laurel had come out and they'd become a family in those weeks before John Adler's death.

He simply wished that had been the only funeral he'd had to attend.

He didn't know the hows and whys. Big Tag didn't talk about ops outside of his team, but Mitch knew that whatever had gone wrong had left McKay-Taggart changed forever, and he only hoped they could rally after losing one of their own.

"Who needs coffee?" Flynn slipped in, carrying a tray. "I've heard you will live off of caffeine for a very long time."

"Thanks, I'll take it. I don't want to sleep. I just want to hold him." He didn't want to let his son go.

"Well, I want to hold him, too." Laurel sighed and sat up, dragging the covers around her.

Mitch stood. "Momma gets dibs. She spent hours giving birth to you."

She looked tired but radiant as he gently transferred the baby to her arms.

"If she's going to breast feed, I'm going back out to the lobby," Flynn promised.

"Wimp," Chase shot back. "It's a normal, natural thing. Baby boy's gotta eat."

"Yeah, well, you're not wired to think it's kind of hot," Flynn admitted.

Chase laughed. "Not in any way. But I'm going to be the best uncle ever."

The kid had turned it around. He seemed happier now, though Mitch knew he missed his father. Mitch often got Chase to talk about their dad.

"I think I'm the best uncle," Flynn argued before putting his arm around his younger brother's shoulder. "Come on. Let's give these two some peace. I know they'll have a flood of visitors soon."

Laurel waved good-bye and then scooted over. "Sit with me."

He didn't hesitate. They'd found a perfect place together over the months of living as husband and wife. They'd continued to play until she couldn't. Mitch had discovered he preferred keeping their D/s life mostly to the club. His Laurel was such a perfect partner he wanted her by his side at all times. And he never, ever held himself back when he was making love to her. He was thinking about doing it now. "You know, after getting caught fucking on a desk by the police, I really think the nurses wouldn't be a big deal at all."

"Oh, you're waiting a while for that, babe." She leaned against him.

He kissed the top of her head. "You're worth waiting for. And the good news is Johnny can go to college. The sale of Dixon Tech went through. Harvey and Frances are making two hundred million each."

"And poor Patrick is making friends in prison. You know it couldn't have happened to a nicer guy," Laurel admitted.

His wife had been a vigilant watcher of Patrick Dixon's trial and relieved when the man had been sent to prison. She was taking some time off from saving the world to spend with their baby, but Mitch knew she would be back at it.

This time, he might help her. After all, he wanted the world to be as perfect for his son as it was for him.

"I was thinking. You know, as long as we're redoing the office at home, maybe I should take a look at your office at work."

He groaned. "You are always changing things. But fine. When you change things, I like them more. And god knows I love you more than my desk."

She smiled up at him. "Oh, no. We're keeping that desk. It's a historical desk. John's lucky he wasn't named Daddy's desk because he was conceived on it."

"We're never telling him that story. He only needs to know one thing about his conception."

"And what's that?"

"That he was conceived in love. I love you, baby. So damn much."

"Back at you, Bradford."

She rested her head against his chest and they watched their son sleep, the world fading around them.

Sign up for the 1001 Dark Nights Newsletter
and be entered to win a Tiffany Key necklace.

There's a contest every month!

Go to www.1001DarkNights.com to subscribe.

As a bonus, all newsletter subscribers will receive a free
1001 Dark Nights story
The First Night
by Lexi Blake & M.J. Rose

Turn the page for a full list of the
1001 Dark Nights fabulous novellas...

1001 Dark Nights

WICKED WOLF by Carrie Ann Ryan
A Redwood Pack Novella

WHEN IRISH EYES ARE HAUNTING by Heather Graham
A Krewe of Hunters Novella

EASY WITH YOU by Kristen Proby
A With Me In Seattle Novella

MASTER OF FREEDOM by Cherise Sinclair
A Mountain Masters Novella

CARESS OF PLEASURE by Julie Kenner
A Dark Pleasures Novella

ADORED by Lexi Blake
A Masters and Mercenaries Novella

HADES by Larissa Ione
A Demonica Novella

RAVAGED by Elisabeth Naughton
An Eternal Guardians Novella

DREAM OF YOU by Jennifer L. Armentrout
A Wait For You Novella

STRIPPED DOWN by Lorelei James
A Blacktop Cowboys ® Novella

RAGE/KILLIAN by Alexandra Ivy/Laura Wright
Bayou Heat Novellas

DRAGON KING by Donna Grant
A Dark Kings Novella

PURE WICKED by Shayla Black
A Wicked Lovers Novella

HARD AS STEEL by Laura Kaye
A Hard Ink/Raven Riders Crossover

STROKE OF MIDNIGHT by Lara Adrian
A Midnight Breed Novella

ALL HALLOWS EVE by Heather Graham
A Krewe of Hunters Novella

KISS THE FLAME by Christopher Rice
A Desire Exchange Novella

DARING HER LOVE by Melissa Foster
A Bradens Novella

TEASED by Rebecca Zanetti
A Dark Protectors Novella

THE PROMISE OF SURRENDER by Liliana Hart
A MacKenzie Family Novella

FOREVER WICKED by Shayla Black
A Wicked Lovers Novella

CRIMSON TWILIGHT by Heather Graham
A Krewe of Hunters Novella

CAPTURED IN SURRENDER by Liliana Hart
A MacKenzie Family Novella

SILENT BITE: A SCANGUARDS WEDDING by Tina Folsom
A Scanguards Vampire Novella

DUNGEON GAMES by Lexi Blake
A Masters and Mercenaries Novella

AZAGOTH by Larissa Ione
A Demonica Novella

NEED YOU NOW by Lisa Renee Jones
A Shattered Promises Series Prelude

SHOW ME, BABY by Cherise Sinclair
A Masters of the Shadowlands Novella

ROPED IN by Lorelei James
A Blacktop Cowboys ® Novella

TEMPTED BY MIDNIGHT by Lara Adrian
A Midnight Breed Novella

THE FLAME by Christopher Rice
A Desire Exchange Novella

CARESS OF DARKNESS by Julie Kenner
A Dark Pleasures Novella

Also from Evil Eye Concepts:

TAME ME by J. Kenner
A Stark International Novella

THE SURRENDER GATE By Christopher Rice
A Desire Exchange Novel

A BOUQUET FROM M. J. ROSE
A bundle including 6 novels and 1 short story collection

SERVICING THE TARGET By Cherise Sinclair
A Masters of the Shadowlands Novel

Bundles:
BUNDLE ONE
Includes Forever Wicked by Shayla Black
Crimson Twilight by Heather Graham
Captured in Surrender by Liliana Hart
Silent Bite by Tina Folsom

BUNDLE TWO
Includes Dungeon Games by Lexi Blake
Azagoth by Larissa Ione
Need You Now by Lisa Renee Jones
Show My, Baby by Cherise Sinclair

Sweet Child o' Mine
A Masters and Mercenaries Extra
Lexi Blake

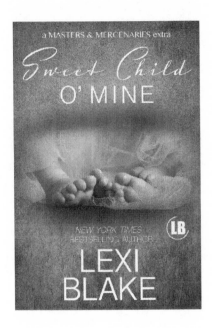

Dedication

To you. Yes, I'm talking to you, dear reader. This one is all for you with my great thanks for all the support and love. Thank you for sharing this journey with me and I look forward to many more adventures.

Chapter One

Ian Taggart frowned as he looked at his childhood friend. Sullivan Roarke had grown up with Ian, Alex, and Sean. He'd worked the same shitty jobs Ian and Alex had worked for the same shitty pay. He'd given Ian some of that pay when Ian had a hard time keeping a roof over his and Sean's head. Sully had never asked for payback.

Until today.

"So what you're telling me is this douchebag lets you film his life and people watch it? Like actual living people who breathe and shit."

Alex, who was sitting beside Sully, groaned. "Ian hasn't developed tact in the decade or so since you last saw him."

Sully sat back with a wry smile on his face. "I wouldn't expect him to. And we don't call Hoover the douchebag. We like to call him the talent."

"Which only proves you have no understanding of the word." Tact was useless in Ian's mind.

"Perhaps, but I've made a lot of money off *Kendalmire's Way*. The network recently reupped us for three years. Do you have any idea how unusual that is? I've been in this business for a while now and this show is my goldmine. If I can get six or seven years out of this show, I'll be set for life and I won't have to do reality shows anymore. I'll be able to move into scripted TV, which is where I want to be."

Thank god. He'd worried that Sully had lost his damn mind. "So you don't particularly want to film douchebag rich kids who think they're DJs and their blonde model girlfriends, who shop and prove the American education system has completely failed?"

Sully chuckled. "Not particularly, but then I suspect you've taken on some jobs that weren't agreeable for the sake of money."

Oh, he'd saved a few people who he would rather have strangled. "True."

"So from what I understand you have to run this by the rest of the team before you take a case?" Sully asked. "I didn't know that or I wouldn't have brought Hoover in today."

Normally, he would present the case to the team and they would decide to take or reject the assignment and who was the best operative to work the case, if they agreed to it. "You didn't just bring Lord Douche. You brought all his douche minions, too."

"The good news is apparently none of them eat because Charlotte offered them cookies and they looked at her like she was crazy," Alex offered. "That's in your favor, Sully. If any one of them had touched Ian's cookies, he would have thrown them down an elevator shaft."

They were his freaking cookies. Sean had recently brought in an assistant pastry chef at his restaurant, Top. Ian was a principle investor so he tended to treat Macon Miles like his own personal bakery. Adam's baby bro didn't seem to mind. He'd kept Ian supplied with sweets. Ian was caught in a never-ending cycle of pain. He got nervous about Charlie giving birth and he ate. He got worried that he was going to end up as big as Charlie and with no actual babies coming out of him, so he worked out. He then worried he was working out too much and neglecting Charlie and he reached for the cookies again.

He was going to be so freaking happy when the demons were all born and life could get back to...

Yeah, he wasn't sure what normal was anymore.

He really wanted one of those cookies followed by a couple of rounds of punching the shit out of someone in the ring he'd set up at the new Sanctum facility. Or he could punch Hoover Kendalmire. That would be fun, too.

"We're taking the case, Sully," Alex assured him.

They were. Because he owed Sully for all those precious ten dollar bills he would slip to Sean for school lunches and for showing up with pizza right about the time Ian's paycheck would run out. "How many times has he been assaulted?"

"Yesterday makes three. It was a really close call. Someone took a shot at him. We have it on camera," Sully explained.

Ian had already looked over the footage. Hoover and his model girlfriend Brie had been filming their very high-end picnic when someone had taken a shot at Hoover with a high-powered rifle. Unfortunately, they'd only managed to hit the bottle of Cristal that had then splattered all over Brie's overpriced shirt and she'd thrown a fit. She hadn't been pissed someone had nearly taken off her boyfriend's head, but damn she wanted to hurt whoever had ruined her designer wear.

Ian wished whoever had tried to kill the fucker had been better at their job. He sighed and leaned forward. "Why don't you go and join your crazies in the conference room. Alex and I will be right out. I want to take one more look at that footage before we talk to…god, I hate even saying his name…Hoover."

Sully stood. "Yeah, his parents had more money than sense. I often think they named him after the vacuum cleaner, which is oddly appropriate since he sucks the intelligence out of any room he enters. But damn that kid's got a million-watt smile. And if you can solve this case without Hoover dying, I can use all of this as a storyline for next season. If the kid dies, so does the show. But you aren't going to let that happen. I know you, Ian. You're going to solve this in no time."

Sully was smiling as he left the office. At least someone was happy.

"I say we set Si and Jesse up on this case," Alex said. "Phoebe and Chelsea won't mind a couple of months in LA. I'll estimate the project at roughly six to eight weeks. We'll need to interview everyone involved and get a feel for what the victim's life is like. I've already been on the phone with LAPD. Derek has a friend in the Threat Management Unit. They're overtasked and apparently Brie and Hoover are difficult to deal with. What a surprise."

Ian flipped a button on his computer and looked over the footage again. The shooter had been roughly five hundred feet away, in a cluster of trees. The shot would have taken off Hoover's head if he hadn't caught sight of his reflection in the bottle of champagne. The dumbass actually picked up the bottle and started to admire himself. His narcissism saved his life.

The cops had found the spot where the shooter had likely stood, but they couldn't determine much. The spot was a hiker paradise. There had been too many footprints to make any kind of guess.

"I'll talk to them. Maybe we should send one of the new guys, too." He'd recently set up a close-cover bodyguard unit within McKay-Taggart. His operatives were almost all family men, and that didn't seem to go well with twenty-four seven close cover. So he'd talked to a friend of Sean's and allowed him to run his business as a subsidiary of McKay-Taggart. "Do you find any of Fisher's men annoying? Because I want to set someone annoying on this guy. Jesse and Si will be too nice. Hey, maybe Chelsea can do some of that rat bastard stuff she used to do to me."

Like putting him on a no-fly list and subjecting him to body cavity searches for months when he flew. It had been a complete dick move and one he respected. He didn't fuck with his sister-in-law much anymore. She was mean and he could understand that.

Charlie could be mean, too, but when she was he would spank her sweet ass and show her who was boss. Well, she was boss and he damn well knew it, but in the bedroom there was no question who topped who.

God, he wanted to top her. Lately, he was too worried to. He looked at that big belly of hers and worried things were going to change again.

"Stop."

Ian looked up. "What?"

"You've got your 'worried dad' face on."

"I do not have one of those."

"You do. It's a little like your 'I'm going to murder someone' face but slightly less happy. You're going to be fine, Ian."

He hated this. Hated all this touchy-feely shit. Still… Alex was kind of his go-to guy. If he couldn't talk to Alex, he couldn't talk to anyone. "I have no idea how to raise girls. Why couldn't they have had penises? I know what to do with a boy. Shove 'em out in the backyard and let them free range for a few years. They'll build their own cabins and become self-sufficient. I don't think I can do that with girls. Speaking of complaints. Why two? One I could maybe handle, but now it's a freaking girl gang at my house. Do you think they're pulling a fast one on dear old dad? Maybe they're hiding their penises and laughing their asses off in utero."

Alex laughed, the sound lightening the mood. "This has been a fun nine months for me, brother. I can't wait for the rest because there are no penises and that gang of girls is going to be so much fun for me to watch when they get to be teens."

Ian shuddered. He didn't want to think about teens.

Alex leaned forward, that sensitive I'm-about-to-give-you-words-of-wisdom-because-I-watched-a-lot-of-Oprah-in-my-time look on his face. "You're going to be fine, Ian. I know you think because your dad walked out that you won't know what to do, but Sean would disagree. Sean would tell you you've already been a great dad. There's only one rule."

"Don't kill the children. Charlie already made me promise." He didn't like the fact that Alex was right. Or that the idea of Sean thinking he was going to be good at the father thing made him a little soft on the inside.

Alex rolled his eyes. "God, you're a pain in the ass."

"What?" He wanted to know. "What's the one rule?"

"Be there. And let me tell you, Ian Taggart's got that one down. So relax. You're going to be a pro at this in no time. And I think you're going to look good in the pink sling Eve bought you."

"Oh, that was so not Eve, asshole." The baby shower had been a revelation. So much fucking pink.

Alex gave him a shit-eating grin. "I laughed the whole time I was buying it. I tried to find a place that would bedazzle the fucker, but Eve wouldn't let me."

Ian stood. "You know what, I'm going to make that shit manly. You think I won't wear a pink sling? I will rock that motherfucker."

"If anyone can, it's you," Alex conceded. He grabbed his laptop. Alex would deal with setting up the project files and all the administrative stuff that came with a new case. He'd backed off of active duty since he and Eve had adopted a baby boy named Cooper.

Who would one day likely turn that innocent gaze of his on Ian's daughters.

"You tell your boy to keep his hands to himself."

"Oh god. I hadn't even thought about that. You're going to be that dad. You know the one who thinks his girls are perfect angels and all the boys around them are the devil? Can we wait until they're born before you accuse Coop of trying something with them?"

Ian kind of thought Cooper eyed Charlie's baby bump as though he knew something good was going to come out of there. "You're wrong. I know my girls won't be angels, and that's why I intend to keep an eye on them at all times. And they're going to look like Charlie so they'll be gorgeous. No doubt about it. Those girls are going to be trouble."

He followed Alex out into the hallway. It was so weird to walk this hallway now. At one point the floor had been damn near empty. They'd really only needed reception, the main conference room, and seven offices, though when they'd first begun, Ian had claimed they only really needed six because Adam was so far up Jake's butt they should share one.

He still loved giving Adam shit. It was one of the constants in his life.

Back in the beginning they'd closed off half the floor and now he was thinking about buying the floor below him if he could convince those damn lawyers to move out. The back conference room had been turned into a daycare center. Charlie now occupied a corner office where she helped Alex with the administrative stuff and was the chief liaison with clients and the outside world. They'd lost Sean to the culinary arts and the world was a better place for it, but somewhere along the way they'd picked up Simon, Jesse, Phoebe, Erin, and now even damn Tennessee Smith had an office, though he'd put Ten in the back next to the babies so he didn't think this was a forever thing.

He was a little scared he was going to end up with all of Ten's former team on the payroll. Since Ten had been disavowed by the CIA for getting too close to a dirty politician, his old team was slowly working their way out and they all ended up at Ian's office with their hands out. He would send the fuckers away but Charlie kept putting them on the payroll.

"Boss, you can't be serious." One of the newbies was marching down the hall, her red hair flying behind her and a look of righteous fury on her face. Yeah, Erin had obviously gotten her new assignment.

"I'm never serious," he replied. God, he loved parts of his job, and fucking with his employees was one of them.

Especially when he fucked with them for their own damn good.

She breathed a sigh of relief. "Thank god. I was hoping it was a joke."

Alex never fucked with anyone. He was practically Captain America. "It's not a joke, Erin. You can pick up your tickets with Grace. You and Theo are set to fly out early Thursday. You have a meeting with the security head of the hospital on Monday, so rest up. It's a long flight and you've got a half a day's layover in Frankfurt. Grace gave you a nice long layover so you don't miss that flight to Monrovia. Also, since your cover is that you're an ex-military, down-on-her-luck girl looking for work, we put you in coach. I'm really sorry."

Ian snorted. Damn, maybe Alex did fuck with the employees. That flight to Liberia was a killer. "But we made sure Theo's got the seat right beside you. After all, a Master always looks after his precious submissive."

Erin's face went a bright red that could have been anger, but unfortunately her T-shirt was thin and that showed the truth. Poor girl's nipples had gone rock hard and it wasn't cold in the building.

Really, he should get extra for playing cupid to the clueless.

"Send someone else with me," she said, her shoulders straight and her feet planted like she was standing at attention. You could take the girl out of the Army, but Erin hadn't yet figured out how to get the Army out of the girl. "Send me in with Chase or Hutch or Michael Malone. I understand that I'm the only female operative who can handle this mission. Hell, I believe in this mission. I want to take out Senator McDonald as much as anyone, but I don't think Theo is ready."

Was that how she was going? "In what way? Is his SEAL training not sufficient? Was his time as a CIA operative too short for your liking? Or is there something else you would like to tell me? Has he harassed you?"

He hadn't considered that. Theo had been attracted to Erin from the moment he met her. There was sexual chemistry between them, but also his half-brother seemed genuinely fond of her. He tried his damnedest to take care of Erin, though it was obvious she was scared of Theo. But if Theo had been doing something he shouldn't, Tag would shut that shit down, brother or no.

Erin's eyes slid away. "No, Sir. You know he's actually very kind. I don't know how to handle it. I would be more comfortable with Hutch."

Because Hutch treated her like one of the guys. "Hutch is incapable of looking like he's in love with you and he has zero training in D/s. Faith McDonald has been in the lifestyle for longer than you have."

"Longer than Theo, too." It was obvious Erin wasn't giving up.

"But Theo has been training day and night." Theo seemed to have figured out what Erin needed, and he was trying hard to be able to give it to her. He'd been working with Ten under Tag and Alex's tutelage, and he'd come a long way. His brother was more than ready for this assignment. He was the best man for the job. Tag liked to fuck with his employees, but he took his business seriously. "Theo is perfectly prepared for this mission and you're the right operative to get close to Faith McDonald. You'll be her personal bodyguard and you can bond over giggling and tea and whatever girls bond over."

Erin flipped him off. It was a good sign. He suspected she had some serious shit in her background having to do with authority figures. Flipping the boss the bird meant she was comfortable he wasn't going to hurt her. Now she simply had to figure out Theo wouldn't either. "I'll take care of Faith. I actually kind of admire her. She's smart and seems to be trying to do good in the world."

Unfortunately, her father was an evil fuck who sold out servicemen for a buck and made his fortune off keeping the wars going. Faith McDonald could be Mother Teresa and he would still use her to take down her father. "Don't go into this expecting a lifetime friendship. She's the target. Talk to her. Convince her to come to Dallas with you so she can meet a new Master. She's single right now, but the word is she always indulges during her off time. Get her back here with you and Ten will handle the rest."

"And Theo?"

Did he have to figure out everything? "Don't sleep with him. It's just your cover. Sometimes operatives don't use their covers to get a little something something." Ian scratched his head, trying to think of an example. It was hard. His operatives were the worst when it came to sleeping with their partners—Simon and Chelsea, Jesse and Phoebe, Alex and Eve—or being stupid fucks and falling in love with their targets—Sean and Grace, Li and Avery. Hell, Jake and Adam had married their freaking client. It could be their new slogan. *McKay-Taggart: We Don't Keep It In Our Pants.* Oh, well, there was one he could think of. "Alex and I went undercover once and we did not sleep together."

Alex shrugged. "He tried but I wanted someone a little more tender. Li used to go undercover with Karina and he's never once slept with her. Then there was that first mission we sent Jesse on at the strip club."

Ian cleared his throat. He was pretty sure Jesse had slept with about ten of those strippers, but that had all been before Phoebe.

Alex shook his head. "JoJo, Eboni, and Misty Rose weren't his partners. Simon was. Si swears up and down they've never cuddled. Not once. So you're safe, Erin."

"You're all jackholes, you know that, right? And Liberia? Really? I left the damn Army so I didn't have to spend all my time in the world's shitholes." Erin was shaking her head as she walked away. "Simon gets to go to Venice. Li's biggest op was in London. I get fucking West Africa."

"Don't forget the Ebola," Tag called out. "You're welcome." He shook his head as she disappeared around the corner. "They're totally going to do it in Africa."

"Oh, they will so do it, but then that's your plan." Alex started toward the conference room again. "You know she'll probably end up being your sister-in-law. Your girls will call her Auntie Erin and she'll teach them how to make homemade grenades or something."

"Yeah, well, I can't seem to get rid of anyone anyway, so I might as well minimize the damage. God only knows who Theo would drag home if he wasn't all moony over Erin. I'm pretty sure Case is going to show up with some chick he scrapes off the floor of a bar. That boy can drink." He had to smile because the light of his fucking life stepped out of the break room.

Charlie Taggart. The sight of his gorgeous wife made his heart speed up. He knew she was due to deliver their babies in five weeks, but damn he wanted to fuck her long and hard. She was stunning, a freaking super-hot fertility goddess who made his dick stand up and cheer every time he thought about her. She had a grin on her face as she caught sight of him. "Hey, those people from LA are completely insane. They asked for spring water but nothing filtered by modern hands or from any country with a dictator or not approved by Angelina Jolie. They also asked for water without carbs. Seriously. They think water has carbs. We could make so much money off these people."

It would be a miracle if he survived the afternoon. "How does Chelsea feel about heading to LA for a couple of weeks?"

"Months," Alex said. "This could take months and Sully has

promised to pay top dollar."

Charlie frowned. "I don't know that I want to be so far away from my sister after the babies are born. I kind of hate that idea."

"I'll figure it out." If Charlie wanted Chelsea, who was the single least maternal woman he'd ever met, around their babies, then Chelsea would be there. "Maybe this once, Jesse can work with Michael."

She went on her toes and kissed him. "Thanks, babe. And have you come up with a name yet?"

"Rocky." It was a joke between them now. "Or Rambo. Hey, maybe you'll name yours Rambo. I think they're perfect names for twins."

She made a vomiting sound and slipped her hand in his as they walked down the hall. "Over my dead body."

"Is he still doing this? What was it last week?" Alex asked.

Ian saw the conference room up ahead. It was full of Sully's "cast." Apparently, it wasn't Kendalmire's way to travel with less than an entourage. "Chuck. Girls can be named Chuck."

"Not if they want to have any kind of a social life. Ian, they'll be here soon. Mine is Kenzie. Her sister needs a name that wasn't plucked from an action movie." Charlie gave him her death stare but it was really softened by the hand on her belly. She smoothed it over as though soothing the babies inside. "We can talk about it after the meeting."

He stepped inside, and Sully was talking to his people.

"This is all going to be over soon and it won't disrupt your schedule." Sully spoke in silky tones, like he was calming down an unruly child. "Trust Mr. Taggart. He's got a sixth sense about this kind of thing. We'll have you safe in no time, Hoover."

Hoover Kendalmire stood at the back of the conference room, his likely expensive loafers tapping against the floor. "My life isn't safe, Sully. There's nothing about this life that's safe, and I'm going to put it all into my music, man. You'll see. I'm going to be the new Eminem. Except way more attractive and less angry. Why so angry, dude? But seriously, I'm going to be the Eminem of Malibu."

Sully sighed. "Well, we can get right on that as soon as we get back to California. We'll be out of here soon."

An emaciated blonde flipped her hair back. Ah, the girl who modeled. According to her press kit, Brie Westerhaven was the daughter of a minor rock star from the eighties and a groupie who didn't know how to use birth control. The show chronicled her attempts to make it big on fashion runways while her dunce boy attempted to take on the music business in absolutely the most superficial of ways. They were surrounded by hangers on. Hoover's two brothers, his producer, who looked heavily invested in dental gold if that grill he was wearing was real, two personal assistants, who looked like they really wished they'd finished college and gotten real jobs, and the chick with the crazy eyes.

Ian looked over at Alex, who shook his head.

"You can't know that," Alex muttered under his breath. "Don't, Ian. We should follow procedure."

"Do you see those eyes?" It was all so clear to him and he'd spent two seconds with these people.

Alex's mouth firmed stubbornly. "It could mean nothing. Let Jesse handle it. He'll follow procedure and we'll actually make money off this."

Brie shook her head as she paced. "God, I hope we get back to Cali soon. This is so boring. I thought Texas was one of those not real places. You know what I mean."

She glanced over at a woman who stood by her side, staring up at the model as if she was the second coming of the Virgin Mary. "I do. You're so smart, Brie. I didn't think Texas was real either. I mean who would? Sully, we should tape this scene. Brie is so funny."

"Dude, anyone who's seen Dallas knows it's real, hello." Hoover waved a hand through the air as though it was all too much for him. "Don't you watch TV and shit? Where do you think J.R. came from? It's a brilliantly ironic television show about global warming."

The pixiesque woman by Brie shot the DJ a look Ian had seen before.

Damn, Sully had really lost his touch. He used to be good at understanding the people around him. Alex wasn't going to like it, but Ian really couldn't stand the thought of even having these people as an open case halfway across the country. It was time to shut this shit down.

He pointed at the girl because despite the fact that Sully was willing to pay by the hour, if these people didn't get out of his office he was going to launch a grenade at them. "It's Crazy Eyes. She's a closeted lesbian in love with Dimwitted Blonde, and she tried to kill Douchebag."

Damn, didn't they know it was always the bitch with the crazy eyes?

His wife turned, about to yell at him—yeah, he knew that look—but Crazy Eyes saved him from the inevitable lecture about giving peace a chance and shit by pulling a forty-five out of her outrageously large handbag.

"You don't deserve her!" Crazy Eyes shouted as she pointed the gun at Hoover.

All hell broke loose, but then it wasn't really a day at the office without a little chaos.

Chapter Two

"Crazy Eyes, I swear to god if you fire that fucking gun in my conference room, I will kill you myself, and you won't like how I do it," Ian swore. His heart was going to beat out of his fucking chest. Charlie was in here. If the bullets started flying, she could get hit. The babies could get hit. Damn it, they were supposed to be safe here.

Brie had a hand over her chest as though protecting herself. "Marcy, what are you doing?"

Sully put out his hands and eased toward Crazy Eyed Marcy with the calm movements of a lion tamer. "Marcy, honey, there's no need for this. Hoover wasn't trying to be mean. You know how he is. Let's calm down and talk about this."

Hoover had ducked behind the dude with the grill and was currently peeing his pants, if the smell was any indication.

Yeah, Sully was going to pay for that.

"Charlie, get out of here." He didn't like how shaky Marcy was. And she'd already proven herself entirely incapable of hitting her target.

"It's fine, Ian." She didn't move, merely watched as the chick with the gun pointed it her way.

"Don't move," Marcy said, her voice thin and reedy.

"God, Marcy, you're such a drama queen." Brie huffed and sat down in one of the chairs and started to look at her nails as though the rest of the action bored her.

"Marcy, honey, why don't you give me the gun?" Sully asked.

"Wait, it was Marcy?" One of Hoover's brothers scratched his head and seemed to be trying to the figure the situation out.

"Dude, I thought you slept with her," the other brother whispered in a too loud voice.

Marcy pointed the gun toward Tweedle Dee and Tweedle Dumb. "I only love Brie. I would never sleep with any of you."

Alex leaned toward him. "You get Charlie and I'll take down the girl."

Ian nodded. He had to be careful. Normally he would simply hit Charlie with the force of a steamroller, forcing his body over hers so if a bullet came their way it would take him out instead of her. But her body wasn't her own. Her body held their babies. His girls. All three of his girls were in danger. His heart pounded in his chest, adrenaline coursing through his bloodstream. Normally he went ice cold in these situations. Charlie was deadly all on her own. His wife could take care of herself, though he preferred to handle the dangerous stuff. She was competent, but she was almost nine months pregnant. God, if anything happened to his girls...

Charlie had died once. Oh, it had all been a ploy in a spy game they'd been playing, but he'd spent five years in hell mourning her. He couldn't do it again. He couldn't lose her again and god, he couldn't lose their daughters. He had a sudden vision of burying all three of them, and it stopped him in his tracks.

"Ian, are you all right?" Alex whispered.

And that was the moment Charlie chose to make her play. Marcy had backed up, moving away from Sully, who seemed to be putting himself between the gun and his star. Unfortunately, it moved Marcy's back close to Charlie, who had her in a choke hold before Ian could scream. The gun fell out of Marcy's hand, clattering to the floor.

"Oh, my god. Something's kicking me!" Marcy said before her eyes closed and she went limp.

Charlie let her drop to the floor and Alex was kicking the gun away before Ian could move. She grinned his way, her hand on her belly. "Ian, the babies just went crazy. I swear to god they could tell we were taking someone down. They're already helping Mommy take out the bad guys." She frowned. "Babe, are you all right? You are really pale."

Ian sat, staring ahead as he tried to get himself under control.

"I think you broke him," Eve whispered to Charlie two hours later.

"I can still hear, you know." He hadn't moved in hours. He was replaying the situation over and over in his brain. The sight of Charlie creeping up on a woman with a gun while she was super pregnant wasn't one that would go away easily.

The Dallas Police had shown up and hauled Crazy Eyes off to prison. She was about to find out just how damn real Texas was, complete with a prison system where she could totally find a new girlfriend since Brie wasn't interested. She hadn't been all that interested in Hoover, who had required a change of pants, either. She had been interested when the press had shown up downstairs.

Derek was going to keep McKay-Taggart's name out of it so they didn't become the go-to security firm for douchebag reality stars. Lieutenant Brighton had tried to question Ian, but all he'd managed to say was something about asking Charlie since she was freaking Superwoman and his babies in utero could kick ass.

Jesus. He couldn't breathe.

"Babe, do you want something to eat? I can have Sean bring something over." Charlie was using a deeply soothing tone on him as she rubbed his shoulders.

"Not hungry." He might never eat again.

"How about some Scotch?" Charlie offered.

"I know Alex has some eighteen-year-old," Eve offered. "Or we could go back to my office and sit and talk. You've been through something traumatic. You need a safe place to discuss your feelings."

That got him moving. He wasn't going to have a flipping session. "I'm fine."

He stood up and started down the hall but not before he noticed Eve taking a twenty-dollar bill from Charlie, who was shaking her head.

"Told you it would work," Eve said under her breath. "Now you need to go and fix him. That man is in serious denial."

He wasn't in denial. He knew damn well there was absolutely nothing he could do. He strode down the hallway. It was utterly out of his control. He hated this. He wasn't in control of fucking anything anymore.

Adam started to walk out of his office and shrank right back in when he saw the look on Ian's face. At least one person was still afraid of him.

He needed more fear from his employees. He should begin routine beatings. Yes, that would make him feel better. He could randomly beat the shit out of people, and then he would have the illusion of control.

Because it was all an illusion.

He'd just sat down in his chair when she came through the door, closed it quietly, and locked it behind her.

What was that about?

"Ian, I know you're mad."

"I'm not mad." He couldn't be mad. She was ridiculously pregnant and that meant he couldn't get mad. He couldn't take charge. He couldn't do fucking anything. He was supposed to be "supportive" and calm, even when she did stupid things like take down a killer with a choke hold.

"Yes, you are furious and I don't really understand how you aren't yelling at me. Come on, babe. It would make you feel so much better. Do you want me to get the paddle out? It's been a while since you gave me a good long spanking. We could both use it."

Yes, he could so use a nice session where he took out all of his frustrations on her gorgeous backside. But again, she was pregnant. "I think you're right. I'll have some Scotch and chill out here. It's not a problem, though I'm sure Alex is pissed I didn't draw this out."

She reached out a hand, and when he thought she would lower herself into his lap, her knees found the carpet and she knelt down beside him. "You always have had an instinct for finding crazy eyes."

"Baby, that can't be comfortable. Let me help you up."

"No, I want to be here. I'm fine. You have got to stop treating me like I'm made of glass. I'm fine. You're the one who's fragile right now."

"I am not fragile, Charlie."

A little glint hit her eyes. "Prove it."

Frustration raced through him like a freight train. When she got that light in her eyes, he was usually in for a hell of a time. His Charlie could take as much as he could give. Their kinks matched beautifully. He topped and she loved to be topped.

If he was honest, he would say his kinks changed for her. He'd been hardcore, dominating women for both discipline and sex. His D/s style had been rigid. Now he was a lovingly indulgent top who spanked his wife more because she liked it than for any real disciplinary reasons.

Though today, he'd definitely wanted to smack her ass for pulling that stunt. She could have been killed. She could have lost the babies. Anything could have happened.

"I'm not going to talk you into punishing me, am I?" Charlie asked, her eyes wide and innocent.

He wanted to, but he didn't dare. She was so close to delivery. She might think she was superwoman, but she was pregnant with twins and he would be damned if he caused her a single moment's discomfort until she was fully recovered.

Then all bets were off and her ass was his.

And he would still have to deal with the fact that he wasn't in control. Two small girls would prove that to him once and for all. He couldn't control those girls. Kenzie and...

One of his babies didn't have a name yet and he couldn't come up with one. He'd been joking about Rambo, but he couldn't for the life of him come up with a name. The one thing Charlie had asked him to do.

"Ian, you're going to be good at this. Everything is going to be fine. I know you're scared, and I didn't make that any better by taking down crazy pants by myself. I think you need to relax. You've spent the last several months catering to my every whim and I really need to pay you back for that." Her hands were close to the fly of his slacks. She was on her knees, that gorgeous mouth of hers trembling. "I need you to top me. I need to know that you still want me. For weeks you've been so sweet and so distant. I know I'm big, but I still need you. I need to be more than the mother of your children. I need to be your wife. God, I miss being your submissive."

And he longed to be her Master. What could it really hurt? If he was gentle, he wouldn't hurt her.

He twisted a hand in her hair, pulling lightly. He wouldn't be too gentle. Charlie wouldn't like that. He pulled just enough to watch her eyes go soft as she began to submit. "You want to play, brat? You want to play after that stunt you pulled? I need you to understand a few things, Charlie Taggart. Your ass is mine as soon as those two girls who are renting move out."

She bit her bottom lip before running her tongue over it. "What are you going to do to it, Master?"

Fuck. He was going to come before she touched him. He took a tight reign on that unruly and desperate cock of his. She was right. They both needed this. He needed a few moments where he could pretend everything was the same. "I'm going to slap that sweet ass silly. Have you seen some of the new toys I've bought for you, my love? Unzip my slacks and take my cock out. You're going to see to me while I explain how bad it's going to get for you in a few weeks."

He let go of her hair and she eagerly moved forward, her hands on the fly of his pants in an instant.

It was one of the things he adored about his wife. She didn't hold back or prevaricate. She loved playing with him and she didn't hold back her affection. It was Charlie's honest need for him that had first broken through his defenses and allowed him to love her openly and with a free heart. God, he fucking loved her.

He was also going to torture her.

His cock popped out as she drew back the band of his boxers. He was already hard as a rock and wanting, but he was going to enjoy this and that meant not shooting off the minute she touched him no matter how much the bastard wanted to. "Lick me. I want you to suck my cock until I tell you to stop, but I swear to god, Charlie, if you're in pain because of the position, you better tell me."

Charlie groaned and her only real reply to him was a long lick of her tongue over his dick. Her hand disappeared and he groaned as he felt that soft palm cup his balls. She rolled them lightly as she swiped at his cockhead, licking up the cream he was already producing. His dick was always ready to go where she was concerned.

So fucking good. His wife knew exactly how he liked it. She leaned over, her strawberry blonde hair flowing all around, and she sucked at the head of his cock. He shifted his hips, trying to make it easier on her. She settled in and started to suck his cock in long passes. Pure pleasure swamped him, but he hadn't forgotten what he promised her.

He settled back and watched his cock disappear between her plump lips. "Once you're recovered, I'm going to take you to Sanctum. It'll take a few months, but it's going to be perfect. I've stocked it with everything I need to torture you. You won't believe the things I've bought. New plugs to open up your asshole with. Pretty clamps for your nipples."

Her head came up. "It might take a while to get to those, Ian. I plan to breastfeed. You know how sensitive they are now."

They were crazy sensitive now. He could lick one and practically make her come. Her whole body had been sensitive lately. After the initial vomiting period, Charlie had been all about getting a little something something, until the final month when she'd been somewhat miserable because she had two extra humans in her body.

Why did his sperm have to be overachieving? Two babies? Three girls. He was going to be so overwhelmed.

He growled and pushed her back to his cock. "I do not need to talk about lactation right now." Although her breasts were larger. Plump and round. Sexy. He knew the reasons for the change, but he couldn't see her as anything but stunning. And his.

"I built a privacy room that's just for us, baby." He wouldn't have to share it with anyone because there were plenty. He'd built them a suite complete with a massive bathroom. The shower and soaking tub were built for the two of them. The tile was heated because her feet were always cold and the towel racks warmed the big fluffy bath sheets he'd ordered for her. The bed was huge and there would be an armoire stocked with everything he would need to torture his pretty submissive. In that room they wouldn't be husband and wife. They wouldn't be partners. They wouldn't be parents. In that room, they would be lovers, Master and sub. Ian and Charlie.

"I can't wait to see it." She sucked the head of his cock, sending pleasure coursing through his system. Her tongue bathed his dick. Over and over, she laved him with affection.

He was a possessive asshole, but he wasn't going to change. She belonged to him. She'd belonged to him since that moment he'd looked across the dungeon floor in Paris and saw her. Back then she'd had dark hair, but that mischievous grin had been the same.

That very night he'd approached her and negotiated a scene. He'd spanked her and they'd been in this very position about two hours after meeting. She'd been on her knees, sucking his cock like she would die without it.

Suddenly, he needed more. As she sucked him, he could see it—their life together playing out in sharp scenes in his head. Those first days when he realized what it meant to go crazy over a woman. He'd never wanted anyone the way he had Charlie. It had been refreshing and terrifying all at one. That first time he'd slid into her body, forcing his way in as she clung to him. *Sweet Child o' Mine* had played throughout the club and they'd taken way longer in the privacy room than he'd signed them up for. He saw her standing there in London as he'd made her his wife and no matter what he did, he would always see her dead. It was always on the edge of his consciousness. He knew what it felt like to lose Charlie.

And to get her back. He could feel himself opening the door the night Alex and Eve had remarried. One moment changed everything. One turn of a doorknob had shifted him into another world—one where Charlie was alive again.

He'd fought her. He'd fought so hard and now he couldn't think of a single reason why. He should have gotten on his knees and thanked the fucking universe for the second chance he'd been given.

There was no one—no other woman in the world—who moved him, who challenged him, who completed him.

He tugged her off his dick. If she went much longer, he would come in her mouth, and that wasn't what he needed. He needed communion. His love for her was sacred and he needed to pray. "No, Charlie. I want to get inside you. I need to be inside you."

He stood, not giving a damn that his slacks slid off. He reached down to draw her up. She was heavier, but that was only because she was carrying their babies. The truth was, she was beautiful always to him. She could gain or lose weight, grow older, change her hair. It wouldn't matter. He would see her one way. He was surprised to find out the Charlie of his dreams wasn't the woman he'd first met. She'd been amazing. She'd haunted his dreams for years, but when he closed his eyes, the Charlie he saw was the one he'd opened the door to. The one who had been smart enough and brave enough to find her way home. The one with strawberry blonde hair. She'd gotten on her knees for him that night, too.

"Charlie Taggart," he said in an authoritative voice as his hands found her hips.

Despite the fact that she was tall for a woman, she had to look up at him. "Yes, Ian?"

He stared at her as though he could imprint his will on her. "Did I ever say thank you?"

Her lips curled up slightly. "You rarely do, but you don't need words to say how you feel. I know."

But she deserved the words. "Thank you for coming back for me."

Her face softened and reached up to touch his, her fingertips sliding along his jaw. "Babe, there was never a question of that. I will always find my way back to you."

"I love you and you should know that if you die on me again, I'll find you. I won't let us be apart again."

"Never again," she promised. "Ian, I'm going to be okay."

She always saw through him. He lowered his mouth to hers. "You better be or there will be hell to pay. I love you."

"Back at you, Taggart."

Her arms went around his neck and he stopped thinking about anything but getting inside her. His tongue plunged deep and met with hers, sliding together. He caressed those sensitive breasts and felt her shudder in his arms. She was right. He'd spent the last few weeks treating her like she was fragile, but his Charlie was strong enough to handle almost anything. He drew her close and circled one of her nipples with his thumb. Even under the cotton shirt and bra she was wearing, he could feel the nipple go rigid, begging for his tongue and mouth. He unbuttoned her blouse and drew the strap of her bra down so he could release one plump breast.

"Please, Ian," she murmured as his hand cupped her. "Please touch me everywhere. I miss this so much."

He kissed his way down her neck, her skin so familiar and yet always so exciting to him. This was his true home. This woman. They could be anywhere in the world and as long as he was with her, he was home.

He leaned over and gently captured that pert nipple between his lips. He was careful with her, licking around the areola before sucking it into his mouth. Charlie shook in his arms, her hands finding his hair and fingernails scratching along his scalp. He fucking loved that. He pulled on her clothes until she was bare from the waist up and he got those breasts in his hands. He dropped to his knees and began to drag the voluminous cotton skirt she wore over her big belly.

"You're sure it's not horrible?" She stared down at him.

She might still get a spanking. He dragged on the skirt until it hit the floor and then ran his hands over the outrageous curve of her stomach, smiling when something kicked back at him. His girls. They weren't calm or patient. They wriggled around as though anxious to get this life going. He kissed her belly. "You are the most beautiful woman in the world, and just for that I'm putting you on the human hamster wheel. No talking shit about my property."

She was his and no one talked shit about his queen. Not even his queen.

He gently eased her back on his desk, his hand running down between her legs. He could already smell her arousal. Sweetest damn smell in the world. His fingers found her, parting her and playing through her labia. So hot. She was already wet for him.

Charlie spread her legs for him. She was supported by his desk, her palms flat behind her so she leaned back to where she could get comfy. Yeah, he could work with this position. He circled her clit.

"Hamster wheel?" Her voice came out in a breathy pant. "You can't be serious."

Oh, he was serious. "Top of the line. And after you're through breast feeding, I'll trade out the little water bottle for vodka."

She threw her head back and laughed, the sound sweet to his ears. Like everything his wife did, she laughed with great enthusiasm. She moaned as she tilted her pelvis up. "That feels so good. And you're insane if you think I'm running on a hamster wheel. Hey, maybe we should get one for the girls. If they're anything like their cousin, they'll be rambunctious. Carys is a little ball of energy. We can let them run on the hamster wheel for a couple of hours a day and then they'll sleep."

And she matched him for deviousness. "Done, baby. I knew Sean was too easy on that kid. He lets her play with Aidan and Tristan. He's asking for her to get involved in some weird ménage thing."

"Yes, right there. Oh, right there." Her head dropped back. "And you have to go easy on the boys. They're infants. They're not trying anything."

He wasn't so sure, but he would keep his own counsel on that one. And he was definitely watching the boys in his daughters' playgroup. He might even have a little man to baby talk with all of them so those boys knew the lay of the land. Charlie had liberal ideas about how girls should be raised. He was thinking about going old school and locking them in a very nice cloister for the first forty years or so.

She was close, but Ian liked to tease. He withdrew his hand.

His wife's head came up, those gorgeous eyes flaring. "Ian!"

He was ahead of her. He lined his cock up and started to work his way in. He spread her wide but kept the penetration shallow. In another two months or so he would take her hard and plunge deep, but he was careful now. "I'll give you what you need, baby."

He found her clit again and pressed down as he thrust inside her.

Something kicked him hard, a sure sign that those girls were going to make his sex life very difficult. Luckily, he didn't let anything get to him when he was fucking. They could kick all they liked. This was his time.

Charlie tightened around him, but he was ready. She responded so easily to him, as though she was always primed to take pleasure from him. He set a steady rhythm and watched as her breasts bounced as she moved against him, trying to force him in deeper. It wouldn't work. He controlled this, but he liked to watch her fight for her orgasm. He pressed hard again, the pad of his thumb tight to her clit, and she flushed. Charlie's body tightened and her eyes went soft. She called out his name and squeezed him tight.

This was what he'd needed. Connection. When he was inside her, everything was right with the world. The rest of it—the worry and fear—it fell away until there was only her and pleasure.

He felt his balls draw up and thrust faster, getting just a bit deeper. It wasn't all he wanted. He wanted to be balls deep, but he would take her any way he could get her. He was addicted to this woman. He craved her.

He let go and his orgasm flooded his system with pure joy. The world seemed softer than before, his troubles further away. He pumped into her, giving her everything he had.

He sighed and reached for her, pulling her close. Her belly was between them and the girls seemed more active. He chuckled as he kissed her nose. He even loved her damn nose with its light dusting of freckles. "That didn't make them happy."

Charlie laid her head on his shoulder. "It made me happy." She draped herself around him. "I swear they're fighting for dominance in there."

He ran a hand over her flesh. "They're Taggarts. What else would they be doing?" He suddenly wanted to stay this way, alone with her, naked with her. "Baby, why don't you get dressed and I'll take you home. We'll take the rest of the week off. Hell, let's take vacation and we'll wait for the babies."

She turned her head up, a little frown on her face. "I really am fine,

Ian."

She wasn't because she obviously didn't understand him. "I wasn't concerned about your health." Though he really always was. "I want to be alone with you. In a few days, there won't be much alone time. I want some peace before the demons show up."

She laughed and lightly slapped him across the chest. "Stop calling our daughters demons, Ian Taggart. They are going to be sweet little ladies."

"So you cheated on me with the UPS guy?" Because his daughters likely wouldn't be very ladylike. Not if they took after their dad.

She hugged him again and then pushed away, getting to her feet. He kept his hands on her, making sure she didn't fall. She looked him up and down. "You are the only man in the world who can have his junk hanging out like that and I still find attractive. Naked is so much hotter." She proved it by turning around and walking toward the bathroom conveniently located a few feet away.

"You didn't let me get undressed, baby. You were too hot for that." He bent over and dragged his slacks up, tucking his shirt back in. His body was humming and the sight of his gorgeous wife walking across the room made him wonder if they shouldn't take a nice long shower before they went home.

She disappeared behind the door.

Why not take the next few weeks off? Alex could handle the administrative crap and Simon could deal with clients and operative questions. They didn't have too much on the docket. Sully had written him a hefty check despite the fact that it hadn't taken him more than a few moments to solve the case.

He could easily spend a few weeks nesting with his wife, and he could start by washing that lovely body of hers off in the shower he'd had installed a few years back. Back then that bathroom had been all about function. He often slept at the office in the early days. Now it was definitely helpful for those times when he and the missus decided to get their freak on.

And he suspected Sean had hauled Grace in here just for kicks. It would serve him right since he'd screwed Charlie on Sean's desk at Top a couple of months before.

The heart wanted what the heart wanted...and his dick definitely wanted her.

He was almost to the door when it opened and Charlie stood there, her eyes wide.

"Ian," she said in a breathless voice.

His heart nearly seized. "What?"

"My water broke."

How the hell did water break...shit.

Normal was over.

Chapter Three

"Do you think they can tell?" Charlie asked when the doctor left.

"Yes," Ian replied. "They can tell you're pregnant, baby. They are really good doctors and they know a pregnant lady when they see one."

She'd lost her damn mind, but he was going to be supportive.

Her eyes rolled and she shook her head as she maneuvered her way to sitting on the hospital bed. "No. I'm talking about sex. Do you think they can tell that we had sex?"

He gave her belly a pointed stare. "Yeah."

She sighed. "I meant recently, Ian. I meant like two hours ago. That kid was all down there looking at my lady bits and I was wondering if he could tell you'd been up in that today."

"Not at all." Probably, but he wasn't about to tell her that. "All they can see is the centimeter thing."

Charlie's whole body stiffened and she reached for him. He moved as quickly as he could, giving her a hand to hold on to as the pain took her. It seemed to last forever, but he knew it wasn't more than a few seconds. His wife was in pain and he couldn't do a damn thing about it. Well, he could.

"Take the epidural."

"I will if it gets to be too much," she agreed. "But right now it would only slow down the labor."

He needed everything to slow down. He needed it to stop. From the moment she'd told him the babies were coming to now seemed like both forever and the blink of an eye.

The door opened and Chelsea strode in. "Hey, sis. Looks like my nieces are eager to get here."

Ian took that as a sign that he could step out for a moment. He kissed his wife and left her with her sister for the moment. Dr. Bates couldn't have gotten too far. He had a few questions he didn't want to ask around his wife.

He walked out the door and jogged to catch the OB who was standing at the nurses' station. Melinda Bates was a lifestyle friendly doctor. There was a small network of them. Dr. Bates had grown up with a mom and dad who were full-on 24/7, and she understood. It made Ian infinitely more comfortable to have her watching out for Charlie. She wouldn't look at them sideways if Charlie forgot and called out for her Master.

"Doc," Ian began.

"Yes, Mr. Taggart? Is Charlotte all right?" Dr. Bates asked.

"For now. Shouldn't we be doing a C-section? And isn't it early? The babies are going to be premature. Shouldn't we have things set up to take care of them?" They would be small. So fucking small. They would be fragile, and if anything happened to them it would be Ian's fault. This was his family. His girls.

"Ian, it's going to be fine." She put a hand on his shoulder, obviously tossing aside formality. "If she hadn't gone into labor this week, I likely would have pushed to induce her soon. The babies are at a good weight, and from what I can tell they're already obedient little girls. They're both in a heads down position and ready to be born. Charlotte's placenta isn't obstructing her cervix. This is a textbook case for delivering twins vaginally. Everything is going perfectly."

"And if something goes wrong?" He didn't even want to think about it. He would almost rather just get it all over with.

"Then we do an emergency C and she's still fine. Look, nothing I say is going to make you feel better. You're out of control and I can't give it back to you. This is woman's work and it always will be. There isn't a man in the world who's watched his beloved labor to bring their child into the world and not felt helpless," Dr. Bates said with a sympathetic smile. "But Charlotte is strong and your daughters are strong. Let them do their work. For now, all you can do is let them know much you love them."

He nodded, but her words didn't really help. All he could see was Charlie looking pale in that hospital gown she'd had to change into.

So many things could go wrong. He could lose them all.

"Ian?"

He turned and Sean stood there. He was still in his chef whites, as though he'd walked out in the middle of prep for tonight's dinner. Which given the time was the most likely scenario. "You didn't have to come up here. It's probably going to be hours."

Sean simply walked up to him. "I wouldn't be anywhere else. My sous-chef can handle Top for the night. I'm staying here with you. Grace and Li stayed behind to close up McKay-Taggart, but they should be here very soon if not already. I think you'll find everyone else is here. They've kind of taken over the waiting room. We are going to be hell on the volunteers."

God, he hadn't expected that. "Tell them to go home, Sean. Like I said, it's going to be hours."

Sean put a hand on his shoulder. "Walk with me. Chelsea's got Charlotte covered for the moment. I want to talk to you."

He stepped back, wary. "I don't need touchy-feely shit."

"Sometimes I wonder why we put up with you," Sean said under his breath. "Fine. I'll go to plan B. Ian, I've got lemon cookies Macon made in the waiting room."

"Oh, I will take those." As long as he wasn't about to get some lecture about the step he was about to take. He didn't want to hear about that. He kind of didn't want to think about that. Sometimes it was best to simply let things happen.

He started to follow Sean down the hall.

"Do you remember the moment you decided you wanted kids?" Sean asked.

Touchy-feely territory. Yep. His brother was trying to get him there, but Ian was good at avoiding the land mines. Usually he would simply walk away, but he wanted those cookies so a little deflection was necessary. "Nope. I do remember the day Charlie said she was no longer on birth control and what was I going to do about it. Here's a hint. I did not get snipped, which was the only option she gave me besides rolling the dice."

"Seriously, that's what you're going to tell those girls?"

He shook his head. "Nah. Charlie really wanted kids. You've seen her with Carys. Besides, Carys deserves family. After you and Grace made the decision to keep her a single, it kind of fell to me and Charlie to give her cousins."

"You make it sound like we did it to spite you," Sean groused. "The doctors told Grace another pregnancy could be very difficult. She wanted to try. I said no. Carys needs her mother more than she does more siblings."

This was the way it was with him and his brother. They worked out their issues through sarcasm. They didn't need the therapy crap other people did. "Well, I think she needs cousins. I will say if I'd known about Case and Theo at the time, I totally would have shoved this duty off on them."

"Don't even say that," Case said, walking up to them.

Theo was at his side with a big grin on his face. "I'm up to the challenge, big brother. Well, maybe not the actual babymaking challenge, but I'm willing to practice."

Case rolled his familiar blue eyes. "He thinks he's getting some in Africa. He's absolutely certain Erin is going to fall into his bed while they're fighting Ebola and stuff."

Theo didn't back down. "I'm optimistic. I'm getting her alone and I'm pleading my case."

"Yeah, she's going to respond by shoving her foot up your ass, little brother," Case explained.

Ian kind of figured that Erin would try to shove her boot up Theo's ass, but he also thought she might not fight him too hard. "Any way I can convince you to go to Africa and just get the job done?"

He'd often found that the people around him did exactly the opposite of what he asked them to, so he employed reverse psychology to get his way. In this case, it wasn't exactly his way. It was Theo's way, but Theo was going to waste a ton of time if he didn't go after that girl and take her down. She wouldn't respond to roses. She responded to a man strong enough to take her shit and protect her from whatever the hell she was afraid of.

Theo frowned. "I'll try, but I gotta be honest. I'm probably not going to try very hard. Something about that woman does it for me. I can't help it."

Case groaned. "I swear I'm going to beat him to death if he bursts into song."

Ian sympathized. "It's disgusting, isn't it? I had to put up with Sean singing about Grace for weeks."

"I did not sing, asshole," Sean shot back.

They continued down the hall. "I distinctly remember you singing and weeping and playing really bad guitar."

"I did none of that," Sean clarified.

"I'm pretty sure Theo's been writing poetry." Case fell in step with Ian.

Theo shook his head. "Never once in my life have I written poetry."

Sean and Theo walked alongside but there was zero way to miss the similarities. Case and Theo might be twins separated by mere minutes, but they were he and Sean all over again.

Before they got to the lobby, Case put out a hand and held Ian back.

Shit. Was Case about to ask him not to send Theo to Africa? Case could be super protective of his younger brother. Another thing they had in common.

"What?"

Case frowned. "I just wanted to say something. I know I was kind of an asshole when we first met."

"You can't help it. It's your personality." He knew what Case was talking about. Case had always resisted acknowledging their connection as anything past a coincidental biological link. He was wrong, of course, but Ian didn't bother to point it out.

Charlie, on the other hand, had been pretty specific with his brothers. They were family and therefore her responsibility, and she didn't care if Case agreed. A while back, Case had broken his leg, and without bothering to ask the boy what he thought, she'd simply moved Case into the spare bedroom and taken care of him while Theo was off in Dubai.

"Yeah, well, it's yours, too," Case shot back. "Look, this is hard for me. Could you please shut the fuck up and listen? I'm sorry I was an asshole. I worried you would come in and Theo would look up to you."

Ian felt for the kid. He remembered what it felt like to only have his brother. "I was never going to take Theo away from you."

"I know, but I think you should also know that I wish it had been different."

Ian could only imagine. "I'll get Charlie to back off. It was never my intention to run roughshod over you, Case. I just wanted to get to know you."

"That wasn't what I meant. I didn't mean I wish we hadn't met. I mean I wish you'd been my big brother, too. All those years...I wish it had been you and Sean and me and Theo."

The Taggart brothers. "You understand I'm going to beat the shit out of you."

"Jesus, man. Is that a tear?" Case looked properly horrified.

"It's manly hug time." He caught his brother and gave him a good pounding on his back. "And now we're done."

Case's mouth turned up. "Thank god because Theo would have drawn that shit out."

Sean popped back out of the waiting room. "What's going on?"

"Absolutely nothing," Ian lied because Sean would drag that shit out, too, and the last thing he needed was a bunch of crying dudes hanging on him.

"Not a thing, brother." Case gave him a nod and joined the rest.

Sean stared at him suspiciously. "Yeah, I believe that." He sighed. "You know you're going to be good at this, right?"

"I'm good at everything." But not this. Maybe he would be awful. He was sarcastic and didn't particularly believe in showing his emotions to anyone but Charlie. He worried that he was going to resent the kids for taking time away from her, and didn't that make him a complete asshole?

"Joke all you like, but in this I'm the leader, brother. I know what this feels like. I know how awful it feels to watch your wife do something you can't help her with. You can't take this burden from her."

Ian shrugged. "Charlie's tough."

"And I also know what it feels like to worry that your whole world is about to change," Sean said, ignoring him completely. "And guess what—it is. Nothing you've gone through prepares you. A lot of people will tell you you've already been a parent to me, and in some ways you were. You took care of me. I know what you sacrificed, but Ian, I wasn't your kid. You have no idea how you're going to feel when they put that first baby girl in your hands, and nothing I say will prepare you for it. But I am going to say this."

"Do you have to? You know I really think those dudes back in the sixties had it right. We should go and sit in a bar somewhere and a nurse will call us and tell us the baby's here."

Sean put a hand on his shoulder. "Wasn't that the life? Sorry. Come in here and you're going to figure something out. I know you say you're not afraid, but I'm going to do this anyway."

He led Ian through the doors of the waiting room, and Ian was shocked at how they'd taken up all the space.

Li and Avery sat with Jake and Adam and Serena. They'd set up a small playpen and the boys were sitting in it while Carys held court between them. Grace was talking to Eve while Alex was pacing the floor and talking on his cell phone.

"Yes, Damon. I'll be sure to call when they're born," Alex was saying. "Yeah, I know. Two girls. They're going to drive him absolutely insane. Say hello to Penny for us."

Simon was sitting with Jesse and Phoebe, and at least half of the members of Sanctum were here, too.

"I know one thing in this world and that's the fact that Ian Taggart knows how to create a family. None of us would be here without you, you sarcastic asshole brother of mine. So go and help your wife make our family a little bigger."

Ian did just that because the last thing he wanted any of them to see was the way his eyes had watered.

They'd come together because they'd all been defeated one way or another. They'd all been broken—by death or loss or failure. Ian hadn't wanted to lose them. He hadn't wanted to lose himself, so he'd started McKay-Taggart in order to give them all something to do.

How had they become more than friends? More than colleagues? Those people had become his family.

And his family was about to welcome another two of their own.

He slipped into Charlie's room, ready to face the future.

Ten hours later, he was fairly certain his hand was going to break.

"One more big push and the first one will be out, Charlotte," Dr. Bates said. "You're doing great. I wish all my twin deliveries went like this."

Charlie grunted and squeezed his hand and seemed to put all her willpower into her task. Then again, she was trying to push two whole human beings out of her vagina. She glanced up at him. "You could say something helpful."

"Nope." He really couldn't. He'd spent hours watching her in pain and not being able to do or say anything that could make it better. He hated this. He hated every part of it. They were never doing this again. These two girls better like each other because they weren't getting siblings. No way. No how. For the first time he actually thought about getting snipped so she would never have to deal with this kind of pain again.

"Wimp." Somehow Charlie managed a smile right before she screamed again. And then with a long sigh, she laid back.

"Oh, hello pretty girl," Dr. Bates said. "Ian, do you want to cut the cord?"

He wasn't getting anywhere near that. He didn't even like the symbolism. "I'll pass."

He needed to stay with Charlie. He needed to make sure she was all right.

"You are lucky, Charlotte," the nurse said. "Any longer and you would have been giving birth to two toddlers. The first twin is five and a half pounds. She's perfect."

"Go and see her," Charlie said.

"I'm fine. I can wait until the other one is out."

"That could take a while," the nurse said. She was holding a tiny bundle in her arms that looked absolutely nothing like a toddler. Toddlers were resilient, if Carys was any indication. The kid could bump all day and not really come to any harm. But whatever was in that little pink blanket, that was a fragile thing.

He was far more used to killing than nurturing.

"Show her to your wife," the nurse urged.

Ian shook his head. "Charlie should hold her."

Dr. Bates looked up from between his wife's splayed legs. Yeah, it was that kind of a day. "No. I think this one is close. Charlotte needs to push again."

Charlie nodded. "I can feel it. This one isn't going to wait. Let me see her, Ian."

Deep breath. He could do this. It was just one tiny baby that had recently been expelled from his wife's body. He could handle one small female. Hell, he was the Dom of Doms. He was the ultimate authority figure.

The nurse placed the little bundle in his arms and Ian looked down.

The baby looked up. Not the baby. His baby. His daughter. She had Charlie's eyes and the sweetest little cap of strawberry blonde hair. There wasn't much of it, but it was there. She had a little bow mouth and a tiny little nose. And a totally misshapen head.

"She looks like an alien." An alien version of a baby Charlie. A gorgeous baby girl with a cone for a head.

"If you don't show me that baby right now, Ian Taggart, I am going to pull your balls off," Charlie growled.

He knew when to obey. Even the baby's eyes had popped open, as though she knew the sound of her mother in a killing rage. "I think this is the one who tried to take out crazy eyes. I'm naming this one."

He lowered his daughter down and watched in wonder as Charlie's eyes softened and she reached to touch her daughter for the first time.

And then her body seemed to seize. "Oh, here comes your sister."

He cradled baby number one in his right arm and held Charlie's hand with his left. He kept switching his gaze between his girls. The baby in his arms was yawning as though the whole event had really been tiring but no big deal.

Her sister was born three minutes later, and ten minutes after that he found himself following his daughters down to the nursery. He stood outside, watching through the glass as the pediatrician began checking the babies over. Baby number one was wrapped in her pink blanket and number two was in yellow. It was a good thing because he couldn't tell them apart by looking at them. He wouldn't let them out of his sight and explained in no uncertain terms that his daughters wouldn't be left there overnight. Charlie had been very specific about it. She was keeping them in the room with her unless they needed to be checked out, and then Ian would be watching. At the time, he'd thought she was being unreasonable. She was surely going to need sleep. He'd been planning on quietly letting the girls go to the nursery.

Never. Not even once was he letting those babies out of his sight. They were his.

This was what Sean had meant. When they'd put baby number two in his arms and he lowered them both down to Charlie, he'd finally understood. He'd protected Sean, but Sean hadn't been his.

These two small things were his and Charlie's. They were proof beyond all doubt that they loved each other. Those girls were immortality, a way for his love for his wife to always live on. In that one moment, he understood what it meant. His love for his wife could be selfish. He wanted things from her. Love. Affection. Sex. Submission.

He wanted nothing from these girls except the right to love them, the right to protect and teach them.

Loving Charlie had made him a man, but these girls made him a father, and that was so much more.

"Look at that," Sean said, coming to stand beside him. The rest had gone with promises to come by in the morning, but his brothers had stayed. Oh, Case and Theo had both fallen asleep in the waiting room, but they were here.

Ian and Sean watched the babies through the glass as the pediatrician checked them out. Kenzie, daughter number two, was lying peacefully while his firstborn had already kicked out of her swaddling and was currently giving the doctor hell. Baby girl didn't like the eyedrops. She didn't like the shot. She didn't like being poked and prodded, and now the whole hospital knew it.

"That one's going to kick a little ass, Sean." He smiled as his daughter screamed her head off. He could already tell that scream wasn't about pain. She was pissed.

And then her sister tuned up with her, as though crying in sympathy.

Damn but they could make a racket.

"Any idea of what you're going to name her?" Sean asked.

"Yeah. I think I got that all figured out," he said with a smile.

Epilogue

"Kala? Isn't that like the goddess of chaos in Hindu mythology?" Adam stared at Ian like he knew something was going on. Adam followed him out on the porch, away from the rest of the team who were now getting ready to sit down to Charlie's welcome back dinner.

She'd only been in the hospital for two days, but Ian had made them wait two weeks before getting together in a big group. Charlie needed peace and quiet, but now she was ready to show the babies off to their family.

Naturally, Kenzie had gone to sleep right after her feeding and Kala had fussed, so Daddy was holding her close, cuddling her so she could rest. His Kenzie and his Kala.

Adam was always far too perceptive. It was precisely why Ian loved to give him shit. "I think you've watched too much Indiana Jones. And no. That's Kali. Kala is a perfect little name for a precious baby girl. In Sanskrit it means virtue."

Adam's eyes narrowed. "You looked it up?"

Maybe he shouldn't have mentioned that part. At the time it seemed like a really good way to throw people off the scent. Charlie had accepted his explanation of Kala without blinking an eye. She'd told him she loved it and that it was perfect.

If only she knew how perfect it was...

"I can look things up, Adam. It's my daughter's name. It's important."

Adam took a drink off the coffee he was holding. This little dinner party was booze free since Charlie was breastfeeding. Sean and his sous-chef had made a grand Italian dinner for the group. The smell made Ian's stomach rumble. "I don't believe you. You're the man who wanted to name them Bruce and Arnold."

Ian shrugged, patting his daughter's back. She seemed to like to sleep on his shoulder for some reason. Kenzie preferred being cradled, but Kala always wanted to be up high. "I have a deep affection for 80's cinema. What can I say?"

Adam frowned. "I'll figure it out in the end. Hey, Charlotte. Did the other little princess wake up?"

His wife stepped out onto the back porch with Kenzie in her arms. "She never sleeps for long if Kala isn't close. We tried to force them to sleep in separate beds, but they cried until we put them together."

He loved to watch them sleep. Honestly, he kind of loved to watch them do everything. He'd never understood until he looked down at a baby that was equal parts him and the woman he loved more than life. He would sit there like an idiot and watch those babies sleep, cuddling together like they had in the womb.

"I'll go see if I can help with the prep work, but I meant what I said, Tag. I'll figure it out and I'll find some way to use it." Adam grinned as he walked back in the house.

It would likely be fitting if Adam was the one who took him down. He gave Adam more crap than all the others, but he was fairly sure his friend wouldn't figure it out.

God, he hoped Charlie never figured out he'd named their daughter an anagram for Kick A Little Ass.

"What was he talking about?" Charlie said, suspicion in her voice.

Ian gave her his most innocent look. "No idea, baby. You know how he likes to torment me."

Charlie laughed and sank into one of the two rockers on the back porch. "Yeah, Adam torments you. That's one world view. Sit down for a minute. Sean will come and get us when dinner's ready."

He sank down beside her. "Too many people? I can throw them all out."

She shook her head. "Don't you dare. That's our family in there, but I wanted a couple of minutes where it's just us."

Us had been him and Charlie, and now that one word meant something more. Us meant two sweet girls who would likely drive their father utterly mad.

He reached for her with his free hand. He always wanted the connection with her. "Think you'll ever want more?"

Charlie's eyes widened. "Eventually, yes. I thought I would have to fight you on it."

He shook his head. "No. I get it. I think I thought if we had kids, I would have to share you and I do, but I also thought somewhere in the back of my head that I wouldn't be me anymore. I'm just a different me. I like this me, Charlie. Best thing I ever did was to open that door and welcome you home."

Her jaw dropped. "You are such a liar, Ian Taggart. You gave me hell."

Sometimes it was good to be him. "Not how I remember it." He was good with his revisionist history. When she started to argue with him, he hushed her. "You'll wake the babies."

The gorgeous gleam in her eyes promised retribution. And he would take it. He would take everything he could get from her and give her back all of himself.

He held her hand and rocked while inside his family waited.

A man couldn't ask for anything more.

About Lexi Blake

Lexi Blake lives in North Texas with her husband, three kids, and the laziest rescue dog in the world. She began writing at a young age, concentrating on plays and journalism. It wasn't until she started writing romance that she found success. She likes to find humor in the strangest places. Lexi believes in happy endings no matter how odd the couple, threesome or foursome may seem. She also writes contemporary Western ménage as Sophie Oak.

Connect with Lexi online:

Facebook: https://www.facebook.com/lexi.blake.39
Twitter: https://twitter.com/authorlexiblake
Website: www.LexiBlake.net

Sign up for Lexi's free newsletter at
http://www.lexiblake.net/contact.html#newsletter

Master No
Masters and Mercenaries, Book 9
By Lexi Blake
Coming August 4, 2015

Disavowed by those he swore to protect...

Tennessee Smith is a wanted man. Betrayed by his government and hunted by his former employer, he's been stripped of everything he holds dear. If the CIA finds him, they're sure to take his life as well. His only shot at getting it all back is taking down the man who burned him. He knows just how to get to Senator Hank McDonald and that's through his daughter, Faith. In order to seduce her, he must become something he never thought he'd be—a Dom.

Overcome by isolation and duty...

All her life, Dr. Faith "Mac" McDonald has felt alone, even among her family. Dedicating herself to helping others and making a difference in the world has brought her some peace, but a year spent fighting the Ebola virus in West Africa has taken a toll. She's come home for two months of relaxation before she goes back into the field. After holding so many lives in her hands, nothing restores her like the act of submission. Returning to her favorite club, Mac is drawn to the mysterious new Dom all the subs are talking about, Master No. In the safety of his arms, she finds herself falling head over heels in love.

Forced to choose between love and revenge...

On an exclusive Caribbean island, Ten and Mac explore their mutual attraction, but her father's plots run deeper than Ten could possibly have imagined. With McKay-Taggart by his side, Ten searches for a way to stop the senator, even as his feelings for Mac become too strong to deny. In the end, he must choose between love and revenge—a choice that will change his life forever.

On behalf of 1001 Dark Nights,

Liz Berry and M.J. Rose would like to thank ~

Steve Berry
Doug Scofield
Kim Guidroz
Jillian Stein
InkSlinger PR
Dan Slater
Asha Hossain
Chris Graham
Pamela Jamison
Jessica Johns
Dylan Stockton
Richard Blake
BookTrib After Dark
and Simon Lipskar

Made in the USA
San Bernardino, CA
12 May 2015